HICKORY, DICKORY, DEATH

Hickory Dickory Death

Cover Design by Emily's World of Design

Editing by Dr. Edith A. Kostka

Formatting by R. S. Williams

ISBN E-BOOK: 979-8-9862189-0-8

ISBN PAPERBACK: 979-8-9862189-1-5

ISBN HARDCOVER: 979-8-9862189-2-2

First Edition: October 2022

10 9 8 7 6 5 4 3 2 1

HICKORY. DICKORY. DEATH

N.D. Testa

Contents

To anyone who has ever
    had their heart broken...
    been taken advantage of by others...
    felt their life was never going to get better...
    and lost hope...

This one's for you...

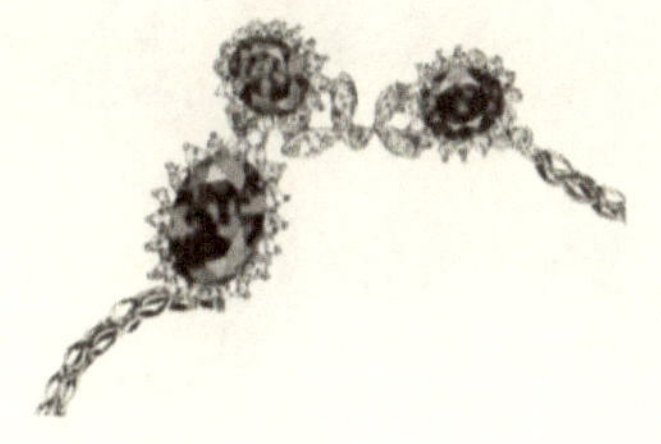

To my sister and best friend Ashley. Thank you for always being here for me. You are the most amazing person I know. I love you!

To Mom & Dad. Thank you for believing in me. I appreciate everything you have done for me. I love you.

To my editor Dr. Edith A. Kostka. Thank you for all your help. This book would not be possible without you. Thank you for being both a friend and family to me. I love you.

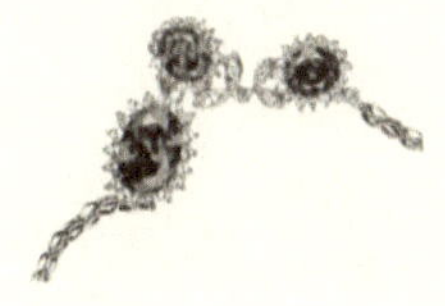

A Note to the Reader

The book contains scenes of violence. Readers who may be sensitive to these elements please take note.

A Soul for a Soul

Death Deals a Ring

I am a lady
I don[1] black
My lover's heart ceased to beat
The wedding is now a funeral

Edward Hall is dead.

October 24, 1880
3:00 p.m.

This date was supposed to be my wedding day, but it is now the day of burial.

I, Adelaide Bennett, have become a widow in my twentieth year before vows have ever left my lips.

Edward Hall is dead. The man I love is dead.

I watched strangers lower his coffin into its grave. Now, I sit at my dressing table and stare at my lifeless expression in the mirror. My body is adorned in black. Hot flashes burn my skin. My green eyes are swollen from tears.

I loved Edward passionately. He had eyes of the deepest blue, a chiseled jawline, and dark hair. Edward found the sunshine when

I could not. He was my light. Now my light has been extinguished.

I weep scalding tears. My heart aches in torment. My soul is hollow.

By the light of the gaslamp I see myself in the looking glass. There is no one there. There is no gold on my finger. There is no love in my heart.

My thoughts are interrupted as my bedroom door bangs open and my aunt enters the room.

"Still shedding tears over that street vendor, Adelaide?" sneers Lady Margaret Thomas throwing a handkerchief across my combs and brushes. "Dry your tears. Edward did you a favor by leaving this Earth. Now you can marry someone of a rank you deserve. I have arranged for a meeting tomorrow with Lord Arthur Wright. That will give you twenty-four more hours to grieve for your ragamuffin."

The tears that leak out of my eyes and down my cheeks stop abruptly. I grip the sides of my chair. Anger boils in the pit of my stomach and flows through my blood to my brain. There are no words to express how much I hate my aunt.

The word "aunt" does not apply to Lady Margaret. She is a vile human, full of greed. She is butter on bacon[2] and cares only for the image she can portray to the community. I would love nothing more than to shove her onto her bustle and stomp the smirk off her face.

I lift my head and glare at my aunt whose image I see in my looking glass. Her image flickers in the light of the lamp.

"Do not speak of my husband that way," I whisper.

"Your husband? I'm sorry… What did you just say…husband? That dying duck in a thunderstorm[3], lally-gagging[4], niminy-piminy[5] impoverished soul you dare call a husband? That is not a husband. That is the scum of the Earth. People of our class do not associate with men like that.

Do not give me that look. You should be grateful I was able to drag you and your mother out of that vile district full of vagrants and diseases."

"I think you are describing your own gal-sneaker[6] of a husband," I hiss surprised at how sharp my tongue is.

Normally I shy away from disagreements with Aunt Margaret. She is a powerful woman, and I have yet to see fully what she is capable of.

"Dear Aunt, you forget how you would still be in the streets if you had not seduced your husband. Or have you forgotten your dollymop[7] ways? You only took us in because you wanted an heir since your womb was incapable of one."

A sharp pain burns my cheek as Margaret slaps me.

"Mind your tongue, you ungrateful brat. You would have nothing if it were not for me. You will meet Arthur tomorrow or your mother's condition might take a turn for the worse."

"You would not dare!"

"I can and I will if you do not do what you are told. Trust me. If I could have borne an heir I would not need you!"

She closes the door behind her in a huff.

I put my hand to my cheek and feel the heat rising through my flesh. Oh, how I hate that woman. My eyes fall on the white handkerchief on the vanity. The sight of it consumes me with rage. I lift it carefully and place it into the flame of the gaslamp. It catches fire quickly, burns brightly, and sears the glass shade.

I rejoice at the sight of the flames. I would use nothing that ever comes from that woebegone woman.

---

1. **Don:** wear
2. **Butter on bacon**: Victorian Era slang meaning too much extravagance
3. **Dying duck in a thunderstorm:** unattractive, lackadaisical
4. **Lally-gagging:** flirting in a sexual way with the opposite sex
5. **Niminy-piminy:** effeminately affected, not masculine
6. **Gal-sneaker:** a man devoted to seduction
7. **Dollymop:** prostitute.

October 24, 1880
5:00 p.m.

I look out the windows into the elegant gardens of the Thomas Estate. The plantings are lush with flowers and shrubbery.

There was a time when I had not been under the crushing grip of my aunt. There was a time I had experienced freedom, but now all I see is Death. I would welcome a visit from Death.

My father died on February 16th, 1871. I was eleven years old. He had been battling lung fever all winter. We lived in a pretty house in a genteel neighborhood thanks to his income as a merchant. When he died, the bank took our home.

My mother and I were left utterly alone. I heard my mother speak of her sister, but no one had ever seen her in person. With no other family to help us, my mother and I were forced to move to the East End of London where we rented a small flat. The East End was home to back-to-back housing, narrow alleys, poor lighting, violence, and robbery.

My mother and I took jobs in the factories making clothes.

We suffered long hours for little pay.

My mother was injured at the factory in January of 1880.

Her condition deteriorated over the months. Unable to afford proper care for a doctor, I began to fear I would add my mother to the list of people who had left me in death.

The first week in August of 1880, Aunt Margaret appeared on our doorstep during our time of need. It was a little too convenient for my taste. When I laid eyes on Margaret, I felt an aura of evil around her. Fifteen years older than my mother, Margaret had the money which we desperately needed.

My mother invited Margaret into the house where the older sister apologized for not staying in touch. Aunt Margaret said she left town when she was eighteen years old. She never knew their parents had died or that my mom had been sent to live at an orphanage. I knew she was lying by the way she lowered her eyes. I kept quiet.

Margaret went on to explain how her husband had passed six months ago, in February of 1880, and as a childless widow she had no heir. According to her husband's will, there needed to be an heir to continue the estate's affairs.

Margaret wanted me to stand in as her heir so she could keep the Thomas Estate. She claimed the estate donated to many charities, and innocent people would lose money. (That turned out to be a lie). My mother jumped at the opportunity and agreed without my consent. She said it was important for me to get out of the East End. I would never have a future there.

I was angry with my mother for offering me to a relative I barely knew. Quietly I decided to accept this arrangement on my own terms.

Mother would come live with me at the Thomas Estate where she would receive the proper care. In return, I would be my aunt's stand-in heir and make a pretense of being her daughter. Margaret agreed, and we moved into the Thomas Estate in September 1880.

Margaret was good to her word. She made sure my mother had the best doctors in all of London. However, I did not realize that being a woman of a refined social society meant marrying a man of respectable position.

Without my consent, my conniving aunt had already chosen a husband for me, but what she did not know was that I already had a future husband of my own choosing. In the privacy of my heart, I was betrothed to a kind and gentle man, my beloved Edward.

I stand at the window, watching the blue sky turn dark. In my reminiscing, I recall a troubling scene with my aunt, a scene that signifies the depravity of her character. The day I told her I would not agree to her wishes...

September 30, 1880

"Do not be vazey[1]," Aunt Margaret sneers in front of the fireplace in the sitting room. "You cannot marry Edward Hall; you are now a lady of gentility."

"I agreed to pose as your heir," I snap back, "but I did not agree to marry Arthur Wright. As you know, I am already betrothed to Edward. We are to be wed in less than a month. You got what you wanted, which was to keep the estate."

"What is the problem? You cannot settle for that ragamuffin."

I fold my arms. I have a sudden desire to push Margaret into the fire.

"Margaret," my mother's weak voice drifts into the drawing room like an angel on the wings of truth. "Adelaide is right. You said you needed an heir to keep the estate. The papers have been signed; the mansion is yours. Who Adelaide marries has nothing to do with your social status as proprietor of this manor."

In a fit of anger, Margaret storms out of the room.

It is hours later in the evening, when my scheming aunt slips into my bedroom. It appears my mother's words have given her a change of heart. She confesses my marriage to Edward has nothing to do with her social position. She even offers for us to hold the wedding in the estate gardens. She says an heir of gentility should have a wedding of splendor even if the groom is a rogue.

Margaret gets up from my bedside and stands in the doorframe of my chamber. "I do hope that Edward accepts the idea of you being worth more money than his fingers would ever touch. You do know that a man's ego is extremely fragile. It is important for a man to be seen as the breadwinner of the family. That is why I have suggested you not marry Edward; I worry for the man's sanity. The embarrassment of knowing he cannot live up to his wife's status could make a man lose his mind."

I stare at Margaret for a moment. She is in her late fifties but still dresses as if she were my age. Her burgundy dress is too cheerful for her disposition. She always wears a turban around her head to hide the signs her youth has left her. Who knew so much evil could be packed in such a tiny frame?

"Edward does not care about money."

Margaret shakes her head, "Let me warn you that marriage changes a man. I saw it happen with my own husband. Nevertheless, I shall get started on your wedding details tomorrow. Good night."

I lie down to sleep, but slumber evades me. What did Margaret mean when she said money and marriage can change a man? Edward is not like that. Even though he is without a fortune, he is the most amiable and optimistic soul I have ever known.

How could I have foreseen that he would take his own life?

---

1. 7 **Vazey:** stupid

November 9, 1880

Edward has not even been dead a month and I am married to Lord Arthur Wright.

Lord Arthur Wright is a man of social distinction whose family has been associated with my aunt and uncle since his childhood. In truth, Arthur is only three years older than I. But he is not Edward. There is something dark in Arthur's eyes as if he holds secrets his soul would not dare spill.

Oddly enough, Aunt Margaret paid for Edward's funeral and burial arrangements. She felt it was the least she could do. I am grateful to Margaret for the gesture even though I know it would eventually come at a price.

I am broken. My heart is broken. The only man I have ever loved is dead. Dead by suicide the authorities ruled.

The police had been called to an alley on the East End, hours before dawn on October 23, 1880, the day before our wedding. They found Edward with his wrists slashed, a knife in his hand, and a note in his pocket.

The note was addressed to me. It stated how he knew in his heart that he would never be a good husband. I deserved so much more than he could provide for me. He knew that I would never leave him, so he would leave me through death. This way I could find a more suitable husband for the station I had inherited.

Post mortem results claimed death by suicide. I was not convinced. Edward was a happy man. Happy with our love. He would not take his own life.

However, the authorities ignored my protest. They said that the note, knife, and the cuts on his wrists all led to the conclusion Edward had taken his own life. Clearly I had been unaware of some mental instability he had cleverly disguised from me.

To make matters worse, when I approached Margaret and told her I would not marry Arthur, she threatened to revoke my mother's care. My mother had been making progress since coming to live at the estate, but in the past few days her health had declined again.

My hands were tied. I could not lose my mother who was the only family member I had left, so I gave in to Margaret's demand.

On November 9th, 1880, I stand at the altar in my aunt's garden and say my vows through clenched teeth. Only my vows are not spoken to the man I loved but to Lord Arthur Wright. I glare at my aunt as Arthur slips the ring onto my finger.

There she sits, the devil in her elegant silk dress, a smirk on her lips, and satisfaction all over her face. It is then I am sure she has been responsible for Edward's death. I want to kill her, but I have no idea how.

November 10, 1880

After our wedding I move into the Wright Mansion which is adjacent to the Thomas Estate. It seems I can never be free from my parasitic aunt.

Arthur has agreed to continue Mother's care, so she has the best doctors in the country looking after her. In time I move my mother to Lady Mary Taylor's comfortable townhouse near us on the same avenue. She is a widow and will make sure Mother is cared for.

Thankfully it seems Arthur is more interested in the idea of having a wife as a symbol rather than actually spending time with her. This arrangement is agreeable to me.

Every night Arthur leaves our home at dinner hour. I never

question him and am happy to watch him leave. When he returns, it is well past midnight.

November 12, 1880
10:00 p.m.

I sit near the fireplace reading *The Scarlet Letter* by Nathaniel Hawthorne. It is a suitable tale for my life. Arthur has left for the evening. Good riddance!

Adelaide

I raise my head.

Adelaide

I hear a voice that does not belong to my husband.

"Arthur, are you home?" I call out. "Did you forget something?" I swear if that fool decides to stay home with me, I am going to be very annoyed. I have plans of my own.

Adelaide. The ghostly voice calls again. It comes from Arthur's study.

In the light of the gaslamp, I see the flicker of a man's silhouette in the hallway. Strangely. it resembles Edward. I see him in the dim light and I rejoice.

My heart quickens, and goosebumps rise on my skin as I follow the silhouette to Arthur's door.

Eerily the door opens although nobody is there.

From the light of the sitting room, I see Arthur's desk. Edward's silhouette becomes clearer as one of the drawers flies open. I blink and Edward is gone.

I place my hand to my chest to calm my racing heart. I bend over the drawer. Inside is a piece of paper. I pull it out and walk toward the light. I can now read the elegant script. It is a contract written twenty years ago between the Thomas family and the Wright family. Sir John Thomas, Margaret's deceased husband, had made some poor business investments and owed Arthur's parents a small fortune. The contract stated that Arthur's father would forgive the Thomas debt if the Thomas family produced a daughter to marry his son. Such a marriage would join two great families in matrimony.

"Aunt Margaret never cared about my happiness. She never loved me. That selfish wench has used me to line her pockets with money!" My thirst for revenge begins my one unquenchable desire.

November 13, 1880
12:30 a.m.

The day a person is able to leave the East End is a good day. No one ever goes back. However, I go back. Every night.

I spent almost a decade of my life there, and I met many people who had been kind to us when my mother was ill. When Arthur goes out for his "business" ventures, I wait thirty minutes then leave for the East End. I have saved one outfit from the time I lived in that dreadful part of town. That way I blend in. I have my own business to take care of. I take the gifts Arthur has given me: jewels, trinkets, money, and other items. I give them to the people of that neighborhood who helped us during our time of need despite being poor themselves.

I roam in and out of the alleyways and streets like a ghost. No

18

one ever bothers me, but I am always prepared. I take a pistol from Arthur's gun collection and keep it in the pocket of my gown. If any man decides to give me trouble, a glimpse of the shiny barrel sends him on his way.

It is especially dark tonight. I am walking down Cavell Street. I have just left Mrs. Kelly's flat, a plump red-haired Irish woman with nine sickly children. When my mother was ill, Mrs. Kelly took care of her. Now I take care of her. I try to drop her off money once a week. Up ahead I see a figure stepping out of a nearby flat. I dart into the alley and hide behind a stack of crates.

The person coming out of the house is my husband! Arthur! Even though he is adorned in a dark cloak, I recognize that slight limp. My jaw clenches and my muscles tense. Business meetings my foot! No man of wealth would ever be caught dead in the East End except for one reason. The time of night and the woman standing next to him gives me my answer. The lady wears a shabby dress, with her hair in blonde ringlets. Arthur places an envelope in her fingers, then gives her a kiss on the lips. My eyes widen and my hands turn to fists.

My aunt has forced me to marry this cheating miscreant. I have given this man loyalty and respect, yet here he is showing his unmentionables to all of the East End while the man I love is grinning at daisy roots.[1]

"She is not the only light-skirt your husband sees," a voice says.

I whirl around to see a little old peddler woman standing behind me. A black shawl covers her shoulders and her white hair is covered in ashes. She gives me a wink. A chill runs up my spine. I fear her.

"Adelaide Bennett," she says. The lines crease deeply in her face. She holds a staff that resembles a serpent.

"I'm sorry I do not know you, and it is Adelaide Wright now," I reply. In all my years living in the East End I had never seen her before. And yet I feel she has been a constant visitor to this place of woe.

"No, your name is Adelaide Bennett. He does not deserve you to have his name, that skilamalink[2] gal-sneaker" the woman replies. "I am called Persephone. You do not know me, but I know you. A young woman whose real husband was taken from her in this very alley."

"Edward?" I whisper. "You knew Edward?"

Persephone nods. "And your current husband uses you for his shield while he lurks in the bedrooms of the East End.

And you Beautiful One, you have given away your happiness so your mother's health can be restored."

She peers closer at my face from under her ashes. "You are a kind woman. You grew up here, and yet you have not allowed your advantages to change you. Instead, you come back and help others. This is why I am going to help you."

Persephone pulls from her bag a small box and holds it up. I feel a terrible foreboding from this woman. She is not of this world. I sense she comes from a place of Death.

I look at her gift.

"This will unleash your ability to be strong against the ones who have deceived you. You will find strength in the face of weakness. You will find courage in the face of fear. With this ring you can bring the past to the future." She places the box into my hands. "Guard it well, for it has the ability to alter life. But there is one caveat. It takes a soul for a soul. Life always comes to an end. In every end there is a new beginning."

Once again I look down at the small black box wrapped in gray ribbon. "Thank you. But I do not understand." I look up. Persephone has disappeared.

----

1. **Grinning at daisy roots:** dead
2. **Skilamalink:** secret, shady, doubtful

November 14, 1880
10:00 a.m.

"He did not commit suicide, Mrs. Wright," the medical examiner Dr. Grace Smith whispers to me.

"I would prefer Miss Bennett," I reply. Dr. Smith looks at me strangely but I ignore her.

Morning has risen with a biting bitter wind, and clouds steal the sun. Arthur has gone to work, and I have made my way to the place of the dead. Dr. Smith had been the one to examine Edward's body. She signed off on the suicide confirmation. But after a hefty sum from me, she reveals the truth.

"I knew it," I whisper. "He was murdered. Why did you lie?"

"I did not want to," continues the doctor. She goes into the back room and unlocks a drawer in a tall cabinet. She carries a paper file and gives it to me. "My original analysis was murder. When I pulled out Mr. Hall's stomach contents I found traces of arsenic in the food he had eaten."

"Someone poisoned him?"

Dr. Smith nods. "Yes, he was poisoned. The slash marks to the wrists were made after he was already dead. When I brought that fact to the attention of the commissioner, he told me to write suicide. When I told him that was not the correct analysis, he told me that Mr. Hall had taken his own life, and if I wanted to keep my job, I would do as I was told. He reminded me that women doctors are not welcomed in our modern world. I hid the file away before it could be destroyed. You may keep it; but you cannot tell a soul how you got it."

"No, Dr. Smith. You do not have to worry. Your secret is safe with me."

I hide the file in my purse and leave. Already the gears are turning in my brain. The only reason the commissioner would lie would be if he had been paid a high price by someone with money. I know of only one person who would wish Edward dead.

November 14, 1880
11:15 p.m.

It is eleven-fifteen in the evening, I stand in the alleyway where Edward died. I open the box. Inside is a gold ring. It shines with an eerie light. It seems to have a kind of magic. I remember the words Persephone whispered *"a soul for a soul."* With shaking hands, I slip the ring onto my finger. In the nearby street, the gas lamps flicker as if an ill wind has touched them.

Immediately my head begins to throb as if my brains are being beaten by a hammer. I fall to my knees and my surroundings spin like a carousel. Then everything stops. The cloudy sky is now lit by a full moon and I see a silhouette stumble into the alleyway holding his stomach. He is gasping and wheezing. The man is Edward. Edward stumbles forward onto the cobblestones and lies still. I clutch my hand to my heart; tears of anger prick at my lashes. The ring on my finger burns hot. Two men step out of the shadows. They crouch over Edward, and one man places a finger to his throat.

"Is he dead?" The first man asks. His voice is pitched like that of a woman.

The second man nods.

"Guess we better get to work." The first man shoves a note into Edward's pocket while the second man pulls out a knife.

The scene shifts before me. Now I am standing in Aunt Margaret's study. She cannot see me through the veils of this vision. Aunt Margaret sits in her chair looking very smug. A man stands before her.

"Is it done?" Margaret asks.

The man nods. "The police are taking his body as we speak. They should be declaring suicide very soon." Margaret nods. "I'll pay the commissioner a visit in the morning."

"Ruperta was persuasive in convincing the cook to poison the food," says the man whose voice seems strangely familiar.

"Once you are married, you had better stay away from the East End. We do not need a scandal being put out. A married man frolicking with a lady of the night. Heavens," says Margaret. "And you better stay away from Blanche Thompson, too. I know you favor her for marriage, but a deal is a deal."

"Yes, Margaret," the man replies.

My heart pounds as I watch the man step into the lamplight which illuminates his face. The man is Arthur!

November 15, 1880
11:55 p.m.

I sit staring at my reflection in the mirror. My eyes are different. They hold a deadness coupled with the light that is almost frightening. The clock ticks behind me declaring the time eleven fifty-five in the evening. I feel nothing but rage. I reach into the drawer and pull out the box Persephone has given me. I open the velvet gift and look at the gold ring on the satin cushion.

You will become strong in the face of weakness. Persephone told me.

25

As a woman I am considered weak. I have no voice and no choice in my actions.

I pick up the ring and place it on my finger. I take a deep breath then snap to attention. My green eyes have turned black. My hands grip the sides of my chair. Warmth flows through my body, feeding my muscles, and lifting the fog from my brain. I know what I have to do. I put on my dark cloak, pull my veil over my head, and leave the house.

The leaves blow on the ground in time with my pace. I let my feet take me to a particular door. I lift my fist and knock.

"Who is it?" a familiar voice calls. The door flings open, and there stands Aunt Margaret. "Who are you?" she demands.

"You did it!" I speak. I push my veil back so she sees my face.

"Adelaide!" she snaps. "What are you doing on my doorstep at this ungodly hour of the night? Go back home and go to bed with your husband." She attempts to close the door on me, but with one hand I push the door back so it smashes into the wall. I am strong now.

"My husband is dead," I say in a low voice, "because you killed him." I push Margaret. She stumbles back into the wall. I enter the house and slam the door behind me.

"Adelaide, what are these lies escaping your lips?" asks Margaret holding her shoulder, a grimace on her face.

I begin to speak. The golden ring gives me the truth through its gentle pulses. "You are evil. When your husband died eight months ago, you were delivered a letter from the Wright's attorney. The letter stated you had to provide an heir to marry their son. This you agreed to many years ago. Otherwise, you would have been forced to return all the money your husband owed them. Since you are insanely greedy, you remembered your sister who had a daughter would be of marriageable age. It was then you put your plan into place.

"Adelaide, you clearly have lost your mind. Do not make me call Arthur to come here and get you."

"Arthur is currently in the East End sharing a bed with one of his ladies. We have about five hours until he returns."

Margaret tries to get past me to escape, but I give her a swift punch to the mouth, and she falls onto the settee holding her jaw.

"You paid the factory owner to tamper with the equipment that would injure my mother. You paid the doctor to give her medicine that would make her sicker than she really was. Then like a savior you showed up at our door."

"You cannot prove any of this you little tramp," hisses Margaret.

I walk over to her bookshelf. The gold ring whispers to me to pull out the leather-bound book Mary Shelley's *Frankenstein*. Margaret's eyes widen; the smug look on her face disappears.

"You knew you could not commit this murder alone, so you called on Arthur to help you. You knew he liked to visit the East End at night to have his little fun. You had him follow Edward and found out he liked to eat his dinner at a particular pub. Arthur had his mistress Ruperta Morris seduce the cook and add arsenic to Edward's dinner.

Once the meal was consumed, the high amounts of poison began to take effect as Edward walked home. Arthur and his other mistress, Blanche Thompson, who was dressed as a man, followed. When Edward died in the alleyway, they slit his wrists and placed a note in his pocket. You paid them a hefty price to kill Edward. You paid a forger to write a note in his handwriting. Then you paid the commissioner to classify Edward's death as a suicide. That is also why you wanted to pay for the burial because you wanted to make sure there was little time to examine the body."

I pause to listen carefully to the ring. Its whispers are so clear to me. I open the book to see pieces of paper spill out. It is receipts.

"Here are all your payments. Proof that you are nothing but a murderess."

Margaret's eyes narrow. "You ungrateful mongrel. After what

I went through to make sure you were a lady of quality instead of living in that vile district."

"Coming from a lady who walked those streets herself is ironic," I hiss. "You do not care about us. You only care about keeping your money." I pause. The ring whispers deeper secrets. I look at Margaret. "Not only did you kill Edward but you killed your own husband as well."

Margaret lunges forward and opens the drawer in the deal table beside the settee. I know she is going for her pistol. However, I am faster. I grab the fire poker and swing with all my might at the side of Aunt Margaret's head. She falls to the floor dead, blood seeping from the wound in her skull. I take the poker with me and walk out the door. I have a long night ahead of me.

November 16, 1880
12:45 a.m.

I knock on the door of a filthy flat in the East End.

"Arthur, I do not have time now. I have a customer coming in fifteen minutes," Ruperta Morris opens the door.

"Oh, you do not have time," I reply as I overpower the woman and enter the flat. I close the door behind me. "But you had time to seduce a cook then poison a dish to kill a man. Just like your client Arthur Wright requested."

"Who are you?" demands Ruperta. She is a woman of slight build with voluptuous curves. Ruperta adjusts her corset and twists a blonde ringlet around her finger. Her face is covered in defiance which tells me she does not like her territory invaded by another woman. However, I am not here for fun, I am here for revenge.

"I am the fiancée of Edward Hall, the man you were paid to poison. I am also the future widow of Lord Arthur Wright, the man who comes to visit you every night." I hiss.

Ruperta grows silent. "I do not want any trouble."

"Oh, but you already requested trouble when you agreed to murder an innocent man for money."

Ruperta tries to run but I am faster. My hands wrap around her throat, silencing her for good. Then I throw the poker on the floor.

November 16, 1880
1:45 a.m.

An hour later, I do not even wait for Blanche Thompson to open the door. I simply burst right through it; the ring tells me that her husband is away on business. Thompson Mansion has let all their servants go for the night. Blanche is alone.

I float up the stairs like a phantom. I feel my soul leave my body and watch from afar while the emotions of revenge and betrayal take control of my actions.

I enter the bedchamber of the lady who conspired to kill my husband. She is asleep. She wakes as I throw a vase against the wall.

She screams and jumps out of bed, "Who are you?" How ironic to hear that question echo yet again.

"Your guilty conscience," I reply. I come closer until we are face to face. The ring whispers the truth. "First you break your marriage vows to your husband by sneaking around with Arthur Wright. Then you allow your lover to persuade you to dress as a man and help kill an innocent human being. You are the forger who was paid by Margaret Thomas to write a suicide note."

I throw another vase against the wall.

"Is that not so, my dear Mrs. Thompson?"

"I-I love Arthur," stammers the frightened woman. "He told me if I helped him with this, he would find a way to leave his wife and we would be together."

"Have you forgotten you are married yourself?"

She scoffs, "Arthur has promised to help me get rid of him."

I roll my eyes, "And you really expected Arthur to leave me after all the trouble he went through to kill my fiancé? I am his wife. I can tell you your plan has failed."

Her brown eyes narrow and hatred spreads across her face. "If he could not find a way to leave you, I was going to find a way to kill you myself. I already have one murder blotched on my soul. What is another?"

"Interesting." My voice is slick. "So, you believe you exchange one soul for another to get what you want?"

I feel the enormous power of the ring.

I reach for her throat. My fury is fierce; my strength is ferocious. I squeeze her breath, her life, her soul out of her body. On my finger the ring glows with a brilliant fire as its magic strengthens.

I walk out of the Thompson Mansion. Satisfaction creeps across my face. The grand finale is about to begin.

November 16, 1880
3:45 a.m.

I am a raging thundercloud as I throw open the door of our home.

"Where have you been?" asks Arthur getting up from his chair near the fireplace in the parlor.

"I could ask you the same question," I reply. "But I already know the answer. Every night you go out for business which is getting your desires taken care of in ways I dare not speak. However, this night has been different. You have been to see Ruperta Morris in the East End, but she did not answer. Then you have been to see Blanche Thompson, but she did not answer, either. So, you have decided to come home and play the role of a loving, loyal husband when you are nothing but a gal-sneaker!"

"How do you know that?" His skin pales and his eyes widen. He taps his pipe against his thumb faster and faster. In light of the fire, I see the fear in his eyes.

"I know everything."

I knock the pipe out of Arthur's hands. It has been irritating me.

"Just as I know that you and your mistresses plotted with my aunt to kill my husband Edward."

"I am your husband, Adelaide," stammers Arthur, backing up as I move forward asserting my dominance. Beads of sweat line his forehead.

"Not for long. You only helped my aunt because she paid you a lot of money. Your family money is held in trust. Use of it can be traced. My aunt's money cannot be traced. I know you, Arthur. I know you keep many mistresses."

"Adelaide, that is not true," Arthur stumbles a little but regains his balance.

I feel the heat of the ring on my finger. "It is true," I speak.

"Darling, you do not understand. I did this for us. Addy, Edward could never give you a good life. You know this. I can give you what he never could."

Heat from the ring nearly burns through my skin. Anger surges through me like fire.

"You lie, Arthur. You lie, you cheat, you kill. There is darkness in your soul."

"So true, my darling Adelaide, so very true. Your aunt knew this - that is why her and I work so well together."

Arthur's back touches the wall. He is cornered as his lies slowly strangle him.

Gasping for breath he calls out, "Beloved, I could never harm you. Let's end this whole argument. You know I love you."

"Liar," I hiss.

From the folds of my gown, I pull out a knife. I chose a knife because a gun would be too easy. I want this to be personal. I want my face to be the last thing he sees before Death takes his soul. I want him to feel the power of this ring. I know he killed Edward.

I lunge forward. The knife penetrates his flesh. His heart stops.

The magic of the ring deals justice. Soul for soul.

November 16, 1880
4:15 a.m.

Vindication! Vindication!
Much to do before the night is through.
My husband lies dead in a pool of blood.

Cold November air sweeps through my lungs as I rush down the stairs into the darkness. All is quiet in our neighborhood. On the wind I hear a call. Chilling. Frozen. Like Death.

Only a few steps lead me to my aunt's door. I rush inside. She, too, is surrounded by blood.

The ring burns my finger; it brightens. I hear Persephone's voice: *souls for souls call forth the souls.*

The golden ring allows me to summon the souls of Arthur, Ruperta, and Blanche to join my aunt and me at the Thomas Estate. By the magic of the ring their bodies appear at my feet. I see their souls.

A gaslamp burns innocently nearby. Its light casts deep shadows across death.

I reach for the lamp flickering on the table and clutch it as if it were a throat. I raise my arm and smash it against the curtains at the window. Flames burst forth. Fire quickly consumes the entire wall. Soon the whole room will be ablaze.

I head out the back door. The ring tells me I have innocent souls to claim.

November 16, 1880
5:00 a.m.

As the light of dawn touches the morning sky, I stand in the graveyard in front of Edward's headstone. My emotions of revenge and resentment have been fulfilled. The only emotion that needs justice is happiness. I hold my hand out in front of me. The moonlight makes the ring glow brighter.

With this ring you can bring the past to the future, Persephone's voice whispers in the wind. *Soul for a soul.* I kneel forward and place my hand on the tombstone.

"This soul I claim. Come back to me," I whisper.

I blink. The gravestone is gone.

"Addy," a confused voice calls. I turn around to see my love, Edward, standing before me. He looks just as he did the last time I saw him before he died.

Tears of joy prick my eyes, and my heart sings with happiness. "Edward."

I call his name and run into his arms. He hugs me tightly and I plant my lips on his.

"Why are we here?" asks Edward. "A graveyard is no place to be the night before our wedding."

"Actually, it is November, my love," I reply. "We had to postpone the wedding. Circumstances beyond our control."

"My darling Adelaide. I do not remember." Edward scratches his head and looks confused.

"You have not been yourself lately," I respond.

Edward nods. "Shall I walk you back to your aunt's estate?"

"No."

I smile. The ring on my finger cools.

I run among the tombstones until I find a special one. I place my hand on the stone and whisper, "This soul I claim. Come back to me." The marker disappears.

"Adelaide?" a voice calls.

I turn around and smile. My father stands before me and I run into his arms.

October 24, 1881.

Thomas Estate burned to the ground. It was ruled an unfortunate accident as a consequence of the fireplace left unattended.

As Margaret's only heir, I have inherited her entire fortune. I also have inherited the Wright fortune. I am now a very wealthy woman.

No one has questioned the revivification of Edward nor of my father. By the magic of the ring everyone has forgotten the people I love were ever dead.

I have sold the Wright Estate and Thomas Estate. Both of which have made me an even wealthier woman. I have my own lavish property deep in the countryside of Surrey, far away from London. My mother and father now live with Edward and me. I married Edward Hall in a modest ceremony in the gardens of my mansion.

It is now a year to the day since all the phantasmagoria has occurred. Instead of sadness I am filled with joy. The box with the gold ring is in my hand.

"Thank you," I whisper to the ring. "Thank you for making me happy again."

I close the lid of the box. I open the drawer of my dressing table and place the box inside. I close the drawer and lock it.

Someday when the right person comes along, I will pass the ring onto another soul in need.

I get up from the velvet bench and head downstairs to join my husband Edward and my parents in the gardens for lunch. I walk down the hall; the diamond in my wedding ring catches the light from the window. It sparkles with contentment.

"Adelaide Hall," a voice whispers.

I turn to see Persephone appear beside me. Her wrinkled lips turn upward into a smile.

"Did you get exactly what you wanted?" she asks.

"Yes."

Her hand unfolds and the gold ring appears in her palm. "Then I believe we can pass this gift onto the next soul who needs aid."

I nod, "Yes, we can. Thank you."

Persephone laughs. Her laugh is light and airy at first, then turns into a cackle. The ring begins to glow, then is transformed into a long scythe. A black cloak and hood appear around her. She gives me a wink, then disappears. I stand alone in the hall.

My lips part into a smile. Death has dealt me a ring.

The End

Death Nabs a Necklace

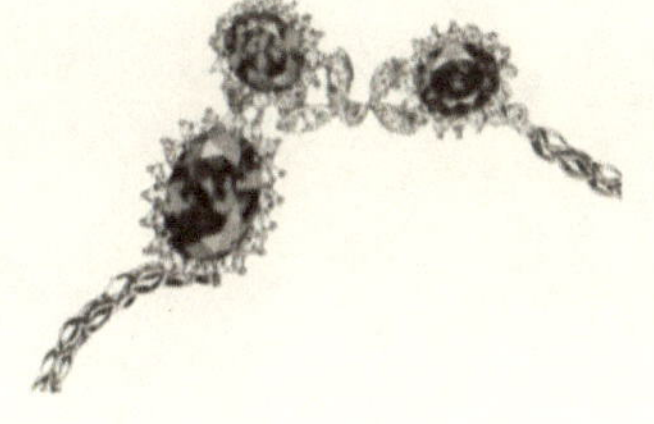

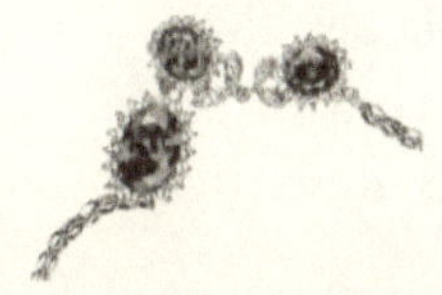

September 20, 1884
12:00 a.m.

Bells toll the hour I find him.

Nervous - angry - confused - heart-broken - words fail me, but what can one say when you come home to find your husband stabbed with a corn dryer?

I wrap my fingers around the farming tool and pull it from his chest. Holding it up to the light of the gaslamp, I stare at the rod with five prongs covered in blood - my husband's blood.

My poor Theo lying there before me. What had been his thoughts as he inhaled his last breath? Who could have been so cruel? And why?"

Whoever inflicted this heartless act will feel my revenge for taking my husband's life.

"Anna Cooper," a voice echoes. It is soft, as if it bids me no harm. Like an old friend from years past coming to call.

My eyes move back and forth. Most of our small house is cast in darkness. Shadows leap on the walls from the single gaslamp that burns on the table.

"Who speaks?" I yell. "Show yourself!"

"Anna, really," the voice calls. "This is how you treat guests to your home?" A figure steps out of the shadows into the parlor.

"Who are you?" I ask. My sweaty palms grip the corn dryer closer to me. Its prongs are ready for attack.

"Ah, not enough light."

The voice is female. The intruder clicks her tongue as the clock chimes. An owl hoots outside bringing bumps to the surface of my skin.

My mysterious visitor walks to the fireplace where a pile of logs rest on the grate. Waving her hand, flames emerge from the dry wood and grow taller. In seconds, a roaring fire crackles, throwing light onto my trespasser.

A woman in gray stands before me. A handkerchief wraps around her short white hair. A black shawl covers her shoulders. She winks and the creases in her face deepen as she smiles at me. It is as if she has known me my entire life.

I do not know how the sight of an elderly woman could instill so much fear in my heart but it does. My legs tremble and my breaths increase.

"Do not be afraid, dear Anna, I bring you no harm." Folding her arms, she circles around me. "You are a kind woman, Anna. Always putting others before yourself. This is why I am going to help you."

"You are not of this world?" I whisper.

"Perhaps yes and perhaps no; it depends which world you

believe in," replies the woman. "Death is a ritual of life; however, there are cases when it comes before the right time. When others think they can play a role that is not meant for them. When people choose to step into that forbidden caveat, they must be prepared for the consequences that follow." She stands in front of me. "Much of our lives are spent concealing emotions that are improper to display. There is evil in us all waiting for the right moment to be unleashed"

She holds her hand out to me. In her palm appears a black box wrapped in gold ribbon. "Take it," she commands.

I place the wrought-iron corn dryer on the floor, then reach forward to take the gift.

"Thank you, but I do not understand."

"I am sure you can understand that when the dawn breaks, you are about to become the number one suspect in your husband's murder." The woman's eyes flash and her dark pupils transfer the serious nature of the predicament that seems to have caught me in its snare. "Nothing in this room has been touched; it does not look like a robbery, and you have touched the weapon that took your husband's life."

"What? I would never kill Theo! I love him. We want a family." I cry.

"None of that matters when murder is involved. Passion and love are the most powerful motivations for seeking unholy death. Open it."

With shaking hands, I unwrap the ribbon and raise the lid. Inside is a beautiful necklace. A statement piece consisting of multiple oval rubies and diamonds. It is the most exquisite piece of craftsmanship I have ever seen in my life.

"I do not understand," I can barely utter the words, for my tongue seems frozen in my mouth.

"This necklace placed upon your neck will unleash your inner emotions. The feelings you have held dormant in your heart will finally be free. With this newfound strength, you will find the courage to face the one who has wronged you. In doing so, you will restore the light that has been extinguished in the one you loved most. But you must tread cautiously, for exchanging a soul for a soul is dangerous work. If you take the wrong soul, you might lose more than you ever imagined." The woman replies. Shadows from the flames dance on her face, and her eyes sparkle with a secret only she knows.

"I do not understand. Who are you?" I cry.

"My name is Persephone, and do not worry, child, we will meet again shortly. Now get some rest. When the clock strikes five, the police will arrive."

I glance at my beloved on the floor and the blood beneath my feet. When I look up, Persephone is gone.

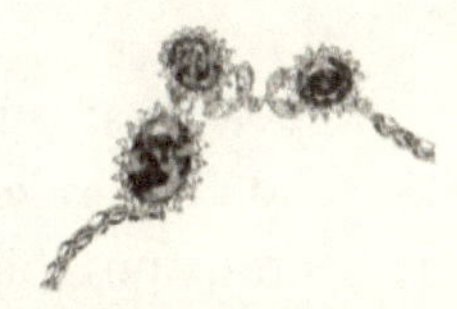

September 20, 1884
6:00 a.m.

Lips move in front of my face, but I am unable to comprehend them as my heart beats a tattoo against my eardrums. The policeman narrows his eyes and glares at me. We are at police headquarters and I wish more than anything I was back home in my bed.

How dare he look at me so accusingly! Does he not understand that I loved my husband dearly? We had been married five years and were eager to start a family. Yes, it was taking longer than we expected, but how dare he suggest I blamed my husband for not giving me a child? How dare he level charges that I wanted to rid myself of useless baggage by murdering my husband? How dare he suggest such a vile accusation?

The ruby necklace against my skin feels warm, and I am not

certain whether it is the jewels or the burning desire for revenge that is creating so much heat.

How I would love to take this corn dryer sitting on the constable's desk and smash it over his head.

I grip the handles of the worn wooden chair where many a wicked criminal has sat before in the face of doom. *What thoughts are these that consume my mind? This is not who I am.*

The door behind me opens and a voice calls into the room. "Constable, are you planning to charge Mrs. Cooper with the murder of her husband?"

Looking behind me, the policeman strokes the edge of his thick mustache. "We must follow the rules of evidence. As the situation stands now there is strong possibility that Mrs. Cooper has killed her husband. However, as there are no eyewitnesses and no blood on her hands, there is cause for reasonable doubt. I completely empathize with Mrs. Cooper, and I may not fault her for doing what needed to be done. With that being said, Mr. Cooper is dead. We need to find the person who took his life. There is a chance that in time Mrs. Cooper might be confined to an asylum if we find that she indeed is a murderess.

"I am not insane!" I burst out. "How dare you! I did not murder my husband. As I have stated before. I was asleep, and when I woke, Theo was not in bed. I went searching throughout the house and found him in the sitting room... dead."

"Do you have any hard evidence?" The voice continues.

"Not at this time. Given the state of affair, Mrs. Cooper, you may go; but I must advise you not to leave town. And if it turns out that you did kill your husband, you will be headed for the gallows."

I glare at him. I feel a presence come behind me and a hand is placed on my shoulder. I turn to a cloaked figure who has reached out to touch me. The visitor beckons me to follow.

How I wish I had that corn dryer in my possession.

The mysterious visitor leads me out of the police station and onto the streets. We pause at the top of the steps, and I watch the horse-drawn carriages ride by. Everywhere there is the bustling of pedestrians, and vendors on the corners selling their goods. I hear the hooves of the horses clomping on the cobble-stones and the ringing of the harnesses on the carriages they pull. Whistles are blowing and bells are clanging. People are chattering to one another as they walk by. The scent of chest-nuts, eels, pudding, and pies from the nearby street fill my nostrils. This fast-paced city-life is how I grew up. After I married Theo, we moved to a house on the better side of town. I enjoy the quiet.

"I told you we would meet again, my dear," The figure lowers her hood and I look into the face of Persephone.

"What are you doing here?" I whisper. I could have sworn I dreamed her. Yet here she stands before me smiling as if I am a pawn in her game of trickery.

"Is that any way to greet the woman who stopped you from getting thrown in jail? Really, Anna."

I stare at her, my eyes unblinking. Is this what madness feels like? No, I cannot be mad. My senses are keen and I am observant of what is going on. However, in my heart lies a plan of attack that I have yet to unfold. For when I find the murderer, I shall do to that person what has been done to my husband. I can think of nothing but finding this miscreant and watching him die!

"The police officer makes a valid point. If I was sleeping, how could I have not heard the sounds of someone killing my husband?" I hear the words leave my lips but I do not recognize myself saying them.

"Maybe it was because Theo did not want you to know," replies Persephone.

"What do you mean?" I ask.

"Perhaps he gave you something so you would stay asleep," she hints.

"My husband tried to kill me!" I cry.

"No, he had a meeting that night, and he did not want to risk disrupting your dreams while he engaged in secret mischief. He did not want you to hear his conversation. Did you drink anything before you went to bed?"

"Yes, I always have a cup of tea before bed."

A bottle of capsules is held up before my eyes. "What is that?" I inquire.

"Chloral hydrate. Sleeping pills. Your husband carries a dark secret within his soul. One he wishes you may never discover. Everyone has graveyards within them. Hauntings of the past they wish never to be revealed. You must dig up the mystery, for it is the only way you will find the person you seek to take your revenge."

I blink and she is gone.

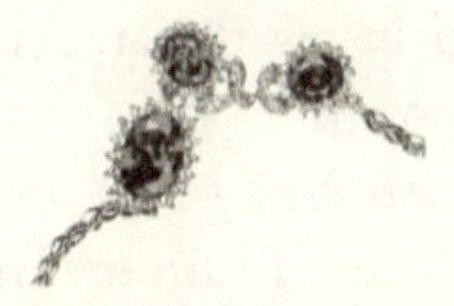

September 21, 1884
11:00 a.m.

I pace back and forth in front of the fireplace. I spend most of the morning scrubbing my husband's blood from the floor. The house is lifeless and empty without Theo's laughter ringing through the halls. At twenty-five, I find myself a widow and childless. A predicament I never anticipated within the bonds of a happy marriage. Why would my husband drug me? What was he hiding that he did not want revealed?

Suddenly I hear a knock

A woman's face greets me as I pull back the oak door. I do not fancy company. I want to sit here with darkness as my companion and discover whose heart needs to be stopped, just like my husband's.

It is Olivia Evans. Blonde and beautiful, she stands before me clutching a folder. Her eyes waver back and forth. The paper trembles in her grasp.

"Anna. I am so sorry to hear about what happened to your husband. May I come in? I have to tell you something."

I grip the knob of the door tightly. I do not want visitors. I do not wish to be entertained, or pitied. I am wrongfully suspected of murder! I have half a mind to tell her today is not the day, but before I can get the words out, the beautiful ruby necklace tightens around my neck. My eyes widen, I cannot breathe! I nod. My words are strangled in my throat. As Olivia steps over the threshold the necklace loosens.

What bewitchment has been placed on this jewelry? I gesture for Olivia to sit on the settee. I turn my back to her and look at myself in the mirror. I work on removing the necklace but the clasp is stuck. Try as I might, I am unable to remove the beautiful lavaliere that hangs like a noose.

"Are you alright?" asks Olivia.

I decide to try to remove the necklace later and I sit down beside her. "I really do not know." I reply.

Olivia and I were long-time friends. We used to work in the textile mills when we were barely out of childhood. Then she went to work for the Carmichael's as a maid, and I married. I have not seen her for a very long while.

"I was cleaning up Miss Carmichael's room and I found this." She hands me the folder. "I knew you would want to know." She stands. "I must go. I cannot risk anyone seeing me here. If Miss Carmichael discovers I took anything from her, I will lose my place."

"Thank you, Olivia." I clear my throat. "You know you do not have to work for Miss Carmichael. I have the means to assist you in securing other employment. I can help you to find something more worthy of you."

"My options are slim, Anna." She smiles. "No one will pay me as well as the Carmichael's. It will all work out."

I close the door and sit on the settee. A new corn dryer leans next to the fireplace. It stares at me. Mocking me. This is the second corn dryer I possess. The first one was taken by the police. I have a small garden behind the big house and corn was Theo's favorite vegetable.

I do not know how long the corn dryer and I glare at each other. I look at the floor, once stained with my husband's blood. The sun begins to set, and I am clothed in darkness. Then a single gaslamp lights behind me by what I imagine are invisible hands.

"Anna," a voice calls. I feel the necklace warm my neck. It is Persephone.

"Really, Anna, I help you evade jail and this is how you return my favor by sitting there wallowing in misery?" The old woman stands before me.

"I do not know who murdered Theo," I hiss.

"Well, of course you do." Her wrinkled hands snatch the folder on the coffee table and place it in my lap. "Your friend Olivia gave you the answer." She places a long dark nail on the paper. "You have found the graveyard. In two days when the moon is full, there will be the opportunity for you to rid yourself of an oppressive weight."

Persephone is gone. Only the flickering flame in the looking glass is proof that I have not gone completely mad...yet.

I sit with the folder on my lap. I do not have time to read. My husband's body lies in the morgue. I need to see to the funeral arrangements. It has been two years since I went through this with Jack. I never thought I would have to bury a loved one ever again.

Anna! Open the folder! An eerie voice calls to me.

"Who is it?" I reply. The voice causes bumps to rise forth along my skin.

Reveal the graveyard!

Is the corn dryer speaking to me? I hope not.

My fingers touch the smooth paper as I pull open the folder. A document looks up at me. Holding it to the light of the gaslamp, I see it is a report from a private investigator. The report is addressed to Mildred Carmichael. The focus of the paper is a history of my husband's mysterious past.

My eyes move over the typed print, as each word makes my heart beat in an agony of memory. Theo had told me his parents had died and he had been raised by his wealthy paternal grandparents who once owned the house we now call home. According to this document, Theo's father had died from influenza. But his mother is still very much alive and currently residing in the Brixton Asylum in London. She had murdered seven men.

The paper slips from my fingers and flutters to the floor. *Seven men!*

I shuffle through the remaining bundle of papers. The report states Theo's mother had a mental instability that had never revealed itself until after she had given birth to Theo. She left his father and worked the streets of the East End of London where she lured men to her flat then killed them. Eventually she was caught for her crimes and deemed insane. After Theo's father had died, his grandparents worked tirelessly to erase any existence of Theo's mother by spreading the rumor that she had died in childbirth.

But why did Mildred Carmichael hire a private investigator to look into my husband's past?

I stare at the flame dancing in the gaslamp. The ruby necklace against my throat warms. A jolt of heat runs through my veins as a forgotten memory surges forth. Long ago my husband said before he met me, he had courted a woman named Millie. But surely it was not Mildred Carmichael, whose father was a wealthy businessman who owned multiple factories and textile mills throughout England?

My necklace tightens slightly and murmurs that my thoughts are true.

I hear voices in my head as the lavaliere reveals the secrets my husband had wanted to take to his grave.

Millie! I cannot marry you. I do not love you. My husband's voice speaks from the darkness.

You leave me for a woman who works in factories! I hear Mildred Carmichael's voice speak. A man of your pedigree needs a woman who is of high station by your side.

I love Anna and we will be married.

Then you leave me no choice, Theodore. I cannot have my family's reputation tarnished by a suitor abandoning me for someone of a lower class!

I shove the papers back into the folder. The edge of the document cuts my finger but I do not feel it. I watch the blood bubble to the surface and drip onto the floor. I feel nothing except anger. Mildred Carmichael wanted my husband.

The necklace murmurs it has more to tell. The wind from the open window extinguishes the light of the gaslamp, and I am cloaked in darkness. I have no fear. Voices in the shadows start again, and the lavaliere tells me I am about to hear a conversation that happened three years ago from today's date.

"What is this?" I hear my husband's voice say.

"I hired a private investigator, Theodore." Mildred's voice hisses. *"I am sure your wife will be pleased to know that her husband's mother is a murderer and insane. What a dishonor to your grandparents' legacy. I am certain the community will be overjoyed to hear the wealthy and respected Coopers have tainted blood. Imagine your children having the consanguinity of a murder running through their veins."*

"You wicked woman" hisses Theo. *"What do you want?"*

"You, Theo," murmurs Mildred. *"Leave your wife and be with me and no one has to know about your past."*

"No! I will not accede to your malicious desires. I do not love you. I will not leave Anna."

"You truly are going to choose that woman of lower class over me! Well then, since you refuse me, you can pay me money every month until either your wealth runs out or you choose me to wed! And you can shred that copy all you want, Theo. I have duplicates."

I stand and walk to the gaslamp. Striking a match, I relight the wick. Mildred Carmichael has been blackmailing my husband for years. This wealthy woman who is engaged to be married to a powerful politician wants to bleed my husband dry.

I grip the sides of the table, the gaslamp in front of me. I look up into the mirror on the wall. Shadows from the flames dance on my face, the rubies in my necklace glow. I look different. The expression on my face I do not recognize, and the deadness in my eyes frightens me.

Voices in the darkness behind me are not finished. The lavaliere tells me they speak the secrets of what happened the other night. I see two shadows standing before me in ghostly form. One is my husband and the other is a man.

I will not pay anymore of Millie's blackmail. It has been three years. She is about to be married, and she still wishes to carry on this charade. My husband's voice shakes. He stands in this very parlor facing his attacker.

These are the conditions of Miss Carmichael's agreement. You pay her a monthly sum, and she will not report her findings to the papers. If you wish not to pay anymore, then rid yourself of your wife and marry Mildred, instead. Now where is the money? The unfamiliar voice is Gus Bobellon who the necklace tells me is Mildred's cousin. He collects the money each month. He is large, bald, and intimidating.

I do not have it. And I will no longer be paying. You can go back to Millie and tell her that I'm sure her fiance would love to know that she has a habit of blackmailing married men to leave their wives.

The ghostly image that is Gus picks up the poker by the fireplace and swings it at my husband but as he is great of girth, Gus is slow. My husband is agile and avoids the blow. Theo yanks the poker out of Gus's hands.

Go tell her what I said. Theo continues. He rests the poker against the side of the fireplace. *There will be no more money.*

Theo is distracted and does not see the rage creeping over Gus's ghostly face. For I realize Mildred has never needed that money. It was her cousin who had the need. The necklace adds that since Gus was the collector, Mildred gave her cousin the majority of that money which he squandered on drinks and women.

Gus snatches up the corn dryer that I had left on the coffee table. Before Theo can react, he is impaled by the corn dryer and falls to the ground. I scream and the ghostly shadows disappear leaving me with only the gaslamp as my witness.

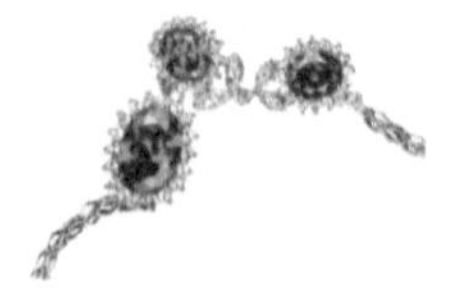

September 23, 1888
12:00 a.m.

I spent the prior day taking care of my husband's arrangements. I see the sympathy in the eyes of some people and the accusations in the pupils of others.

I lie in wait. My bed feels cold without Theo by my side. My soul feels empty. The blankets are pulled up to my chin with my body fully clothed beneath. Persephone's words dance in my mind.

Death is a ritual of life. When people choose to step into the role of taking a life, they must be prepared for the consequences that follow.

I am the consequence. Vengeance salivates on my tongue, waiting for the blood of the ones who have taken what is mine, to quench the thirst.

Much of our lives are spent concealing emotions that are improper to display. There is evil in us all waiting for the right moment to be unleashed. Persephone's voice echoes throughout the room.

I am ready.

The clouds part the night sky to reveal the full moon. Its rays flood through my window making a pattern on the floor as the bells chime midnight. The necklace burns my skin. Throwing the covers off, I rise to my feet. I am cloaked in black. I may be a woman in mourning, but I shall not mourn alone.

Storming into the parlor, I grab the corn dryer and catch sight of my reflection in the mirror. My eyes are dark, my hair is undone, and my face can no longer contain the emotions I have been holding back for so long.

I throw open the door and step out into the night. They wish to accuse me of murder. Then I will live up to the reputation. The full moon is all about releasing what we do not want, and I am about to get rid of everyone!

I am a woman
A necklace my weapon
I release my emotions
And the evil within

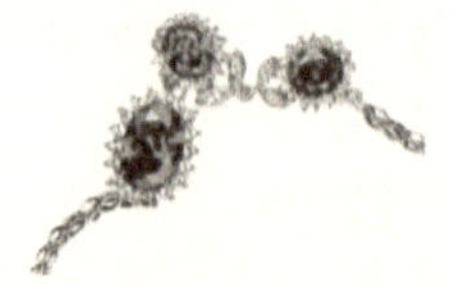

September 23, 1888
12:30 a.m.

Gus Bobellon is so intoxicated he does not hear me break the glass of his back window with the corn dryer and climb inside. I creep silently up the stairs to his room where I now watch him.

I stand in the darkness like Death. My back is against the wall of his sleeping chamber. I watch the murderer snore in his drunken state. I hear his heart beat. Its pulsations thrill me. For in moments, I will still that irritating racket as he stopped the heart of my beloved.

I am like a carrion bird standing close to the future carcass of my husband's killer.

I click my tongue. The drunken fool is so oblivious, he left the fireplace unattended. I stare at the flames flickering in the hearth, and the fire tells me that two hours ago Gus was not alone. Female companionship quenched his desires as surely as I will be quenched by his death.

He sleeps like a baby with no guilt in his soul. No remorse for what he has done. All he cared about was money. Our money! Our money he used to buy this house. Our money he used to get drunk. And our money he used to pay women for sinful acts.

The necklace glows, telling me to be patient. Like a lion stalking its prey, I hunt my victim.

I kick over the pedestal against the wall. The vase perched on its marble structure crashes to the ground. Water spreads over the floor and around my shoes. Roses litter on top of it, baring thorns.

The racket is enough to wake Gus. Rising to an upright position, he opens his eyes. In the moonlight that floods in from the large window, I see his pupils. I grow furious as I gaze at the gray irises, the portals to his cold and greedy soul.

He was the last person to see my Theo alive. He watched my husband take his last breath.

Snorting, Gus looks around the room in a daze. He squints and seems unsure if I am a figment of his intoxicated state or a real person. With my cloak over my head, my features are obscured.

I see his heavy lids close over those eyes. The beer takes control and he falls back against the pillows.

Deep in my bosom I have the urge to say something, but I know that words are of no use. He is not the one with whom I need to speak. He is a pawn in the master plan of someone of higher intellect.

My feet take control and my pace quickens as I grip the rod of the corn dryer. I am at his bedside. His snores anger me, ringing on my ears like a mockery of how this man got away with murder. Well, this time, the ending will be different.

I raise the corn dryer high over my head and bring the prongs down into his chest penetrating his heart. The blood spurts through my fingers, the vindication of a soul that has been taken in the heat of revenge.

Pulling a knife from the folds of my cloak, I cut out his heart. I do not know what has come over me, but the necklace tells me I am a conduit for justice. I feel an impulse I cannot ignore.

The fist-size glob is warm yet silent in my hands. I squeeze it and pull my arm back to my ear, then I thrust forward launching the heart into the fireplace flames. Falling onto the charred logs, the organ is hungrily consumed by the greedy blaze. The sight of the orange and gold flickers tearing apart the flesh of my husband's murderer fills me with joy.

I rejoice, but my work is not yet through. I look down at my hands stained with Gus's blood. *How unattractive!*

On the dresser, the water basin allows me to wash the horrendous act from my skin.

I feel a tightness around my throat. The necklace tells me our work here is not through. Walking towards the fireplace, I stand before the blaze. The remains of the heart sit on the hearth. They are now black, and chunks fall beneath the grate mixing with the ashes.

Whispering to me, the necklace assures me that I will not be burned, for I have unleashed the evil within my soul that has been longing to get out. I reach into the fire and pull on the flaming logs with my bare hands. I feel no pain. The sparks merely tickle like the tongue of a dog lapping my skin.

Turning, I throw the log onto the bed with the corpse. I throw another log onto the oriental rug and a final one at the far wall. The flames move from the burned timber to their new meals. Slowly, the conflagration takes over the room. I close the door, waltz down the stairs and exit the back doorway into the darkness of the night.

It is time for me to see the malefactor of this whole scheme.

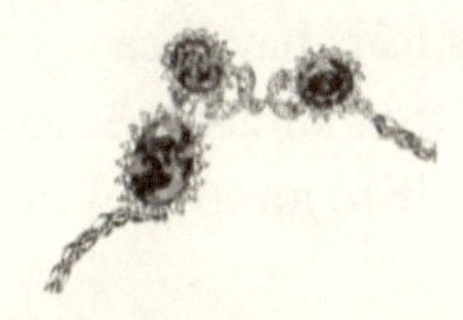

September 23, 1888
1:00 a.m.

Church bells chime as I make my way across town to my final victim. The moon is full. My body possesses the speed of horses as I run through the night. Soon the focus will be on the burning of Gus's house and no one will be suspecting what happens next.

At the Carmichael mansion, a different scene is unfolding. Ominous and dark, the edifice stands in silence. My lavaliere whispers that the servants have been given the night off. I am grateful. I do not wish Olivia to be witness to the acts I am about to commit. Mutterings from the necklace also reveal that Mildred's father is out of town on business, and her fiancé is in Scotland meeting a client. The mastermind of the blackmailing scheme, the woman of envy, is inside, and this time I will confront her.

I find the spare key under the mat and let myself in. Breaking glass would not be the best course of action, the necklace tells me Mildred is not asleep. I stand a moment and admire the beauty of the elegant home. Such a shame it will soon be gone.

I glide up the massive stairs and pause before Mildred's door. I sense she feels unsettled. Quietly I turn the knob and crack the door. The room is dark but the French doors that lead to the balcony are open, and Mildred stands against the balustrade. Her figure is basked in moonlight. She wrings her hands. The lavaliere whispers how Mildred's fears have been growing within her soul since her cousin committed an act she never wished to happen. Each noise causes her body to jump forward as she paces back and forth.

I slip into the bedroom and darkness cloaks me from Mildred's gaze.

"What is that?" She whispers. "Oh, it is an owl hooting in the trees. It is a raccoon in the bushes. It is a bat flying past." Mildred folds her arms against her body and looks up at the full moon. "Why did you have to be so stubborn, Theo? You should have just given Gus the money. You should have just married me. Me! I was the better woman."

Poor woman, she is trying to convince herself this murder was justified. But it is all in vain. For Death stands before her in its black cloak waiting to envelope her victim.

I step from the shadows of the bedroom onto the balcony, my body bathed in moonlight. I close the doors behind me.

"Who are you?" whispers Mildred. Her eyes widen.

"The woman of lower class." I reply, pulling back my hood to show my face. Mildred's fear turns to disgust.

"Anna Cooper! What brings you to my bedchamber tonight? How improper this is. But after all, what can you expect from a former factory girl?" Cries Mildred.

My lips part revealing my teeth. "My apologies, Mildred Carmichael. Would you rather my husband keep you company in your bed instead?"

Her eyes narrow. "What are you talking about?"

"I am talking about blackmail. How for years you forced my husband to give you money to keep the secret of his lineage quiet. But what you really wanted was for him to marry you. He embarrassed you by leaving you for a woman of lower rank as you so nicely put it. You cared only for your reputation. You did not care about the money. Your cousin Gus did! In fact, he was the one who invented the idea of a monthly payment. You just wanted a ring. But a ring you will never get."

Mildred moves off the rail and swaggers towards me. We are face to face.

"I was courted by Theodore first, and I would have had him eating out of the palm of my hand if he had not noticed you during an inspection of the factories. I was supposed to be Mrs. Cooper, not you. You may have a ring, but that ring is worthless now. Theodore Cooper is dead. My reputation has been restored. This is why men need to marry women of their own class."

I move to strike but the necklace tightens against my throat cutting my air. The lavaliere tells me to wait, for Mildred is not through confessing the evils that lurk in her soul. The jewelry relaxes and I breathe again.

She takes a step closer to me. "Theodore deserved better than you! You are a worthless woman, five years and you were unable to bear him an offspring of his own. Your only child lies in the grave with your husband..."

Mildred does not get a chance to finish because my fist collides with the side of her face. She stumbles and falls to the ground. I feel strength fill my muscles and run along my veins with a power I have never experienced before. I feel like I could pull this entire balcony off the side of the house if I needed to.

"I am summoning the police. I will have you thrown in jail. Get mad all you want. It does not change the fact that your womb bears death instead of life."

My body freezes before her. *Jack.* Mine and Theo's only child died when he was two months old. No one knew why.

Rubies and diamonds reassure me that there is nothing wrong with my body. The murderer of my baby is in front of me. Whispers in my head reveal to me that when I had gone into town two years ago for an appointment, I left Theo home with the baby. During my absence, Mildred had stopped by to offer her congratulations. She gave Theo some milk for the baby. Just enough for the baby and no one else. The milk had been poisoned, causing Jack to die.

I stare into her vengeful eyes. She fancies herself so proud that she had taken away the two people that meant the most to me. Little does she know those who choose to take life must be prepared to face the consequences.

"You did it," I whisper. "You killed my baby and my husband."

Her smug expression is the only answer I need. Before I can react, she leaps to her feet knocking me off-balance. Grabbing one of the plants on the balcony, she swings it at me. I duck. She runs towards the closed balcony doors, but I catch her before her fingers touch the handles. Mildred screams, but there is no one around to hear her.

Death has come for her soul.

I pull the knife from the folds of my cloak and silence her heart. Then I place her on top of my shoulder and carry her over to the railing where I throw her onto the gravel below. I hear the corpse hit the ground with a thud. Looking over I see Mildred's limbs splayed out at awkward angles and her hair is spread around her head like a ring of light.

The power of the necklace deals justice. A soul for a soul.

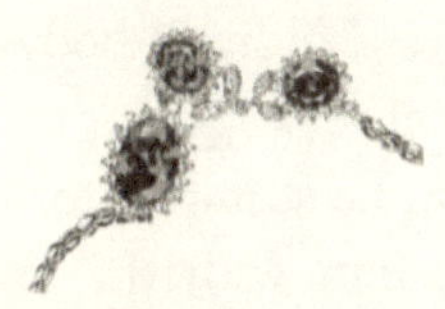

September 23, 1888
4:30 a.m.

Throwing Mildred's corpse off the balcony was not in vain, for I did not wish to drag blood all over the house.

My necklace commands that I must bring her body to the graveyard a few streets away. Her frame feels light around my shoulders and my feet are quick. The powers of the jewelry allow me to run in the shadows so I am not seen by any passersby. But at predawn hours, I do not anticipate anyone being out, only those with evil in their souls like myself.

Vindication! My heart rejoices as the iron gates open, inviting me into the place of eternal rest. The gravestones stand like sentinels while the watchful wind whispers words of comfort to the deceased.

I walk the rows until I find the grave. It is the place where my husband was supposed to be buried in a few days. I drop Mildred's corpse onto the dewy grass.

Touching the necklace, I replay the words of Persephone the day she found me with Theo's body. I have taken the wicked souls. Now I shall be rewarded for my ordeal.

I close my eyes and I see Theo's body lying in the morgue. I call to it.

"This soul I claim! Come back to me!" I cry.

The wind rushes around me in a vortex. It pulls my cloak off my head. I open my eyes. Mildred's body is gone, and standing before me is Theo! He is alive!

His hair is messy and he stumbles forward a bit dazed. I run into his arms and hug him with the love of a devoted wife. "Theo!"

"My darling," says my husband.

What a blessing to hear his sweet voice again.

"Theo," I continue gripping the folds of his lapels. "I know about everything."

His eyes are glazed. "What?"

"I know about your family. I know about your mother. You never had to lie to me, darling. I do not care about your past. I love you for you, and you would never lose me. Not for anything."

A small smile crosses his face. He pulls me close. I feel his weight heavy against me and he sinks to the ground. His eyes close.

A cold sweat breaks out over my body. *Have I lost him again?* Placing my ear to his chest, the sound of his heartbeat soothes my fears. The lavaliere reassures me that reawakening after death can cause the body to go into shock.

I caress his face as he lies peacefully in the wet grass. It is perfect timing for I would have suffered a great consternation trying to explain to him what I was about to do next. I walk along the row of headstones of past family members until I reach the one I seek. I have taken two souls. I have one more soul to exchange. I stand before the small head-stone. It reads:

Our Baby
Jack Theodore Cooper
July 1, 1886 - September 9, 1886

Tears sting the corners of my eyes and a few drops fall onto the Hosta plant that I had placed in the dirt before the tombstone. I kneel and place my hand on the marker and whisper, "This soul I claim. Come back to me."

I do not feel any wind. I look around and I see nothing. Have I done something wrong? I feel my heart sink into my stomach and my legs feel weak. A soul for a soul does not seem to be working. Maybe some souls cannot be brought back.

Trembling, I stand and begin to walk towards my unconscious husband when the necklace tightens against my throat so hard, I stop and grab the chain. It relaxes and I hear a noise. A soft sound, like a whimper, a cry.

I walk back to the Hosta plant and the gurgling increases.

Moving the large green leaves aside reveals a baby wrapped in a blanket. I look down into the child's face and realize it is *my* baby, my Jack.

Scooping the child into my arms, I plant kisses over his angelic face. My child taken from me too soon is now returned to me. I nuzzle my face against his cheeks, breathing in his scent that I never thought I would smell again. Tears mix with my lashes, and I feel my heart will burst with joy.

Running to my husband, I kneel down and shake him. "Theo, Theo wake up!" His eyes open and I help him to stand.

"Where are we?" He asks again, running his fingers through his hair. "Have we been out all night?"

"It is a long story but we decided to take a night stroll to help our son fall asleep." I pass the blanket over to Theo, and he takes it as if Jack has been here all along.

I realize the necklace also has the power of obscuring time. Theo does not remember his son as dead. Only I have that memory, and it is the ghost of an illusion I wish never to relive again.

As the sun begins to rise over the hilltops, we walk home together, a family, happily united in the arms of love.

September 30, 1888
11:00 a.m.

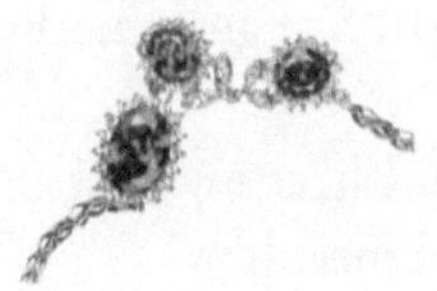

It has been about a week since the incident and the magic of the necklace has worked wonders. No one remembers Jack or Theo ever being dead. The fire at Gus's house which resulted in his death was ruled as accidental caused by an unattended fire. Mildred's body magically returned to the house after the exchange and her knife wound was concealed by the magic of the necklace. Her death was also ruled as accidental from the fall off the balcony.

There are no words to describe how happy I am. My soul is finally at peace. Theo is out for the day ,and I stand at my son's cradle watching him sleep.

"Hello Anna," a voice calls.

I turn to see Persephone step out of the shadows. "I see we meet again, under different circumstances this time." She stands before me. "Did you get everything you wanted?"

Smiling, I nod, "Yes, everything I wanted and more."

Persephone's lips part into a grin. "Wonderful!" She holds out her hand to me. "Then I believe we can pass this onto the next person who needs aid."

"Oh, I cannot remove it," I reply, running my fingers along the rubies and diamonds. "The clasp is stuck."

"Not anymore."

I reach my fingers behind my neck and unlock the little clip. Placing the beautiful lavaliere in Persephone's palm, I feel a mixture of sadness and relief. Gemstones sparkle in the old woman's hand, and transform into a long scythe. A black hood and cloak clothe her body. She gives me a wink and I am alone in the room.

The door opens and I hear my husband call my name. I pick up baby Jack and walk to meet him.

I had my dance with Death! Now it is time to live!

The End

Death Bashes a Bracelet

October 1, 1888
2:00 p.m.

I *never thought my life would turn out like this.*
I sit on the park bench and pull the tattered coat closer around my body. The chill of Autumn whips through the park taking control of the kites as the children giggle and laugh.

My stomach growls.

I do not know where I will sleep tonight. I have spent a few weeks on my friend Alfie's couch but that ended last month. I could not inconvenience him any longer. I am embarrassed as a twenty-three-year-old man to be in this predicament.

Years ago, my mother died unexpectedly. I miss her every day. Then I injured my arm at the factory and could not work. This resulted in me losing my job. I could not afford the rent on my flat and was forced to vacate. To make matters worse, my fiancée

Jessica, broke our engagement and ran off with my best friend Bart.

Heartbroken, homeless, and hungry, I lurk the streets in search of a bite to eat and shelter. People in the East End of London are kind and give me what they can. I found a group of homeless people who live in the alley between Cavell Street and Park Street. They let me stay with them some nights under the make-shift tents of blankets and sheets.

During the day, I work odd jobs to make a few coins. I am limited by the injury to my shoulder and arm. The pain still ebbs and flows, making work difficult. I have no family, barely any friends. I have no one to rely on except myself.

This is not how life was supposed to be. I should have a profitable job. I should be living in my own house. I should be married by now. Is this how the rest of my life is going to be? Am I going to die an impoverished soul?

As if in answer to my thoughts, a chilly wind rushes past me. It blows my dark hair and I feel it seep into my bones through the holes in my coat.

"Life is quite interesting, isn't it?" a cool voice declares next to me.

Turning, I see a woman sitting on the bench beside me. She is an old peddler woman. A gray dress clothes her thin frame. The handkerchief in her white hair is adorned with ashes. She pulls her navy shawl tighter around her body.

"Oliver Gray." Her voice drips sweet like honey but with an icy chill to it.

Goosebumps break out along my skin and shivers run rampant down my spine.

Do I know her? I do not know her. Yet I feel like I know her.

Across her lap lays a staff that resembles a serpent. Her forehead creases as she smiles at me.

"Who are you?" I ask.

"Oh, Oliver, you don't remember me? Why, I have known you since you were a little boy."

I scratch my head. "I am sorry. I don't..."

"I knew your mother, Odessa Gray. May her soul rest in peace. I could not help but hear your plea as I walked by."

I was talking out loud?

"Life is quite the challenge is it not? We grow up having our whole lives planned out. We think about what kind of job we will have, the age we will marry and have children. Then life decides to whack us with a broom and change our whole plan. I feel bad for you, Oliver. All alone, no family, your heart broken by your wretched fiancée. Your best friend betrayed you. You lost your job, your arm injured. Tisk Tisk. This is not how a young handsome man, like yourself, should be spending his life. That is why I am going to help you."

"What?"

The woman brushes soot off her dress. "Yes, Oliver, I am going to help you. Here, have some bread. You look hungry." She pulls from her bag, a tantalizing baguette and places it into my hands.

I thank her and greedily rip apart the loaf like an animal. The tender flaky crust touches my tongue and I realize how famished I am.

"I am going to give you a job. I need you to deliver a package to someone. It will be worth your while."

"Alright, where will I be going?"

"You will leave London tonight. It will be a four-day trip. You will be delivering the package to Lord Homer Harrington at Oakenfield Castle. He is expecting this delivery. Once you have placed this item into his care, I will pay you a hefty sum."

"I agree." I reply covering my mouth with my hands so I do not spit pieces of bread onto her dress. "But who are you?"

The woman's eyes narrow as she looks me up and down. "My name is Persephone. I must warn you this task will not be easy."

"How hard is it to deliver a parcel to a Lord?" *This bread is good.*

"Ah, dear Oliver, the story has only just begun. You will find the outcome from this venture will be worth more to you than money."

Worth more than money? How can that be possible? I need money to survive.

Persephone stands and walks around me, holding her staff in her hand.

"It appears we do have some fixing to do. You have become quite broken for such a young man."

She taps my injured arm with the snake head of her staff. I feel a warm tingle rush from my forearm through my hand, upper arm, and shoulder. It is a calming sensation, washing away the pain and stimulating my muscles. I feel a strength penetrate into my blood. Youth and good health have returned to me.

I gasp and pull back my arm. *No pain.* I move my elbow back and forth, then up and down. Nothing. I am healed.

"What did you do?" I ask.

"Just an old remedy. You must be ready to fight, so I cannot have your injuries make you vulnerable."

"What are you talking about? You said I am going to deliver a package for money. Why would I need to fight?" The hair on the back of my neck stands on end. I have a suspicion there is more to Persephone than she is letting on.

"One more thing," Persephone stands next to me and taps the top of my head with her finger twice. A cooling vibration runs down my spine. I look down at my dirty hands to find they are clean. Placing my fingers on my face, I feel smooth shaven skin instead of the grubby beard. My tattered jacket is gone and has been replaced by a black tail-coat and expensive trousers.

I leap to my feet. "What kind of witchcraft is this? Who are you?"

"I am who I said I am. You should be grateful. Not everyone gets this kind of treatment from me. After all, you represent me now, and I could not have you going to see the lord with your previous attire."

"I cannot afford these clothes. I will not steal them."

"So many equivocations, Oliver! Consider them a gift from me to you." Before I can open my mouth she continues. "Do not worry. Soon I shall exact a payment from you. Now, stop dilly-dallying and look at yourself in the pond." She points towards the water.

Hesitantly, I walk over to the shimmering pool. Taking a breath, I bend over and look at my reflection in the water. I see a man. A man in an expensively tailored waistcoat and trousers. A handsome man. A man who looks like he comes from wealth. That man is me.

This is how I always envisioned myself to look, not a homeless man in poverty living on the streets.

I look back at Persephone who flashes me a smile. "How do you feel?"

"I feel..." my voice trails off as I am at a loss for words. I had never been one to pour out my feelings.

Persephone places her hand under her chin and stares at me. "I see. The exterior is not always enough to fix the interior. While you look the part of a man who comes from wealth, it is not enough to mend your broken heart and salve your sense of betrayal from the world letting you down. Do not worry, time heals all wounds. You are very handsome, and I am certain the ladies will be taking notice."

She pushes an envelope into my hands. "Here is the money that will cover your stagecoach fare for the trip, food, and whatever else you will need." She waves her hand and a French Victorian jewelry box appears between her fingers.

I stuff the envelope into the interior pocket of my coat. Taking the jewelry box from her hands, I can feel it is metal, but it's painted in a faux wood finish. The delicate prize is trimmed in bronze with intricate gold designs etched along the top and sides. In the center is a gold lock waiting for a key to open it.

"It is beautiful, is it not?" says Persephone. She touches the box and it becomes encased in brown paper wrapping. She places it into a knapsack.

"Are you a witch?" I ask. "Am I dreaming?"

Persephone chuckles. "I am far from a witch. They are much nicer. You could say I am a bit misunderstood by the population."

"But you just performed magic?"

"I did nothing of the sort. You see only what your mind wishes you to see, dear. Now do be careful with this parcel. It is very expensive. We cannot call attention to thieves. Lord Harrington has the key and he will open the box once you bring it to him. Remember, turn to the left."

"What is inside?"

"Something whose value is worth as much as this life. A great gift that the soul craves, an opening to magnificent treasure. Now, head to the stagecoach depot. You do not want to miss the next departure." She thrusts the knapsack into my hands. Through the opening I see the words *Lord Harrington* scrawled in fancy calligraphy.

"I still do not understand why you want me to partake in this journey." I look up. Persephone is gone.

October 5, 1888
3:00 p.m.

What am I doing? I do not even know this woman? Yet I am putting my trust in her?

Four days on a bumpy carriage have given me plenty of time to drive myself crazy. I have an expensive jewelry box in my knapsack, money in my pocket, and I have no idea who Persephone is, or where a woman with ashes in her hair can offer a gift of such exquisite design and character.

She is a peddler woman! Her clothes are covered in soot, yet she can afford an expensive jewelry box like that and money! I thought. Not to mention the way she changed my clothes with a flick of her fingers. There is something not right about that woman. But I am desperate. I need money.

Thankfully, she healed my arm, so after this whole venture, I should be able to find a decent paying job again.

After crossing a narrow one-way bridge, the stagecoach pulls up to a tall iron gate. Through the bars, I see a path that leads to an enormous mansion. Guards stand in front. As I step out of the coach with only my knapsack, they look at me up and down.

I barely close the door before the driver cracks the reins and the horses take off down the one-way path. As I watch them ride off into the distance, I think about the carriage driver. He was a bit odd. He had not spoken the entire ride.

A wide brimmed hat covered his face in shadows, but I could not see his eyes, for they were sunken. The skin over his cheeks was drawn tight. His hands were bony.

"What do you want?" One of the guards snaps at me.

"I am here to see Lord Homer Harrington. I am here to deliver a package."

Nodding, the guard pulls a key from his pocket and opens the large barrier. He pushes it back a ways for me to scoot by. "Carry on."

"Thank you." I reply. No sooner do I set foot on the grounds than I hear the fence clang behind me and the lock click shut.

An uneasiness quivers in the pit of my stomach but I ignore it. Think about the money, Oliver. You will be able to have a place of your own and find a new job.

I walk down the long path towards the mansion. This is the most beautiful house I have ever seen. The edifice is built of stone blocks with multiple pointy turrets and grandiose arches that stretch towards the sky. The castle looks as if a person of royal rank should be living there instead of a mere lord.

The crimson exterior accents the gothic style architecture. Looking at the ancient and portentous home, I cannot help but feel as if the palace is shrouded in secrecy. There seems to be a cloud of darkness and an aura of phantasmagorical proportions within its walls.

I walk down the cobblestone path past the well-manicured

lawns and flower beds. This castle is set on many acres, but there only seems to be one way in and one way out. More guards line the long stone steps that lead to the door. Their eyes watch my every move, but their lips remain sealed. Two of the soldiers open the door and I step into a long hallway.

The ceilings are arched and high. Large columns sit on either side of narrow windows. A few patches of sunlight create patterns on the floor, but the place is dark and gloomy. Soldiers line the room. They are dressed in red uniforms, and silver swords hang from their sides, awaiting the command to be drawn.

My stomach is in knots. I feel as if I have stepped into another world. I feel I am no longer in London, but grandeur speaks of aristocratic importance.

At the end of the room, three steps lead to a red velvet-covered throne. Sitting on the throne is an imposing figure, a man bald as a billiard with a glint in his eyes. His face presents a brush-like beard, speckled with shades of red and brown. He is wearing a well-embellished tunic with gold stitching and trousers. A robe encircles his body.

"Who are you?" asks the man. "How did you find this place?"

"The carriage took me here, sir," I reply as I walk down the aisle and stand before him. "I am looking for Lord Homer Harrington."

"That is I? Why do you ask?"

"I was sent here to deliver a package to you, good sir." I pull from my knapsack the jewelry box. "A woman named Persephone instructed me to give this to you."

Lord Harrington's eyes widen. He strokes his beard. "Persephone?"

As I am about to hand over the box, an arched door to the right side of the throne opens, and a shadow steps out of the darkness into the dim light.

It is a woman. The most beautiful woman I have ever seen in my life! Long dark hair falls over her slender shoulders to her waist. A yellow dress clothes her body cinching her small torso.

Her lips are red, a diamond headpiece adorned with large rubies is woven into her hair. A single rose is clasped in her hand.

She lifts her head and our eyes meet. My heart thumps wildly against my chest and my mouth is dry. I need water but even more, I crave the mysterious woman's lips against mine.

Oh, how I would love to be that rose in between her fingers!

"The package, Mr...um...what is your name?" Lord Harrington's voice cut into my thoughts.

I turn to look at him. "Oliver...Oliver Gray, sir."

"Well, Mr. Gray, would you be so kind as to hand over this box?"

"Yes, of course, your lordship." I ascend the steps and place the box into his lap.

I look up in search of the woman but she has vanished. *Where did she go?*

Stepping back in front of the lord, I look all around for traces of the beautiful woman. Nothing.

Meanwhile, Lord Harrington's fingers dig into the package, ripping away the brown paper. He shouts when the jewelry box is exposed. "At last! At last! It is finally mine!

But I do not understand. You are not the person who was supposed to bring me this. Never mind. Who you are is not an issue of any importance."

Reaching into his tunic he pulls out a long chain. At the end is a silver key. He inserts it into the lock. There is a small click and the top of the box pops open.

Reaching inside, he pulls out a small velvet bag. Opening it, a gold bracelet drops into his palm. Holding it up to the dim lighting, he squints his eyes and observes the trinket.

"This is not The Tear of Erisa! What kind of trick are you trying to employ?" He yells.

I step back startled by his aggressive outburst. "What are you talking about? I did not know the contents of this box! You have the only key!"

"You are a liar! You must have stolen it! Guards!"

The soldiers come alive from their motionless stances. They surround me.

"Listen, you do not understand," I cry. "I have no idea what was supposed to be in the contents of that box. I told you, a woman named Persephone gave me the package and instructed me to deliver it to you!"

"Persephone? I do not know a woman by that name. Dabria was the one who was supposed to deliver the package to me. Not a man named Oliver Gray! Lock him up in the dungeons until I can figure this out."

"This is preposterous!" I feel the soldiers' hands seize my arm. I try to shake them off but there are too many. They grab me and take me through a door on the opposite side of the room into the darkness.

October 5, 1888
9:00 p.m.

I sit on the dirt floor in my new surroundings. The castle dungeon. Chains anchored to the stone wrap around my wrists. I squint my eyes in the dim light. At the opposite end of the room are steps leading up to a solid door. My chains will only allow me to move very little distance.

I groan and pound my fist into the dirt. *How could I have been so foolish? I should have known better than to let a stranger talk me into doing a job like this!*

A spider crawls near my shoe. I brush it away. In the darkness my thoughts drift to my mother. She would know what to do. She always had the answer to all of my problems. I miss her.

I hear the click of a lock and a shadow appears at the door.

Closing it shut, the figure seems to float down the steps toward me.

"You are in quite a predicament aren't you, sir?" A feminine voice speaks out. The silhouette steps into the light to reveal herself to be the woman from the throne room. In her hands she holds a tray.

"I brought you something to eat," she says, placing it on the floor.

I stand up and nod my head. "Thank you."

Now that she is closer to me, she looks familiar, but I am unsure if she is the same person. Wearing a tight red dress with a plunging neckline, her dark hair is drawn back into a neat chignon with curls framing her face. Pearls embroider her hair.

"It is a shame to see such a handsome man wasting away in this filthy torture chamber." She takes another step closer to me and I take a step back. I feel my body come in contract with the stone wall.

"Who are you?" I ask. "Did I not see you in the throne room?"

The woman narrows her eyes. "You dare compare me to that woman? No, I was too busy to watch Lord Harrington entertain visitors." She runs her finger down my arm. "You are very strong. Just how I like it."

Chills break out along my skin, and I try to evade her touch, but the chains stop me.

"I am Huxleigh," the woman continues. She leans closer to me, her face inches from mine. "I will make sure you get out. You will be quite useful around the castle." She pulls back and leaves the chamber.

I sink down the wall to the floor. I know that woman is not the same one I had laid eyes on in the throne room. But her features are so similar. How could it not be the same woman? Yet this lady has a curious mystique about her. She is beautiful, yes, but beneath her porcelain skin I feel evil runs unbridled in her soul.

A prisoner
Of mind
Body
And soul
I long to taste freedom

October 5, 1888
10:00 p.m.

"Oliver, really, when I told you to deliver the package, I did not tell you to get yourself thrown into the dungeon." A voice calls to me.

I do not know if it is day or night. The faint light of the airless cell dances around me. I open my eyes. I must have fallen asleep.

Persephone stands before me.

"You!" I cry jumping to my feet. I try to run at her but the chains hold me back. "You tricked me!"

"Life can be quite tricky at times if you do not know your purpose. I did not deceive. I merely tested your auditory skills at which you failed," replied Persephone. "Oh, my! It is rather dingy in here."

She waves her hands, and a gaslamp appears in the center of the room. It is a small lantern, but the open flame flickering in the glass floods the entire cell in light.

"I did what you asked. I gave him the box. There was a substitute bracelet in it. He said it was supposed to be the Tear of Erisa. What is the Tear of Erisa?" I replied. My chest heaves as I try to control myself. My life was already in shambles and this woman is doing more harm than good.

Persephone chuckles. "You will find out soon enough, dear."

"Lord Harrington also said that a woman named Dabria was supposed to deliver the package to him, not me."

"How amusing. Homer should be grateful I chose to give him the Tear of Erisa. But there are consequences to every action, which he will find out soon enough," replies Persephone.

"Who is Dabria?" I repeat.

Persephone raises an eyebrow at me. "Oliver, you know I cannot let any random person know my identity. Only a chosen few receive that privilege." She holds out her hands and the box appears in them.

I step back. "You *are* a witch!"

Persephone chuckles. "Far from it." She walks closer to me and points to the box. "I replaced The Tear of Erisa with a bracelet of rather insignificant value to deter thieves." She puts the package in my hands. "Here, open it."

She waves her hand and a key appears in it. She places it into my fingers.

I hesitate as I look at the key in my palm.

"What is the matter? I said open it." Persephone urges.

"Why should I trust you?" I reply. "After all, I am in this predicament because of you!" Shifting the box to one arm, I use my free hand to gesture toward the dark chamber to emphasize my current situation.

"Well you are in quite a jam. I do not see any practical way for you to get out except with my help." Persephone glances down at the chains fastened to my wrists. "My, you do always find yourself in quite a pickle don't you, boy." She places her hands over the cuffs and the chains fall onto the floor. I am free.

"Now do you trust me?" She asks.

I move my wrists in a circle. They feel tight. "Thank you," I reply. At this point, I know better than to ask Persephone about her bewitching ways.

I sigh. Persephone is infuriating. But she did free me. I have no choice but to trust her. I insert the key into the lock and turn it. The lid pops open and I see an empty velvet interior.

"There is nothing in here," I reply.

"That is because you are turning the key to the *right*. You did not listen to me when I gave you the instructions. I told you to turn it to the *left.*" She reminds me.

"Locks do not turn to the left."

"I said, turn it to the left," repeats the mysterious woman.

I close the lid and reinsert the key into the lock. I turn it to the left expecting to be met with a block but instead, the key moves smoothly and I hear another click. A hidden compartment pops out and inside is a bracelet.

It is a gold bangle bracelet that is covered in blue sapphires cut into the shape of teardrops. The jewels are surrounded by old rose cut diamonds forming the shape of a flower.

"This is the Tear of Erisa." Declared Persephone. "Many times in life, thinking realistically and logically is not always the best way. Sometimes we have to take a leap of faith and follow our heart."

"What is the Tear of Erisa?" I ask.

"It is a long story. But now is not the time. You will later learn the importance of this ornament."

She moves closer to me and looks into my eyes. "You miss your mother, don't you?"

I look at her and my eyes widen. It is as if she had read my thoughts from earlier. I nod my head. "Yes. I wish illness had never taken her."

"Was it really an illness?" Persephone tilts her head and places her hand on my chest. "Your heart is broken, too."

I look away. I do not wish her to see my emotions, but somehow I feel she can see into my soul.

"You are a good man. You deserve to love and to be loved. I have a gift for you."

She opens her palm and in it is a gold bracelet. I lean closer and realize it is a gate bracelet.

The chain is thick and made of a series of interlocking gold links. Each panel is coated in tiny raised diamonds. At the base of the trinket is a large heart-shaped lock. Intricate designs are engraved into the precious metal.

"A gate bracelet?" I ask. "For me?"

Persephone nods. "Do you know why the links on these bracelets are called "gates?" Originally they were supposed to mirror the fences of the English countryside, but in reality, they represent the gates that block our chances at finding True Love. Doubt, jealousy, hatred, betrayal, and pain are only some of the challenges that prevent ourselves from letting our hearts love fully.

I shake my head. "This is a bracelet for women."

"Not really, Oliver," she replies. "Yes, women are known to wear gate bracelets more often than men. But it is a bracelet for lovers. For anyone who desires True Love."

Persephone moves closer to me. "I see the pain in your eyes, Oliver. You must let it go. Jessica was not your true love. She did you a favor by running off with your best friend. Neither are worthy of your loyalty or love."

I wipe my eye pretending it is dust.

"Do you know how a gate bracelet works?" continues Persephone.

"It is meant for lovers when they are to spend a long period apart."

"Exactly. One person wears the bracelet while the other one holds the key. Once the bracelet is on the wrist and the padlock-style fastening closes, the ornament cannot be opened until the key is inserted into the lock. This is why it is in the shape of a heart, for true lovers hold the key to each other's souls."

I huff and roll my eyes. "That kind of legend is meant for fairytales."

"Actually, I think it is quite romantic," replies Persephone. Before I can react, the trickster woman wraps the gate bracelet around my wrist closing the heart-shaped lock.

"Persephone! What have you done?" I cry as the links jingle on my wrist. "Where is the key?"

"I do not have it."

"Well, how am I supposed to remove this?"

"You cannot. Your true love is the only one who can release you from this imprisonment."

"I do not have a lover," I hiss.

"Everyone has a lover," states Persephone.

"Indeed! Who is she?" I demand.

"You haven't met yours yet. You and your true love have been apart for too long. Your soulmate is the one who holds the key. And as the tale states, the bracelet can only be removed when the lovers have returned to each other's arms." She sighs. "In my line of work, you do not get to see romance every day. Loneliness can be quite depressing."

"What exactly do you do, Persephone? Who are you?" I seethe. This ridiculous bracelet has made me a prisoner. I can only imagine how I would look once I return to the city. A homeless man with an expensive heart-shaped bracelet around his wrist.

The old woman chuckles. A smile spreads across her lips. "You will find out soon enough, my dear. What if I told you I know a way for you to get back everything you have lost?"

"What do you mean?" I narrow my eyes. This peddler woman has done nothing but make my life more difficult. I should have gone back to the alley and stayed with my homeless companions. My mother was not joking when she said money could make a man do crazy things.

"In life we must give a little to take a little. All the important things in your life that you have lost can be restored, but you must do an exchange."

I tilt my head. "What kind of exchange?"

"A soul for a soul."

"What on earth are you talking about, woman? You must be mad."

Persephone smirks. "You heard me, Oliver. A soul for a soul. To return a life, a life must be taken." She walks to the gaslamp burning on the floor. Reaching her fingers inside the looking glass she touches the flame.

My eyes widen and I tense my body to rush forward to stop her, but her skin does not catch fire. From the flames she pulls out a knife and walks toward me.

"I am going to resolve everything for you now, but please, dear, try to stay out of trouble. Remember, a soul for a soul," Persephone whispers.

Before I can comprehend her words, she sticks the knife into my gut.

October 6, 1888
6:00 a.m.

I feel satin against my cheek and something brushes my chin. I groan.

Ugh. That blasted woman stabbed me. Why did I choose to get mixed up with such a bewitching lady like Persephone? I do not even know her last name. I do not know where she lives. I know nothing about her... I pause in my thoughts. I am wounded yet I feel no pain. Excellent. I think to myself. I must be dead.

I open my eyes to the loveliest sight. A woman sits in a chair near me. My eyes rove around the room. I am no longer in the dungeon cell. I am in a canopy bed. A fireplace is nearby with flames crackling in the hearth.

Blinking my eyes, I squint to look at the woman sitting in the chair. It is the woman from the throne room. Her black hair falls

96

to her waist obscuring her face as she looks down at the book she is reading. *Strange Case of Dr. Jekyll and Mr. Hyde.* Interesting choice.

She bites her red lips as she gazes intently at the pages. Her diamond headpiece glistens in the light of the gas lamps.

The events of last night come to me, and I slide my fingers down to my stomach. I rub my palms against my skin. There is no wound, no bandage, and no pain. I am healed. But I could have sworn Persephone impaled me with the knife.

My stirring causes the beautiful woman to look up. She snaps the book shut and moves closer to my bedside.

"You are awake." She reaches over to the basin on the dresser and takes a wet washcloth. She places it on my head.

"Who are you?" I stammer.

The woman smiles sweetly at me. "I am Averie. I am Lord Harrington's daughter. She takes a glass of water off the bureau and hands it to me.

"You must be thirsty."

Nodding, I take the water and raise the glass to my lips. I hear a jingle. Looking down I see the gate bracelet on my wrist. A reminder of the prisoner I now am.

The glittering object has also caught Averie's attention. "That is a beautiful bracelet," she remarks.

Before I can reply, the door bursts open and Lord Harrington enters the room with two guards by his side.

He strokes his beard. "I see you are feeling better, my good man." He stands next to my bedside. He must have seen the confused look on my face because he chuckles. "You collapsed in the throne room after handing over the package. Journeys that last for days can take a lot out of a person. Dr. Morris said you must have been suffering from dehydration and lack of food. He will come visit you for another examination in a bit."

Lord Harrington walks to the door and pauses, his hand on the door handle. "Thank you for your help delivering The Tear of Erisa safely. I thought Dabria was assigned to deliver the box, then

I remember she sent me a message stating that as her assistant, you would deliver the parcel instead. You are welcome to stay as long as you like. We do not get many visitors out this way. Averie, come along. Let the man rest."

With a nod. He walks out of the room. The guards follow behind him.

Averie stands up from her chair and smooths out her skirts. She gives me a parting glance with her chocolate eyes. A small smile spreads across her face. My heart skips a beat. She follows after her father.

I settle beneath the covers as the door closes. It appears Persephone has repaired all the damage, but I still do not trust her.

October 6, 1888
10:00 p.m.

Rain beats against the window panes and the wind howls. I lie on my back with my eyes closed. I am asleep but not quite asleep. Visions roll through my mind: the death of my mother, the betrayal of my fiancée and best friend, and the beautiful woman Averie.

I hear a creak of a door opening. However, I am too tired to raise my head and open the burgundy curtains that surround me. I feel the bed bow from the weight of something.

"Oliver" a voice hisses.

I take a deep breath and ignore it. All I can think about is running my fingers through Averie's dark hair.

"Oliver, wake up." the voice commands.

Groggy, I open my eyes as I feel cold steel against my throat.

Sitting on top of me is Huxleigh holding a blade exceedingly close to my jugular vein.

"What in the world.." I gasp.

Huxleigh's eyes are dark as she glares at me. "Where is it?"

"Where is what? Why have you taken that most unbecoming attitude? And kindly remove that knife from my person."

Smiling a glittering flash of her canine teeth, she withdraws the weapon and plays with its edge between her fingers. "It is gone."

"What is gone?"

"The Tear of Erisa."

I clear my throat and hold my hand to my neck. I am grateful to feel the skin still intact.

"The bracelet?"

"Yes, the bracelet. It is not just any ornament. That trinket is the key to finding the treasure."

"I believe it is in Lord Harrington's possession now," I reply.

Huxleigh leans closer to me until her lips are inches from mine. "It is gone. Someone has stolen it." She reclines back on her heels as thunder cracks outside the window. "You are going to help me find it" She glances at the blade.

"Otherwise, I am going to kill you."

A shiver runs down my spine. *Did she just say she is going to kill me?* Before I can reply, she hops through the curtains and off my bed. I hear the door slam shut.

My heart is in my throat and I clasp my hands to my chest. The reality sets in that I could have had my throat slit a few minutes ago. I sit up and look at the curtains. *Have I been dreaming? Nothing feels real.*

I roll onto my side. First thing tomorrow morning, I am getting out of here! At this point I don't know who is more mad, Huxleigh or Persephone.

October 7, 1888
7:00 a.m.

*B*ang!
The door to my chamber bursts open and a guard yells, "Wake up! Put on something decent and report to the throne room at once!"

What is going on?

I change back into my elegant attire. Snatching my knapsack and throwing it onto my back, I walk toward the door. *As soon as I find out what Lord Harrington wants I am out of here.* My fingers grasp the knob tightly and I pull open the heavy oak barricade. A guard stands against the wall. He escorts me to the throne room.

As we arrive into the massive chamber, I see several of the staff carrying something on a stretcher past us. The object is covered by a white sheet.

Lord Harrington is pacing in front of his throne. Built into the wall next to the regal chair is a black box with a turn dial. It is a safe. I do not remember seeing that before.

I witness other members of the castle staff coming into the room. Everyone stands before Lord Harrington, confused looks on their faces. I see Averie enter through the side door.

My stomach flutters and my heart beats faster. Her beauty captivates me. The jewels in her headpiece sparkle in the morning sunlight.

Oh, I wish to be a diamond in her hair.

Lord Harrington's face and ears are redder than his beard. He clenches and unclenches his fists as he takes deep breaths. When the last servant appears, he lets out a yell.

"Last night during the thunderstorm there was a robbery and a murder!" His pupils flick back and forth to each one of us. Narrowing his eyes, it feels as if he is trying to see into our souls.

"Someone entered the throne room and killed the guard standing watch over the safe. Then the perpetrator proceeded to steal The Tear of Erisa!"

I feel my heart sink into my stomach and my palms begin to sweat. My mind replays the dream I had of Huxleigh holding a knife at my throat. It had not been a dream. Someone had really taken the treasure I had traveled so far to deliver.

"Did anyone see anything last night!" The owner of the estate's voice breaks my thoughts.

We look at each other shaking our heads. Everyone seems to be oblivious of the crime.

"Someone took it!" yells Lord Harrington. He folds his arms and stares accusingly at all of us. "And when I learn who has stolen my property, that perpetrator will pay the high price of death. I have waited too long for this prize, and it will not be taken from me. No one is allowed to leave the castle until the bracelet is found!"

"No one can leave the grounds anyway, Lord Harrington," one of the guards declares. "The storm last night rose the river and it washed away the only bridge that leads in and out. It will take a few days to repair."

Lord Harrington nods. "Anyone who finds the thief or the bracelet will be rewarded quite generously. I will have the guards start a thorough search of the castle, so make sure your rooms are open or we will break in. You are all dismissed." Without another word, he storms out of the throne room with the guards following his lead.

The other staff shake their heads and go about their duties. I see Averie still standing next to the far door. She smiles and beckons me towards her. She disappears. I follow her.

Stepping into a corridor with a wall of windows overseeing the grounds, I close the door behind me. Averie leans at the window. She smiles when I approach her.

"Hello." She says.

I watch her red lips move, revealing her white teeth and tongue. I almost forget to reply back.

"Um, hello."

"I see you are feeling better, Oliver," she continues.

I nod. "Yes, yes, much better. I thought I would be able to leave today but it appears that my plans are delayed."

Averie turns and stares out the window. "Father is quite passionate about the bracelet. He searched for many years to find it." She pauses. "It is beautiful, isn't it?"

I lean closer to her, baffled by her response. I look out the window. Beyond the panes, I am greeted with a panoramic view of the estate. The well-manicured lawns span outward toward a tall stone wall that surrounds the premise. Beyond the barrier are thick dark woods that lead into the mountains. The leaves are bursting with colors of red, gold, and orange.

"It is a gorgeous sight," I reply. "However, it is nothing compared to your beauty." The words slip out of my mouth before I can reel them back in.

Averie turns away from me to hide the pink tinge that is creeping across her face.

"Forgive me for being so forward," I add. "Why is your father so concerned about The Tear of Erisa?"

She turns back to me and tilts her head to the side. "Shouldn't you already know? After all, you were the one who delivered the package."

"I was merely the messenger. The purpose of the ornament was not informed to me by my benefactor." I press my lips tighter as I finish saying the word *benefactor*. The thought of Persephone as my superior is not pleasing at all. The woman has still not paid me my money, and all she has done is make my life more difficult than it needs to be.

Averie walks down the hall, her hips swinging from side to side. "My father traveled to Greece a few months ago. He had been corresponding with a jeweler for a year about The Tear of Erisa. It was there that he met her. She was an older woman named Dabria. She didn't have The Tear of Erisa, but after he showed her a drawing, she reassured him she would be able to find it and deliver it to him. A letter came about a week ago stating that we would be visited by a messenger who would bring us the bracelet."

We walk down the stairs and out the door into the courtyard. Averie gestures towards a marble bench and we sit down.

"This is a spectacular estate you have here," I reply.

Averie crinkles her nose. "It is not what you think. It is drafty and lonely. I have never been past the gates. Father does not let me go anywhere. We have everything we need here: a doctor, a chef, a lawyer, and many staff. He says I should be grateful, but I want to see the world."

I would love to have a home as beautiful as this instead of a tarp in an alley.

"I heard the bracelet leads to a kind of treasure." I change the subject.

Averie takes a section of her hair and twirls it around her

finger. "Yes. There is a legend that surrounds this house that hidden somewhere within its chambers is a grand treasure. A long time ago there was a Countess named Yelena. She was desired for her beauty throughout the land. Men from all parts of the world came to court her and showered her with expensive trinkets hoping to win her hand in marriage. However, Yelena desired one man, a man with a good soul, but poverty ran through his veins. Naturally, that infuriated her father who felt his daughter should marry someone of her rank. Yelena disobeyed his orders and married the man anyway.

"A great illness spread across the land and took her husband. This pleased her father because he felt now Yelena would marry someone of her class. He already had in mind the man for Yelena, an earl from the south. But to his dismay, Yelena was pregnant with her husband's child. This is where the legend becomes unclear. Some people say when Yelena gave birth to a daughter, her child was taken from her. Distraught and upset, she ran away and took up residence in this Oakenfield Castle that was owned by an old wealthy Viscount. The two struck up a friendship, and when the Viscount died, he left everything to Yelena.

"Still broken-hearted over the disappearance of her child, Yelena took all of her treasures and locked them somewhere in the castle. She had a bracelet made which would be the key to opening the vault where the treasure was hidden. She named the bracelet The Tear of Erisa for that was her daughter's name. That is the bracelet that you delivered to my father."

"What a sad story," I muse. "Did she ever find her daughter?"

"No one knows. As I said, the ending of the story is very unclear. No one seems to know the truth."

"Do you have any idea where the treasure could be hidden in the castle?" I ask.

"I do not know. That has been the obsession of my father since he bought this estate when I was an infant. He found what is believed to be Yelena's diary from an antique dealer. Some say her diary holds a clue to finding the whereabouts of the treasure.

It is locked in my father's study. Are you planning on locating the treasure yourself?"

I stand up and brush the front of my jacket. "It has crossed my mind. I feel that is the only way I will be able to leave this place. Your father said he will give a reward to whoever finds the bracelet. If I find it and figure out where the entrance to the treasure is, I can finally leave this place."

I could use the extra money from the reward to better my life. Who knows if Persephone will pay me after this disaster? I have a bone to pick with that woman anyway. She is making my life beyond miserable!

"I used to think it was a silly legend until I saw Father take out the bracelet," Averie interrupts my thoughts. "Perhaps the treasure does exist." She pauses for a moment. "No one in the castle knows the location of my father's secret study except me. If you wish to find this treasure, you will need my help. I will assist you on one condition."

"What is that?"

"When you leave to return to the city, I will come with you."

My eyes widen. "I cannot do that!"

"Why not?"

"It would be improper for me to take you to the city without your father's permission!"

"My father keeps me captive here like a prisoner. I am not able to go anywhere. I want to see the world." She stands and faces me.

We stare into each other's eyes, and I feel as if time stands still. I want to lose myself in her brown eyes that seem to look into my soul.

"I cannot do that." I stammer.

"Well, then, I guess there will be no diary for you and no way to get out of here. If I am stuck, then you will be, too." She places her hands on her hips waiting for my next response.

I take a deep breath. "Alright, alright. If we find the treasure, I will bring you with me back to London."

I silently pray for forgiveness for the lie I am forcing out of my mouth. It would be impossible for me to bring Averie to London. I have not known Lord Harrington long, but he seems very protective of his only daughter. I am sure he would kill me before he would allow me to leave with Averie.

"Excellent. We will put the plan in place later tonight...Oh!" She places her hand to her forehead.

"Are you alright?" I ask stepping closer to her.

"It's just my head. I get pains every so often. I am going to lie down." She moves towards the door.

"Do you need me to escort you to your room?" I ask.

"No, no I am fine. I just need to lie down. It will go away after a while. I will contact you when we are going to start the plan."

"What shall I do until you are ready?" I ask.

She places her finger on the knob and looks back at me. "There is much to do around here. But do not get yourself into trouble. Father is looking to take his revenge out on any poor soul."

October 7, 1888
10:00 a.m.

I roam the hall of the castle admiring the portraits. I cannot go back to my room. There are guards posted at the door as they search each of the chambers. Lord Harrington is desperate to have his bracelet back.

In my talks with a few of the staff, I learn that I am not the only guest who is taking advantage of Lord Harrington's hospitality. There are Bryson and Sadie Jenkins, a British couple who live in Southern France.

I walk into one of the drawing rooms to see the couple sitting on the velvet sofa and chairs that surround a roaring fireplace. Mrs. Jenkins furrows her brow and crosses her arms while Mr. Jenkins browses through a pamphlet.

"This is preposterous that the guards are refusing to let us go into our rooms," huffs Mrs. Jenkins.

"You know the reason why, dear," replies Mr. Jenkins, not looking up from his magazines.

"But to even insinuate we took something…"

"They are searching everyone's rooms, darling."

I sit down on the sofa across from them. I am trying not to eavesdrop, but these people are all suspects. If any of them have the bracelet and I can find it, then the reward shall be mine.

The couple fall silent in my presence.

"Hello," I begin. "I am…"

"I know who you are!" Mrs. Jenkins points a finger at me. "You are the reason we are trapped in this ancient prison of stone."

"I beg your pardon." I reply. "My job was to bring the bracelet here safely. It is not my fault it went missing. What is your reason for being here?"

"We are jewelers," replies Mr. Jenkins. "Lord Harrington brought us here to authentic The Tear of Erisa."

"Is it real?" I ask.

"We never got a chance to see it. We were supposed to inspect it in the morning, but you know what happened." Mr. Jenkins shrugs.

"How can you be so calm about this," huffs Mrs. Jenkins.

"If you have nothing to hide, then you have no cause to fret," replies Mr. Jenkins.

"Pssh! I do not appreciate having my time wasted coming all this way to the manor for nothing. Nor do I appreciate being imprisoned in this castle, either. Lord Harrington promised to pay us a fortune to authenticate the bracelet.

Now we will never receive that money. Come on, dear, let's go." Mrs. Jenkin storms out of the drawing room.

Mr. Jenkins gives me a wan smile and follows her. The door shuts behind them.

"Quite an interesting couple," a voice calls out.

I look up to see another person in the room. A man is sitting by the window. He is so quiet I did not notice him. I remember he is the castle artist who goes by the name of Old Man Beige.

He has his easel set up and stares intently at the canvas, his paint brush poised.

Standing up, I walk over to him. I see he is in the beginning stages of a magnificent portrait.

"That is a beautiful painting." I begin. Then I remember my manners. "I believe we have not been formally introduced. I am Oliver."

"Weston Cole," replies the man, "but everyone knows me as Old Man Beige."

I can see why he has earned this nickname. He is old, probably in his early seventies. Long sandy hair with bits of gray fall to his shoulders, and he has a neatly trimmed beard that extends many inches from his chin.

"I heard you are the castle portrait painter. That is an interesting job." I muse.

Old Man Beige chuckles.

"Yes, I am the artist. Many years ago, Lord Harrington's wife hired me to decorate the edifice with my paintings. That was a few months before she died, bless her soul. I have been here ever since. I also do odd jobs around the palace, too. Lord Harrington likes to get his money's worth out of me. Recently he wanted me to paint a portrait of him and his daughter, but I have not had the opportunity given the consequences of 'the incident' some time ago, so I am painting the scenery. It is beautiful around here."

I nod and glance at the clock on the mantel. By now the guards should be finished tearing my room apart looking for the bracelet. I bid Old Man Beige good day and head out into the corridor.

The castle is so big I am forever losing my way. I stand in the corridor debating whether I am supposed to go left or right when I hear a noise nearby.

"Oliver," a voice hisses.

I pause, look around but there is no one. I shrug my shoulders and I begin to walk away when something reaches out and grabs me. I put my arms up to defend myself. As I turn toward the mysterious stranger, I see it is Huxleigh. Her eyes are wide and a sneer has spread across her face.

A shiver runs down my spine. There is not much on this Earth that scares me, but Huxleigh can make the blood run cold in my veins. I stumble backward trying to put as much space as possible between myself and this woman so steeped in horror.

"Good Lord, Huxleigh! What are you doing here?"

Huxleigh stands before me in a black lace dress. The fabric hugs every curve and falls off of her shoulders.

"Oliver, what are you doing wandering these halls?" She says.

"I was heading back to my room."

"Maybe you were trying to hide The Tear of Erisa that you stole?"

"I did nothing of the sort! Where do you come up with these ridiculous accusations, Huxleigh? The guards are searching my room as we speak, and they will be very disappointed to find nothing."

Huxleigh steps closer to me. "Somebody did kill the guard who was guarding the bracelet. You must be careful. Whoever killed the guard might try to kill you too if they believe you are the thief."

"What are you trying to say?" I ask. My heart beats rapidly against my chest. I want to get away from this woman. I feel a wave of mixed emotions from Huxleigh. Part of me feels she desires me, and then another part of me feels she wants to take my life. I want nothing to do with her. I wish it was Averie standing before me instead of this insufferable lady."

"You think you are so clever, Oliver. You took my demand and tried to make it your own. I told you that you were going to help me find the missing bracelet. Now you decide you want to do it on your own." From the folds of her dress, she pulls out a knife and holds it up.

I step backwards and lift my hands up. My words struggle to leave my lips.

"I-I do not want the bracelet for myself!" I cry. "I just want to find the bracelet so that I may leave this deranged castle!"

As Huxleigh approaches me, we lock eyes. It is strange, but in that moment, I see something shift in her brown irises. A softness reflects at me instead of the cruel evil pupils. She hesitates, and I see the blade begin to lower in her hand. Her gesture gives me enough time to lunge forward and rip the knife out of her fingers.

I grab her arm and push her up against the wall.

"I am weary of your knife-wielding threats against me. I would like to know what is your relation to Lord Harrington? Are you family?"

Huxleigh glares at me. "In a way I am. Now unhand me before I scream."

I do not want to release her, but at this moment, I cannot afford another trip to the dungeon. I do not know if Persephone will save me a second time, and I do not want her to stick a knife in my gut again. Reluctantly, I release her.

"You are going to stop threatening my life. It is confounding enough to be embroiled in this untoward situation." I gasp. The gate bracelet heats up, sending a searing pain down my arm. I pull back the end of my jacket, the ornament still fastened to my wrist, its heart-shaped padlock reminding me how deeply enmeshed I am as a prisoner.

Huxleigh steps closer. "What is that around your wrist? A gate bracelet? Why are you wearing a woman's bracelet?"

"It is not a woman's bracelet!" I growl through clenched teeth.

"Who is your true love?"

"If I knew that answer, I would not still be wearing it. You are going to leave me alone! I have reached my limit at finding you popping up all over the place. Good day, madam!" I storm off.

Huxleigh is a thorn in my side. I walk back to my room. Thankfully the guards are gone. I open the bedroom door and slam it shut.

I fold my arms and scan the massive chamber. The sheets have been torn back from the bed. All the drawers have been left open and are off their hinges. The chair in front of the desk is overturned.

I groan. *You think they would have cleaned this place before they left.*

Scooping up a pillow that had fallen to the floor, I flop onto the bed. Staring at the canopy above me, I let my mind wander.

Every person in this castle has a motive to steal The Tear of Erisa. Even if someone could not find the treasure, the bracelet itself is worth a fortune.

My mind drifts back to Avery. She looks so lovely today with her soft lips and beautiful smile. She also has a fire about her which intrigues me.

"You cannot take her back with you to London, Oliver," I tell myself. "As I would love her companionship, that would be improper and disrespectful. Mother raised me better than this."

Ah, how I miss my mother! She would know what to do in this situation. I know she would be upset with me that I struck a deal with Persephone. I should have known better than to trust a stranger.

I silently hope Persephone would appear so I could ask her for some guidance. She had promised me this adventure would be worth my while, but all I seemed to be getting was a headache.

Headache. My mind drifts back to Averie. I wonder how she is feeling. Maybe I should knock on her door and check on her. No, that would not be proper.

I groan and slam another pillow into my face. I am a poor man. I have no job. I have no home. I have no money. What would ever make me think I am worthy of a lord's daughter? But if I found the treasure first, maybe that would make me worthy.

No. I am only going to find the bracelet so that I can get out of here and never do anything like this again.

I close my eyes and an image of Averie appears against the inside of my eyelid. If we find the bracelet, I will be bound to my promise to bring her back with me to London. How could I do that? She told me her father has never allowed her to leave the castle grounds, and she thinks that Lord Harrington is going to let her ride off on an adventure with a stranger?

My muscles feel tense, I also cannot lie to her or lead her on. I do not know what to do.

I reach into the inner pocket of my jacket and pull out the knife I had taken from Huxleigh. A shiver runs down my spine. There is something familiar about that woman but I do not know what it is. I fear her. I get up from the bed and walk towards the door. I make sure it is locked. I do not wish to be disturbed by that malicious woman.

I open the empty drawer of the nightstand beside my bed and throw the weapon in and slam it shut. I take off my coat and hang it on the hook.

The gate bracelet grows hot against my wrist again. I clutch my hand to the ornament.

"Ah, what in the blazes is wrong with this thing?" I wrap my fingers around the links and try to rip it off, but it holds fast and won't budge.

I groan. How am I ever going to get this bloody thing off me? Suddenly the bracelet cools and my skin is able to tolerate its warmth.

I hold the chain links in the light of the gaslamp. The heart-shaped padlock mocks me. A constant reminder that I am not only a prisoner externally but internally as well.

That wench Jessica! Running off with my best friend! If she had been more of an honest woman, I could have been married by now and living a better life than trapped in this mess.

The bracelet heats up again and I double over in pain. I am

merely fooling myself. Jessica was not the right woman for me. I did not love her. The bracelet cools.

I groan. If only I could be happy like everyone else.

Settling into the bed, I wait for slumber to grace me. As my eyelids close, I cannot remove the image from my head that Huxleigh has the same facial features as Averie.

October 8, 1888
8:00 p.m.

Asense of urgency floats through the castle. We are watched like hawks by the guards. They eye our every move. They question us when they see us in the hall. They constantly barge into our rooms and search them. Lord Harrington has barricaded the perimeter so no one can go in or out. He is determined to find The Tear of Erisa.

Earlier this evening, I found a note under my pillow written by Averie telling me to meet at eight in the evening in the corridor near where the Grandfather Clock stands beside a portrait of a setting sun.

I hear the bells chime as I round the corner, and the tall cherry wooden structure greets me. The weighted pendulum swings back and forth behind the glass. Numbers one through twelve fill the circular face. Intricate designs are carved around the perimeter. Next to the clock is a framed landscape portrait of a golden sun setting over a lake. Colors of yellow, pink, blue, and purple swirl together creating a contrast of light and dark between the sun and the background.

I stare at the tall case clock. The soft tick tick makes the hairs on the back of my head stand straight.

"A beautiful masterpiece is it not?" A familiar voice whispers behind me. I take a deep breath to calm myself as I turn to face the owner of the statement. It is Persephone.

She pulls her shawl tighter around her body. "These castle halls can be so drafty."

"I have a bone to pick with you, madam," I begin.

"Oh, Oliver, you flatter me." She wiggles her fingers at me. "You wish to talk to me instead of these young women roaming about the castle?"

I pause to collect my thoughts. This mysterious woman always knows exactly what to say to throw me off guard.

"Where is my money?" I hiss. "You have put me through misery. This journey has been nothing short of hell. First, I was thrown in the dungeon, then stabbed, then magically healed, and now I am trapped in this wicked place. I made a deal that I would deliver the bracelet and I did that. Now I would like to be paid for my suffering, witchy woman."

Persephone places her fingers on her chin. "Yes, you did deliver the bracelet, but now it is gone."

"That is not my fault!"

"It must be if you are trying to find it."

"I am doing this so I can leave! I want nothing to do with this unholy place, and once I escape from here, I will never come back."

"But what about Averie?"

I stop. My mouth is parted to speak but the words die on my lips.

"I see you have grown fond of Lord Harrington's daughter." She smiles at me.

Persephone places her hands on my shoulders and turns me so I am facing the tall case clock. I see the pendulum swinging in a rhythmic motion. The low click click causes goose bumps to form along my skin.

"A beautiful clock," Persephone begins. "The symbol of Life and Death. The seconds precious, the minutes charitable, the hours generous, and the days a gift. Everything in life is temporary, dear Oliver. Nothing stays the same. This section of misery in your life is merely a stepping stone onto the next great adventure."

"But you are the one creating my misery!" I hold up my wrist so the gate bracelet dangles in her face. "Did I forget to mention that I have to wait for a woman to free me?"

Persephone smirks at me, "Your true love is closer than you think." With a wave of her hand, she is gone.

"Oliver, what are you staring at?" Averie appears in the corridor.

I open my mouth but no words come out.

"I have been waiting here for you. What took you so long?" She steps towards me.

"At this point, I honestly do not know, Averie. I do apologize for the delay. What are we doing here?" I reply.

"This is where Father's secret study is." She stands on her tiptoes and opens the door that shields the face of the clock. On the inside ledge is an object which Averie scoops up. It looks like a key. She puts the item in the pocket of her dress.Reaching behind the tall clock case, she pulls something. The blank space of wall next to the sunset portrait moves upward to reveal a large oak door.

Averie's fingers wrap around the brass handle. "Come on."

We enter into a small room with a wood interior. Shelves of books line the walls. There is a fireplace with an oriental rug in front. Two velvet chairs sit on either side. Across the room is a maple desk with stacks of papers. A large mirror hangs next to the entrance.

"My father has a total of five studies through the castle. This is his secret study," says Averie. "He brought me in here one time and made me promise not to tell anyone in the castle about it. He keeps all his special items in here, so I know the diary is in this room." She walks over to the desk and slides the key into the center drawer.

"What is your father going to do when he realizes the diary is missing?" I ask.

"We will have it back before then. This diary is the least of his concerns. He is more focused on finding the bracelet. He will not come back here until he has the Tear of Erisa."

She pulls open the drawer then slams it shut. Groaning, Averie runs her fingers through her dark hair. "Now if I were Father, where would I hide the diary?"

As Averie talks to herself, I feel the gate bracelet warm against my skin. I hear a whisper but I cannot make out what it says.

Stepping away from Averie banging about, I listen. It *is* the bracelet. It speaks in only a tone that I can hear. The ornament tells me that the diary is not in the desk. Following its instructions, I walk over to the fireplace. I admire the engraved mantel and the brickwork that surrounds the grate. The bracelet tells me that it is three bricks down, two across. I place my finger on the slab. It caves inward. A drawer shoots out from the top of the mantel. I duck to avoid being hit. Inside the tiny draw is a leather-bound book.

Reaching my hand inside, I pull it out and open the cover. On the first page in fancy calligraphy are the words *Countess Yelena*.

"I found it." I call.

Averie's head pops up from behind the desk. "Thank God. I was thinking we were going to be here all day."

She walks over to me. As she reaches forward to take the book from my hands, her fingers brush my skin. I feel a sudden urge to take her into my arms and hold her close.

A clatter outside the door breaks the silence. I hear movement as if someone is trying to get in.

Averie freezes, her eyes wide. "Who is that? It cannot be Father."

The bracelet whispers to me that it is not Lord Harrington.

"Someone else knows of this secret lair," I reply.

"How could that be?" Averie reaches inside the fireplace and pulls at something. The back of the firebox opens to reveal a narrow tunnel.

"Quick," She hisses and crawls inside the opening. I follow her lead.

Once we enter into the dark passageway the back of the fireplace moves into its place. At the same time, I hear the door to the hidden lair open. I cannot see who it is.

On our hands and knees, we crawl through the channel.

"How did you know this was here?" I ask.

"Father does not let me leave the castle grounds. I have spent many days exploring the castle. I have found many secret tunnels," replies Averie.

"Where does this tunnel lead?" I blink my eyes adjusting to the darkness.

"To the corridor near the Great Hall," Averie stops and places the diary on the floor in front of us. She sits on her bottom, her back against the wall.

"You took the diary with you?" I say.

"Of course," she replies. "I told you I want to come with you when you leave for London. I want to see the world. I am finished with my father controlling my life."

I open my mouth to tell her the truth, but the words are strangled in my throat.

I must tell her. My lips refuse to move. *I am leading her on. Mother would not approve. Maybe with the reward money, I can buy Averie a stagecoach ticket to London. That way she can have a guard escort her there. So I am not really lying.*

Swish

A spark of light appears before me. A small ball of fire. I jump and realize Averie has lit a match.

"What are you doing?" I cry. "Are you trying to turn the tunnel into flames? Where did those matches come from?"

"For Mercy's sake! Do not raise an alarm! I fancy myself a cigarette every now and then. Plus, we need light in this dreary tunnel. Let's take a peek at the diary."

"Here?"

Averie rolls her eyes. "I will return the diary later once we have the clue, understand? Father won't even know it's gone. I promise. Here." She gives me the match. Then she places a box of the firesticks in my hand. "If the fire gets too close to the end, blow it out and light another one."

She begins to peruse through Yelena's diary while I light match after match. After a few minutes, Averie grips the book in frustration and shakes it. "There is no clue."

"Let me look," I blow out the match and hand the box back to her. She gives me the diary then strikes another match. I open the journal and squint my eyes trying to read the ink and fancy script.

The gate bracelet warms against my skin. It commands me to look at the last page. I flip to the back of the book and a blank sheet greets me.

A blank sheet is not a clue.

I move the book closer to my eyes. There is a dried substance at the corners almost as if the page has been sealed shut. Digging my fingernails in between the page and the back cover. I am unsure of what to think until the paper breaks free.

Averie leans closer to me.

I look at the hidden page. On it are scrolled the words:

R.L. Stevenson

10.3.9

22.11.13

50.33.3

60.19.6

"What do you think those mean?" asks Averie.

"It almost looks like some kind of code," I reply.

Averie grips my arm with her free hand. "It is an Arnold Cipher!"

Her words enlighten me. "Of course, a book cipher. Each cluster of numbers is its own code. The first number is the page, the second number is the line, and the third is the word on the line. But what is the book?"

Averie extinguishes the match, throws it on the floor, and lights another one. "R.L. Stevenson, R.L. Stevenson," she mutters to herself then gasps and the match drops from her fingers onto the floor. Quickly, I stomp on it before it can catch fire.

"Let me light it," I take the box of matches from her. "What is it?"

"Of course," continues Averie. "R.L. Stevenson has to be Robert Louis Stevenson, the author of *Strange Case of Dr. Jekyll and Mr. Hyde.* That is the book!"

I tilt my head to look at her. "That makes no sense. You told me Yelena and The Tear of Erisa is a centuries-old legend. That book was written a few years ago. How could it possibly be the key?"

"I don't know," huffs Averie "but that is the only book written by someone with the same name and initials. Maybe Yelena was never the one who set up the clues. Maybe it was someone more recent."

"But who? You said you have lived at this castle your entire life. How could someone form a clue that is based off a book published a few years ago?" I scratch my head.

"Oliver, stop thinking so negatively." Averie grabs my arms, and I raise my hand up higher so I do not burn her with the match. "The book is the first clue. Who cares who designed it? Come on, let's get out of here."

Extinguishing the match, I follow her as she moves into the darkness.

"Weren't you reading that book the day I was bedridden?" I ask.

"Yes, I was."

"So, you have it in your room?"

"No, I do not," Averie calls over her shoulder. "I returned it to the library."

We reach the end of the tunnel and a wall stands before us. Averie puts her ear against it and listens. Then she knocks her knuckles three times against the wall. A section of it opens and we step out into another corridor. Then the wall returns to its original state behind us.

"We are on the southside of the castle," begins Averie.

She brushes off her dress. "Tomorrow we will meet at the library. I am going to return the book to father's study. We cannot raise suspicion."

"What about the intruder?" I ask. "What if he is still in the study? I will go with you."

"I am sure the person is long gone. Maybe we imagined the noise. I will be fine. I trust you know the way back to your room?"

"Of course," I reply even though I have no idea where I am.

She smiles at me then presses against the wall so the door reopens. Before I can protest she disappears into the darkness with the diary, and the wall seals shut.

I take a deep breath and try to make sense of my surroundings. The gate bracelet warms against my skin but does not speak. As I walk, my mind flutters with various theories. The last owner before Lord Harrington had to be at least twenty years ago or more.

I stop and look at the portraits on the walls. *Is this the right way?*

Before I can collect my thoughts, I feel something hit the back of my skull. Everything goes black.

October 9, 1888
9:00 a.m.

Am I dead? I find myself surrounded by darkness. Something soft is under my head and against my body. I hear voices but my eyelids are too heavy to open. My temples are throbbing and I feel my heartbeat in my brain.

"I found him in the hall, lying there," a voice says. The resonance sounds so familiar. I know it.

Huxleigh!

I try to move but my body feels heavy.

What is Huxleigh doing here? Why does this woman always appear whenever something happens?

"He seems to be regaining consciousness," another voice replies.

"I am not sure what he was doing in that hallway. No one really goes down there," continues Huxleigh

"Whoever it was must have been searching for the lost treasure."

At that moment a searing pain runs from my head down my neck. I cry out and grab the back of my skull. My eyes fly open.

A man stands before me. He has wild blond hair and a thin beard that frames his face. He is scribbling on a notepad.

There is no one else in the room. Huxleigh is gone or was she even there? I know I heard her voice. That woman seems to follow me like a mouse to cheese.

"Ah! You are awake," declares the man not looking up from his notepad. "I was not sure if there was actual brain damage from the bashing or simple fainting from fright, but the fact you are waking rules out the possibility that you suffer the effects of madness."

"Who are you?" I ask. I struggle to sit up but my muscles scream in agony. I fall back against the pillows.

"I am the physician of the castle. My name is Dr. Steven Morris. The guards brought you in a few hours ago. It appears you have suffered a blow to the head."

Before I can reply, the door to the room bursts open and Lord Harrington storms in, flanked by four guards.

"Oh good, you are alive I was about to think that we had another murder on our hands," the regal man begins.

"I do not understand," I reply.

"The guard who was guarding The Tear of Erisa. Apparently his skull was bashed in by a vase." Lord Harrington walks closer to my bed. "What were you doing in the Carolina Hall?"

"What?"

"The hall. We have so many of them in this castle we had to give them names. No one ever goes in that area. Why were you there?" He narrows his eyes at me.

"I-I..." my brain cannot seem to comprehend and I feel disoriented. "I was exploring."

"Did you see who hit you?"

"No, I did not."

"Lord Harrington, this is not the time to be asking the victim questions. He has suffered a crushing blow to the head. He needs to rest. His brain is unable to understand what you are saying," replies Dr. Morris.

The red-bearded lord scowls. "I still haven't found that bracelet. It appears someone else is after my treasure and willing to kill for it. I will not be robbed of what is mine!" He storms out of the room.

I settle into the bed. I hope Averie has returned safely to her own chamber.

Glancing around the large room, I see there are four other beds besides mine. An open door on the opposite side reveals a small office. There are shelves on both walls that are lined with an assortment of bottles filled with colorful elixirs and odd-looking chemicals.

Dr. Morris moves closer to my bedside and places a glass of water next to me. "I am going to keep you here overnight for observation. Tomorrow you will be able to leave if you are feeling better. Do you want me to give you something for your head?"

"I am alright." I reply.

Dr. Morris adjusts a pile of books next to the gaslamp. "Did you see who hit you?"

I am not sure why I keep getting asked the same question over and over. The gate bracelet awakens and warms my wrist. It urges me not to reveal too much. Guilty consciences are at work.

"No," I answer.

Holding a pen a few inches in front of my face, the doctor asks me to follow it with my eyes as he moves the pen side to side. Then he asks me to hold my arms out in front of me.

I do as he says. His lips tense as he glances at the bracelet on my wrist sparkling in the light of the gaslamp.

"What is that?" He asks.

"It is not the Tear of Erisa," I reply.

"I know that. I have never seen such an intricately crafted bracelet before. Where did you get it? May I see it?"

"It is a long story and I cannot take it off. It appears I have misplaced the key."

Dr. Morris opens his mouth to reply, but before the words can escape his lips, the door opens.

Averie walks into the room. Her hands are clasped and close to her chest. Her brow is furrowed. She sees me lying there in the bed and she exhales slowly, her eyes lighting up. My heart thumps faster against my chest.

"Lady Averie, what are you doing here?" asks Dr. Morris.

"I came to check on the patient," she replies.

"He appears to be spending a lot of time in bed. First passing out from exhaustion and now he is suffering from a brain lesion. You should not be here, he needs to rest," declares Dr. Morris.

Averie steps forward towards him. That emerald dress hugs her body nicely. A gold chain hangs from her neck. I do not know what the pendant is, for it disappears into the scoop of her neckline.

"If Mr. Gray is suffering from a lesion, as you say, he needs to be watched constantly. Mr. Jenkins is complaining that he is not well. He is requesting to see you. Go to his room and I will watch Mr. Gray until you get back." Averie crosses her arms and raises an eyebrow at him.

I cannot help but feel a sense of tension between the two.

"Very well," replies the doctor. He picks up a small leather bag from a nearby chair and marches out of the room.

As soon as the door is closed, Averie walks over to me and sits on the edge of my bed. She reaches forward and brushes my cheek with the back of her hand. "You are alive," she whispers.

My tongue feels thick in my mouth, and I can no longer form words or process my thoughts correctly with her hand against my cheek. I fight the urge to pull her into my arms and hold her close. My only reply is a nod.

She pulls back her hand. "How could you have been so

stupid?" she hisses. "How could you let yourself be attacked? You could have given us away."

I blink. Once again words fail me. I cannot keep up with this rollercoaster of emotions Averie continually thrusts upon me. One minute I sense she is fond of me, then in an instant, her mood changes. Now she seems angry with me.

"I do apologize, I do not have eyes in the back of my head. No, I did not see who attacked me," I add, reading her mind before she could open her mouth. That question seems to be an ongoing discussion.

Averie looks down at the sheets and grows quiet. "I am glad you are alright. I do not want to see anything happen to you, Oliver. When did Dr. Morris say you can leave?"

"Tomorrow."

"Good. I want to be the one to find that treasure. Then Father will come to trust my judgment and permit me to leave this dreadful place and go to London with you."

My throat constricts my words. I bow my head.

She reaches forward and takes my hand, her eyes on the bracelet. "You never did tell me why you have a gate bracelet on your wrist? Are you married?"

"No," I reply.

"A girlfriend, fiancée?"

"No...er...I did have a fiancée. She left me for someone else, but this bracelet has nothing to do with her. It was a trick gone bad. I was deceived by an old woman and now I am stuck with this."

Averie tilts her head to the side. "Why would she do that?"

"Oh, she said my true love would remove the bracelet. Odd. She knew very well I do not have anyone." I clench my teeth.

Averie has a faraway look in her eyes as she touches the heart-shaped padlock of my bracelet. "I had a gate bracelet once a long time ago. It did not end well."

"Do you want to go to the library now and find that book?

That way we can get ahead on the clues?" I ask changing the subject.

Averie shakes her head. "No, we will go tomorrow when you are better. We are in this together. Besides, I am nervous now after your accident. The person who attacked you must be the person who has taken The Tear of Erisa. If only we knew who it was."

"It is not as if there are many people at this castle. I mean, there is myself, you, Lord Harrington, Mr. and Mrs. Jenkin, Old Man Beige, Dr. Morris, and Huxleigh." I reply.

"You forget there are at least fifty staff members, chefs, maids, gardeners, and over a hundred guards. Any one of them could have stolen the bracelet," replies Averie.

A searing pain throbs in my head. I wince.

"You need to rest," Averie pulls the covers up to my chin. "Tomorrow we will go to the library and look for the book." She hesitates for a moment then leans forwards to kiss the top of my head. She scurries out of the room before I can speak, passing Dr. Morris as he reenters the chamber.

October 10, 1888
9:00 a.m.

I follow Averie as she leads the way down the winding twists and turns in the castle. Dr. Morris had told me I was free to go back to my room after examining me, but he cautioned me not to over exert myself. I still feel a bit woozy, but I will not let any more time pass. This castle fills me with great foreboding.

Averie pauses in front of two large oak doors. She wraps her fingers around the brass handles and pulls them back. I rush forward to assist her.

We enter the library and I am taken aback by the beauty of this knowledgeable place. The ceilings are dome shaped with wood trim. There is a large fireplace with chairs next to it. Tables and more chairs are placed around the room. Row after row of wooden shelves filled with books meet our gaze. Large windows reveal the beautiful woods and mountains that surround the palace.

By one of the large windows a man sits in front of his easel painting the landscape on his canvas. It is Old Man Beige.

Averie and I exchange looks. We were not anticipating another person taking refuge in the library.

"Ah, Averie and Oliver. What a pleasant surprise." Old Man Beige calls from his seat. "Oliver, my boy, are you feeling better? I heard you had a nasty accident yesterday. Good to see you recovered."

"Yes," I reply. "I am feeling much better. What are you doing?"

"I am dabbling in landscape images. I felt experimental and I thought the work would pass the time. What are you two doing here?"

"We stopped by to get some novels to read." I reply.

We walk down the rows of books and away from Old Man Beige.

"I do not like this," I whisper.

"What?" replies Averie.

"People seeing us together. It is not proper. Rumors of our acquaintance together might start people talking, and your father already does not like me."

Averie scowls, "What are you trying to say? You do not like spending time with me?"

"I do." I whisper. "But you know how people are, and your father is a lord. What is he going to think about you going back to London with me if we find this treasure? He is not going to be happy."

"Do not worry about my father. I will handle him," hisses Averie. She glances down each of the isles as we walk past. "I know I put it somewhere. Ah! Right this way."

We round the corner into a new aisle and we stop, frozen at

the sight that meets our eyes. Averie grabs my arms and lets out a scream before covering her mouth.

Mr. Jenkins lies before us in the middle of the aisle. A book is clutched in his hand. Blood drips from a head wound onto the floor.

"What is going on?" yells Old Man Beige.

"Call for help!" I cry. "Mr. Jenkins has been injured." I kneel next to the older gentleman and feel for a pulse. It is faint but he is alive.

Old Man Beige calls into the hall for the guards and five rush into the chamber and surround Mr. Jenkins. One of the guards comments that Dr. Morris is being fetched.

"Quick! Let's get out of here," whispers Averie. "We do not want to attract suspicion."

"What about the book?" I reply as we leave the library.

"I got it," she replies. She holds up the book and I see the title *Strange Case of Dr. Jekyll and Mr. Hyde*. "It was clutched in his hands."

She leads me up a nearby staircase and down a long hall to an intricately carved door. We step into a bed chamber decorated in white and gold. There is a fireplace before which are graced oriental rugs, satin chairs, and a canopy bed.

"Where are we?" I ask.

"My bed chamber," replies Averie.

My eyes widen and my heart beats faster. This is forbidden ground! I look at the dressers and closets where Averie keeps her clothes. I look at the bed that Averie sleeps in. What I would give to be a pillow or a blanket on that bed right now. This is too much. I turn to leave.

"Where are you going?" asks Averie.

"You know I cannot be here. Your father will kill me if he finds me here."

"Relax, this is the only place where we can have some privacy. Besides, everyone is too consumed in the Jenkins accident, and if my maid comes, I will send her away. She knows to knock first."

She leads me over to the settee and places the book on a delicately-carved tea table. Pulling out a piece of paper, she hands it to me. I open and see the codes.

"Read the numbers to me and I will find the corresponding letters. You can write them down." Averie hands me a pen. I nod.

I state each of the codes to Averie. After writing down each of the clues, I look at the word the four letters make.

S.O.U.L.

"Soul?" asks Averie as she leans next to me and reads what I have written. "Soul will lead us to where the treasure is hidden? That does not make any sense."

"We still need the bracelet, too," I reply.

"I do not understand."

"I do not get it either, but at least we have the clue." I take Strange Case of Dr. Jekyll and Mr. Hyde from her. "I will return the book."

"Are you sure?" replies Averie.

"Yes. You stay here and rest. I am certain the guards and your father will be coming to question you and me, too."

Clasping the book in my hand, I leave the room as quickly as I can. The desire to take Averie into my arms and never let her go has become too strong.

As I walk down the hall towards the library, I pause and question my surroundings. I must have taken a wrong turn. You think after days of being in the castle I would get a sense of my bearings, but I still do not know.

I take a right and recognize this hallway. It is the corridor that leads to Dr. Morris' infirmary. As I walk closer to the door, I hear voices.

"I have to check on Mr. Jenkins, my dear. That fool decided to go and get his head bashed in. He will live and I will not be long." A voice is that of Dr. Morris.

"Did you see the book?" A second voice replies. It is Huxleigh!

"No, I was too busy trying to save a man's life in front of the squadron of guards. But Mr. Jenkins will be alright. I have to give him some medicine for the pain and change the bandage."

"Does anyone suspect we have it?" Whispers Huxleigh.

"Don't worry sweetheart, no one suspects anything. I have it here for safekeeping until the time is right. Soon we will be rich," replies Dr. Morris.

What are they talking about? I think. *Do they have The Tear of Erisa?*

I hear the sound of lips locking then a lock turning. I hide behind another tall case clock that stands in the hall. I see Dr. Morris leave his office and walk away. A few minutes later the door opens again and I see Huxleigh step out into the corridor. She looks left and right but does not see me. I see her back as she disappears around the corner.

Huxleigh is a mystery to me. She seems to disappear and reappear like a ghost. It also dawns on me that Huxleigh and Dr. Morris appear to be having a secret affair. I shiver at the thought.

An idea consumes me. The Tear of Erisa could be in the infirmary, and this could be my only chance to get it!

My heart thumps loudly against my chest as I race over to the office door. My sweaty palms turn the knob and I slip into the room.

The light outside illuminates the dark. I walk into Dr. Morris' office where a gaslamp has been left unattended. I watch the flame flicker in the glass as I try to calm my thoughts. I do not know how much time I have.

Now if I had stolen a bracelet where would I keep it? I think.

I begin to open the drawers of his desk. Then I move the books on the shelf. As I turn, my hip hits the side of the desk and some papers fall over. Cursing, I bend over to arrange the pile. I see a piece of paper on the top that draws my attention. I pick it up. I see the name at the top.

Averie Marie Harrington
Born on the nineteenth day of September one thousand eight-
hundred sixty-seven

I skim my eyes across the paper. It appears to be a medical analysis on Averie dating from the time she was a child to her current age now. The big words confuse me, but at the end of the document I see the words

Disassociation with reality, M.P.

What does that mean? The report was written by Dr. Morris. What was the matter with Averie? She seems perfectly fine to me.

I cannot be distracted. I continue to rummage through the drawers. The center drawer of Dr. Morris' desk is locked. This must be where their secret is hidden. I grab a pin from a cup on the shelf and pick the lock. A trick I learned living on the streets.

The drawer opens and I see a book in the center. I hold it up to the light of the gaslamp. The title reads: *Strange Case of Dr. Jekyll and Mr. Hyde.* A piece of paper is stuck in the side. I finagle it from between the pages and see the numbers for the code written on it.

I reach into my coat pocket and pull out my copy.

There are two books.

Huxleigh and Dr. Morris are after the treasure, too. But how did they get the codes? There is no time left. Sighing, I place the second copy back in the drawer and hustle out of the room. With the hallway clear, I walk toward the library, the book hidden inside my jacket pocket. The bracelet was not in the infirmary. Maybe Dr. Morris and Huxleigh had hidden it elsewhere or maybe they did not have it at all.

I think back to the memory of Averie and me finding Mr. Jenkins unconscious near the floor. He had the book *Strange Case of Dr. Jekyll and Mr. Hyde* in his hands. Averie had taken that copy and that book was now with me. Was he looking for the treasure, too?

Entering into the library, I see Old Man Beige painting near the window as if nothing had happened. His back is turned to me.

"Hello, Oliver," he replies. "Back so soon?" He raises his paintbrush and stares intently at his canvas.

I place the book on the nearby shelf as Old Man Beige turns to look at me, his eyes twinkling as if he knows something everyone else does not.

"You are not the only one who seeks to find the Tear of Erisa." Continues the artist.

"What are you talking about?" I reply.

"I hear things. Most people do not pay attention to an old man painting. But outward appearances can be deceiving. The Jenkins are jewelry appraisers. Do not think they would not love to get their hands on the treasure, as well. Many people would."

"Except you?" I ask.

Old Man Beige shrugs, "When you become an old man like me, you will soon find the things you desire most are the things that money cannot buy."

I look at his canvas. It is not the landscape portrait he was painting earlier. Instead, it is a painting of swirls and twirls of various colors. "What are you painting?"

"I call it Inside of the Soul." He chuckles as my eyes widen.

At this point I believe Old Man Beige can read my thoughts.

The painter points his paintbrush at the bracelet on my wrist. "Interesting choice of accessories."

"It is a long story," I sigh. As much as I try to cover the bracelet with my sleeves it always seems to catch the attention of someone.

I bid him a good day and after returning the book to the proper shelf, I leave the library with my mind spinning. Old Man Beige is hiding a secret, and I feel the mystery links in with all the other strange events.

His words ring in my brain. *Outward appearances can be deceiving.* An idea forms in my head. Lord Harrington has been tearing apart the castle for days and has come up empty.

Maybe it was all an act. Maybe he was trying to hide something. The guards have looked everywhere in the castle, but have they searched Lord Harrington's room?

The Gate Bracelet warms against my wrist. It was an absurd idea, but it might just work.

October 11, 1888
8:00 p.m.

"This is insanity, Oliver," whispers Averie.

We stand feet from Lord Harrington's door. Two large statues keep watch on either side of the entrance trimmed in gold.

"You are saying my father fabricated the whole incident and killed the guard himself?" Hisses Averie.

"I am not saying that. I-I do not know. I just have a feeling if the bracelet is anywhere, it will be in Lord Harrington's room. That is the only place the guards have not looked."

Averie looks down at the marble floor. "It makes sense. My father is not a very likable man. He has committed terrible sins in his life."

"Let's not jump to conclusions. Distract your father while I search his room. If we do not find the bracelet, then we know Lord Harrington has been telling the truth."

Averie nods and places her hand to her forehead.

"What is wrong?" I ask.

"My head hurts again."

I move towards her but she holds up her hand. "I will be alright."

I hide behind another statue in the hall.

She rushes to the door and pounds her fists against it. "Father! Father!"

A minute passes before Lord Harrington opens the door. "What is it, child? Why must you disturb me? You know I have not been feeling well."

"Come quickly! Someone has been in my room! I-I heard noises when I returned to my chamber and many of my precious treasures have been moved."

"Call the guards. I really do not have time for this!" replies Lord Harrington.

"Father, come on!" Before he can continue to protest, Averie grabs his arm and drags him down the hall. He attempts to close the door, but it does not shut all the way. With Averie tugging at his arm, he seems not to notice, which is good for me.

As soon as they are out of sight, I dash into the chamber and secure the lock.

My jaw drops as I take in the extravagance of this room. The opulent furniture is trimmed in gold. Walls are painted ruby red, and the ceiling looks like it should be in a church with its elaborate designs and carvings. Portraits in brass frames cover the room. The intricate style reminds me of the canvases of Old Man Beige's masterpieces, and I wonder if these are his paintings. A large marble fireplace takes up the far wall. A maple desk is nearby, and behind it is a safe built into the wall. A large canopy bed is against the other wall. Bouquets of ostrich feathers tethered to the bed posts add an exotic ambience to the atmosphere in the room, and thick ruby curtains fall down in waves around the bed.

Oh, to be rich like this!

I hurry over to the desk and open the drawers. Nothing. Next

I shuffle through the papers on Lord Harrington's desk. It appears he was in the middle of a task, and he did not have a chance to organize before Averie disturbed him away.

A leather-bound book catches my attention. I open it and waft through the various documents. I peruse one particular paper, and I see it is an adoption record.

For Averie!

What!

The paper says twenty years ago, a man named Noah Cole had signed away his rights for his one-year-old daughter to Homer and Olivia Harrington.

Averie never mentioned she was adopted. Maybe she does not know.

I see another document. It is a written agreement that ownership of the Oakenfield Castle is transferred to Homer Harrington. It is dated about twenty-five years ago.

The bracelet whispers for me to hurry.

Across the room, I spy a portrait of Lord Harrington looking at me. Old Man Beige must have painted it. I walk closer and notice a hinge hidden on the side of the frame. Wrapping my fingers on the edge, I pull the painting to reveal a wall safe.

The bracelet tells me the secret combination, and with trembling fingers, I turn the dial. I wrap my fingers around the handle and pull down. It opens.

My heart leaps into my throat as a drawstring bag meets my gaze. I do not have to open it. The gate bracelet tells me what I desire is already inside. I hear voices approaching. Snatching the bag, I slam the door shut.

The gate bracelet tells me to go to the bookshelf and take hold of the small statue of a lion. I run over and reach for the sculpture. It appears to be fastened to the top shelf. It pulls forward and the bookcase shifts to the side to reveal a secret tunnel. Quickly, I rush inside and the book rack snaps shut as the door to the chamber opens.

I stumble through the tunnel as my eyes adjust to the darkness. Once Lord Harrington finds his prize possession missing, he will tear apart the castle from top to bottom. One certitude I do know is that Lord Harrington cannot admit that the Tear of Erisa was stolen without admitting he deceived everyone from the beginning.

Reaching the end of the tunnel, I fumble with the latch and step out into the corridor near The Great Hall.

Walking as fast as my legs can muster without looking suspicious, I head down the labyrinth of passageways to get to Averie's room. I must tell her what I have discovered.

"Oliver," a voice calls behind me.

I turn and see Huxleigh step out of the shadows. Her eyes are dark and she glares at me. A chill runs down my spine.

"Yes, madam," I reply. In the light I cannot help but notice how similar in appearance she is to Averie; however, her eyes have a deadness to them which frightens me.

"You have it," she hisses.

"Have what?"

"The Tear of Erisa," she moves closer to me.

"No, I do not," I reply.

"Yes, you do! Give it to me!" She reaches for a nearby vase and throws it at me. I duck and it hits the wall shattering glass everywhere.

Pulling a knife from the folds of her dress, Huxleigh raises it over her head and runs towards me. I extend my arms and grab her wrist, holding her hand clutching the weapon away from me. With our faces inches apart, I stare into her eyes, and I see something change. Eyes of fury and evil have become fearful and afraid. Huxleigh breaks out of my grasp and runs down the hall.

I throw a quick glance back at her and then run down the remaining hallways to my bedchamber. I slam the door and snap the lock into place.

I lean against the carved wood. I close my eyes then open then again. My chest heaves as my lungs try to inhale as much air as possible. I see Huxleigh's face in my mind and the knife raised.

Her aggressive manner, her demanding tone, is she the one who has been bashing people in the head? Then I see the fear in her eyes, the confusion, I cannot help but think of Averie.

I want to share my findings with Averie, but that will have to wait. I have no desire to leave my room. Walking over to the table, I open the drawstring bag. An object falls into the palm of my hands. I see the diamonds and sapphires glittering at me. It is the Tear of Erisa.

As the bracelet touches my skin, the ornament around my wrist grows hot and I wince at the heat. My bracelet whispers the secrets surrounding the trinket in my fingers. My head feels woozy and heavy. I stumble backwards as Huxleigh appears before me. My heart hammers against my chest, and my muscles tense to flee. Her image wavers before me, and I realize she is a vision. The Gate Bracelet and Tear of Erisa are trying to speak to me.

Next to the vision of Huxleigh an image of Averie materializes.

Averie

My heart flutters at the sight of her loveliness. I wish to pull her close and inhale the scent of her hair into my lungs.

Now that the two images are side by side, I cannot help but note how similar they are. Even though Averie has a softer expression, I cannot deny their hair color, eyes, facial features, and body structures are identical.

Averie looks at Huxleigh who looks back at her. Huxleigh walks over to Averie and steps into Averie disappearing into her form.

I see the medical document from Dr. Morris' office appear before my eyes.

Disassociation with reality, M.P.

The words leap out at me. M.P. The Gate Bracelet whispers the name *Multiplex Personality*. When one soul is really two souls. Two personalities in one body.

My legs tremble beneath me and goosebumps break out along

my skin. Like Dr. Jekyll and Mr. Hyde, the same occurrence resides at Oakenfield Manor.

Huxleigh and Averie are one in the same.

Averie, lovely Averie, is cursed.

I fear I cannot handle anymore truth, but the Gate Bracelet wants to keep talking. Another vision of a document comes before me, and I see it is the adoption record that I uncovered in Lord Harrington's room. Averie's real father is named Noah Cole.

Noah Cole...Cole...

A memory forms in my brain. I see paintings on the wall. I believe they were painted by Old Man Beige. I walk closer to them. In the bottom right-hand corner, I see a scribble of a signature. W.C. *Weston Cole.*

Didn't Old Man Beige introduce himself as Weston Cole? I place my hand under my chin. *Old Man Beige was here for more than just painting pictures and I needed to know.*

Placing the Tear of Erisa into my pocket, I storm out of the chamber. The Gate Bracelet guides me to the door of Old Man Beige. It opens at my touch and I see him sitting by the window looking at a canvas.

He raises his head and nods as if expecting me.

I close the door and walk over to him.

The painter's eyes scan my face, reading my expression. "You know," he says.

I nod. The Gate Bracelet warms against my wrist and whispers to me.

"You told me your real name," I begin. "You did not tell anyone else that. They only know you as Old Man Beige. Why?"

"Because I can see how in love you are with my Averie," the artist replies.

"How are you related to her?"

He moves his brush along the canvas. "I am her grandfather."

"She does not know who you are?"

Old Man Beige shakes his head. "No. I took a job at the castle as the painter so I could be closer to Averie and find out more about the monster who adopted her. His wife died from influenza many years ago. Harrington never wanted children, so Averie spent most of her time raised by the servants in the castle. Harrington does not let Averie leave the castle because she is not in her right frame of mind. His protective nature is a facade. He cares more about his reputation than his daughter.

I already knew that.

Old Man Beige sighs and looks out the window. "My son Noah was a bit of a wandering soul. He was always drinking and gambling. We had a falling out and did not speak for years. During that time, Noah married and had a child. His wife died in childbirth, and Noah resorted to more drinking and gambling. One of the people he owed money to was Homer Harrington."

"Homer Harrington?" I repeat.

"Yes, Homer Harrington, Lord Harrington as he calls himself. It is all a fabrication. He is not a lord. He gets his money from illegal gambling establishments. Noah owed him a great deal of money, and I guess Harrington's wife wanted a baby, so Harrington made a deal with Noah to give him his infant daughter and his debt would be settled."

"How do you know all of this?" I ask.

"About fifteen years ago I hired a private investigator to find where Noah was. It turns out my son was dead and I had a granddaughter who had been given away. I feared if I revealed myself to Averie, Harrington would have me thrown out of the castle and I would never see her again."

He strokes his beard and looks at me. "Your last name is Gray, correct?"

"Yes."

"I am sure you know the story surrounding the Tear of Erisa. From my research, the last living descendent of Yelena wanted to sell the estate. Her name was Clementine. Lord Harrington wanted to buy the castle, but so did another woman. Her name was Odessa...Odessa Gray...I think."

My heart leaps up into my throat. *My mother?* I do not

remember much about my mother. I know she died when I was a child, but I do not remember us having enough money to buy a castle.

"What happened to Odessa?" I ask.

"Well, Clementine was going to give her the castle when Odessa died of illness the night before the papers were signed, so Lord Harrington got the castle."

That does not make sense. If my mother had enough money to purchase a castle, where did it go? After my mother died, I had no other family. Our neighbor took me in and raised me as her own along with her two other children. But as far as we know, my mother died a poor woman.

My body feels numb and confusion fogs my brain. I hear myself say goodnight to Old Man Beige, but I do not remember the words leaving my lips.

I stumble out of his room and towards my own. I rely on the Gate Bracelet to lead me down this labyrinth of halls, yet I find myself in a deserted corridor.

My feet stop moving in front of a statue placed on an elegant pedestal.

Based on the engravings and color, I know it is an ancient Egyptian statue made of limestone. The sculpture is the body of a bird but its head is a human with a disk perched on its skull.

"Why are you showing me this?" I whisper out loud to the Gate Bracelet. "What is it?"

The trinket whispers to me that in Ancient Egypt this figure is known as the Ba, the human soul. The Ba leaves the body during sleep, then returns in the morning. Half human half bird.

I think back to the clue from the book. The answer was *Soul*. I pick up the figurine and hold it in my hands. I know I have found the next clue. I just do not know where to go from here.

October 12, 1888
11:00 p.m.

I lie in bed listening to the great clock chime outside my door. It tolls eleven. I have spent all day stuck in my room because Lord Harrington had imprisoned everyone in their quarters so he could search the estate. I know he is looking for the bracelet, but he cannot say without giving away he had it all along. The guards tear apart our rooms multiple times over, but they cannot find the Tear of Erisa. I have hidden it behind a loose brick in the fireplace in my room.

All day I have been pondering the news that Old Man Beige had revealed to me about my mother, Averie's dark personality, and the statue of the Ba.

But it is the murmurs of the Gate Bracelet that drive me to madness. Its pulses spill waves of truth that set fire to my soul.

As the last chime falls into silence, my eyes open. I raise my hand and look at the Gate Bracelet on my wrist. The heart-shaped

146

padlock catches the light of the gaslamp on my nightstand. It twinkles with secrets. I am a prisoner in mind, body, and soul.

For so long life had held me hostage. It had pushed me around, stomped on me, and dragged me through the mud. For so long I had no control over my emotions. It seemed I had been in a constant cycle of sadness and anger over the way my adulthood had turned out. For so long my heart had been broken. This Gate Bracelet was a reminder of the detainee I was, but I would not be held captive any longer.

After staying quiet for a bit, the ornament awakens. I feel sears of hot pain run down my arm, fueling my muscles, penetrating my heart, and filling my brain with knowledge.

From the moment I had laid eyes on Averie, I had fallen madly in love with her. I do not know why, but I hope she feels the same way in return. But like me, she had fallen prisoner to life, captive to her inner demons. Like the story of Dr. Jekyll and Mr. Hyde. There are two souls in one body.

Persephone had uttered the mysterious words that night in the dungeon. To return a life one must be taken. A soul for a soul.

I believe I understand her message now.

I will free myself and in doing so, I will free Averie, as well.

I rise from the bed. I am fully clothed in elegant attire. I walk over to the fireplace and remove the brick. Stuffing the Tear of Erisa into my pocket, I pull open the door and step out into the castle halls. The Gate Bracelet whispers the truth to me. I will seek my revenge.

October 13, 1888
12:00 a.m.

My fingers rap hard on the door of Dr. Morris. I know behind the office is another room that he uses for his bedchamber.

After a few minutes, Dr. Morris appears before me.

"Good grief Oliver, what are you doing..." He does not get to finish his statement for I push him hard against the wall and close the door.

"You did it!" I cry. "You killed her!"

Dr. Morris struggles to his feet. "You are mad, Oliver. Get out of my office at once before I summon the guards."

"Does the name Odessa Gray ring a bell to you?" I snarl.

The color disappears from Dr. Morris' cheeks and he becomes a ghost before me. "I do not know what you are talking about."

"Yes, you do!"

Dr. Morris tries to make a run to the door to summon the guards, but I clutch him by the collar of his shirt and throw him against the wall. He stares at me, his eyes wide, his Adam's apple bobs in his throat.

"You dare lie to me," I hiss. "You know exactly what I am talking about."

"I did not kill anyone!" Replies Dr. Morris.

The Gate bracelet has already spoken the truth to me.

"Yes, you did! Homer Harrington was a grifter and a cheat. You were part of his circle helping him cover up his crimes. Homer Harrington wanted this estate because he had heard about the treasure and wanted it for himself. But he was in competition with another person who wanted to buy this castle. Her name was Odessa Gray." I glare at him.

"Odessa Gray? Um... it sounds familiar."

"Do not play games with me, you fool!" I cry.

"Why do you care?" replies Dr. Morris. "Odessa was an unmarried woman who had just received an inheritance from a dead relative out of the country. She was going to use the money to buy the castle and give her and her son a better life. She wanted to leave a legacy for him to be proud of. Homer tried to dissuade her from buying the castle but she did not listen."

"So when Lord Harrington knew he was going to lose the castle to Odessa, he hatched a plan with you to poison her and make it look like she had died from illness. Then you and Harrington stole all her money. You knew she had no family and no one to make a fuss over her death. Her son was too young. You thought you got away with it."

My fingers wrench his collar so tightly my knuckles turn white. My blood boils hot under my skin. The Gate Bracelet speaks to me.

Dr. Morris thrashes against my grasp. "Odessa was a worthless woman who was not going to amount to anything!"

I snarl at him. "So, you feel women are just easy targets to be taken advantage of? Just like you took advantage of Averie instead of trying to help her! You are having an affair with her alternate personality Huxleigh!"

Dr. Morris turns another shade of white.

"Huxleigh is a grown woman with a separate identity.

They are two souls sharing the same body." He hisses.

"Does Averie know she had a separate personality?" I ask.

Dr. Morris shakes his head. "Huxleigh knows Averie exists, but Averie is not aware of Huxleigh. Stupid girl! She does not know of her multiplex personality disorder. She believes I am treating her for severe headaches. Whenever her head hurts, it means Huxleigh is trying to come out. Huxleigh hates Averie."

"How do you think Lord Harrington would feel knowing you are plotting against him with Huxleigh to find the Tear of Erisa and steal the treasure from under his very nose? You are supposed to be his physician, and you betray him this way!"

Dr. Morris kicks me in the shins catching me off guard. I keel over, losing my grip on him just a little for him to wiggle his way out and run towards his office.

He gets to his desk. As I enter the doorway to the office, he pulls a pistol from the drawer and fires at me. I jump to the side away from the entrance and flatten myself against the wall.

I hear his footsteps coming. I wait as he enters back into the medical room. I rise from the shadows and attack him. We struggle for the gun.

I feel my anger welling up inside my heart ready to spill over. I use all the strength in my body and rip the pistol from his fingers. I look into his killer eyes.

"This woman, Odessa, that you say was a worthless soul!" I scream. "She was my mother!"

I point the pistol at his heart and pull the trigger. His pathetic body slumps to the floor, dead. Doctors are supposed to use their knowledge for good not evil.

I stand in silence, waiting for the guards to burst through the door, but nobody comes. The massive size of the estate and the fact all the rooms are on different floors leads me to believe no one has heard anything.

Perfect for me. I walk to the door with my hand paused on the knob. I listen to the bracelet's instructions.

I have taken one soul and now I have others to claim.

I am a man
I stalk the shadows
I hunger for freedom
My new identity is on the loose

October 13, 1888
12:30 a.m.

Minutes later I stand at the door to Lord Harrington's room. I wrap my fingers and the magic of the Gate Bracelet unlocks the door. Stepping into the lavish sanctuary, I see Lord Harrington asleep in his bed. Locking the door, I walk over to him and wake him from the shadows where he sleeps.

I pull a matchbox out of my pocket and light the gaslamps in the room. The shadows dance across the wall.

I tap my finger against the nightstand.

Tap! Tap! Tap!

Softly at first... Lord Harrington starts to stir. I tap louder. He begins to toss and turn. He is trying to tune out the noise but he cannot. Just like he cannot hide the murders that are blotched on his soul.

My taps turn into a bang.

Bang! Bang! Bang!

Lord Harrington sits up and rubs his eyes.

"What is that noise?" He looks around and sees me in the shadows but he cannot see my face.

"Is someone there? Who are you? Step forward and make yourself known."

I move forward into the light of the gaslamps.

"Oliver? Is that you? What are you doing in my room at this ungodly hour of the night?"

"You, sir, are a facade," I begin.

"What in the heavens are you talking about? I shall call the guard." He throws the covers back and stands before me.

"You are not a lord. You are not a person with a title. You are a lowly rotten thief who cheated people out of their money through poker games and blackmail." I state.

The Gate Bracelet whispers the words of truth to me.

"You wanted to buy the castle because you heard of the legend of treasure hidden somewhere in its walls," I continue. "You wanted to buy this place and when you found out there was another buyer who had more than you, you killed her."

"I did nothing of the sort," replies Lord Harrington.

I move closer to him. "You killed an innocent woman Odessa Gray so you could be the only person to buy this castle. Then you stole all her money and shared it with Dr. Morris who helped you commit this evil crime."

Lord Harrington grabs the gaslamp and holds it out in front of him. "Stay back!"

I continue to move forward, "That woman was my mother!"

I knock the gaslamp out of his hand whereupon it lands onto the rug and shatters. Glass spills over our feet and sparks smoke on the pretty fabric.

"You have blackened your soul, Homer," I cry. "You have lied, cheated, and deceived many people out of their entire fortunes over the years. You are immoral and conniving. You thought you got away with it, but what you put out into the world always comes back to you. Odessa is not the only one you have killed."

The rug beneath us begins to smoke. I see the tiny embers from the lamp mixing with the fibers of the rug.

Lord Harrington grabs the nightstand and turns it over to stop me from advancing on him. He runs over to his desk and grabs a knife. He holds it out in front of him and walks towards me.

"I have had about enough of these accusations, young man," He sneers. "You should have just kept your mouth shut."

"I cannot keep quiet when innocent people's lives have been changed forever. Not only did you kill my mother, but you took an infant from her father to appease your wife when you knew you did not want children."

Lord Harrington raises an eyebrow at me.

"Averie!" I continue, "she is not your real daughter and you do not love her. You keep her prisoner within these walls because you are embarrassed you adopted a child with a mental instability."

The deceitful man strokes his beard, "I can see you are quite fond of my daughter, a little too fond. I will not have my daughter getting cozy with a man like you."

He comes towards me with the knife. "I am going to call the guards and tell them that I found you in my room trying to steal more valuables the way you stole the Tear of Erisa."

"Where is the ornament if you believe I have stolen it?" I ask.

The sinister man remains silent.

"The person who stole the bracelet was you. You wanted to make sure no one would deceive you and take the trinket for themselves. Under cover of darkness, you entered the throne room, you killed your own guard, and you robbed your own safe." I hiss.

"I told you, you needed to learn to keep your lips shut. Now I am going to have to kill you like the others. I am going to tell the guards I caught you in here and you attacked me and I had no choice but to take your life."

He charges at me with the knife but I jump to the side. As he chases me around the room, I grab the nearby bookcase and knock it over. Books spill onto the floor, and one of the leather volumes collides with Lord Harrington's foot. He stumbles.

The moment of distraction gives me the upper hand. I grab the vase sitting on the pedestal nearby and bash him over the head the way he had done to so many others in the past.

He falls to the floor dead. Stems of flowers and water surround his body.

I see the rug still smoking on the floor nearby. I pick it up and toss it into the fireplace. The flames engulf the tapestry and consume it. The sight brings me joy.

The Gate Bracelet whispers to me there is still more to do. I pull the Tear of Erisa out of my pocket and stare at the sapphires and diamonds glistening in the light of the fire.

To free a soul, one must take a soul.

I leave the room and lock it behind. This next interaction is a huge risk and I do not know if it will work, but I must have faith.

Her name is Beauty
The one who holds my heart
The one I desire
An identity split in two
I must set her free

October 13, 1888
1:00 a.m.

She opens the door, seconds after my knock. Her lips part to reveal pearly white teeth. She smiles and my heart fills with joy.

"Oliver," Averie whispers, moving aside so I can step into her bed chamber. "What are you doing here?"

We stare at each other. She is fully clothed. She has not gone to bed yet. I step forward and place my hand against her cheeks. She leans into my palm.

How can this beautiful angel have two souls trapped in one body?

"I was wondering what happened to you earlier after I distracted Father." She continues.

"I am sorry to have caused you worry, but we must hurry. We have to do this tonight." I say.

Her eyes light up. "You found the bracelet?"

I pull the elegant relic from my pocket and place it into her hands.

"Father had it all along. Why would he do that? Why would he take the bracelet and pretend someone stole it?"

This poor woman. She has no idea the past of this monster who claims to be her father.

She places The Tear of Erisa back into my hands.

"Follow me, I know where the treasure is." I hold my palm out to her and she intertwines her fingers with mine. My heart flutters with excitement and guilt.

We walk through the halls. Moonlight shines through the tall castle windows, and our shadows dance on the walls. The Gate Bracelet whispers to me the correct location.

Rounding the corner into the abandoned hallway, the ancient Egyptian statue greets me.

The Ba, the soul, leaving the body throughout the night and then returning again. The soul was the next clue in the riddle and right now, it was my mission to take the souls of those who were evil.

I pick up the bird sculpture and turn it over in my hands. Underneath is a circle carved into the base.

Reaching into my pocket I pull out the Tear of Erisa. I slip the ornament into the engraving. It fits perfectly. I place the statue back onto the pedestal and wait.

Averie clasps my arm, "Nothing is happening? Did we make a mistake?"

"Soul is the key to the treasure," I reply. I squint my eyes. There is a faint red light surrounding the Ba. Slowly the glow grows brighter and the pedestal begins to tremble. The Ba begins to move in a circle, faster and faster it spins until it disappears into the ground.

Averie covers her mouth with her hands and looks at me as a crack in the plain wall appears before us. The line snakes its way along the plaster making the shape of a door. It parts before us to reveal an opening of darkness.

As we step over the threshold, the torches that line the walls of the secret passage light up in flames. We descend down a spiral stone staircase, and I hear the opening close behind us.

The stairs open into a hexagonal crypt. The gas lamps hanging on the walls glow, a modern touch to this ancient domain. As the room is illuminated in light, my eyes widen at the sight before me.

The room is filled with the most spectacular items. There are multiple chests filled with different gold chains, silver antiques on shelves, and intricately woven tapestries laid on the floor at our feet. There are jewels upon jewels and fine plates. Silks, furs, paintings and weapons line the room.

It is the treasure of Yelena with The Tear of Erisa as the key.

"You did it, Oliver," cries Averie. "You found the treasure!"

Alone surrounded by beauty and expensive items, the Gate Bracelet whispers to me *it is time*. I have taken two souls, but this one might be the hardest to snatch.

"I am sure Huxleigh will be pleased." I begin.

Averie stops and stares at me. "Who is Huxleigh?"

I walk closer to her. I take a deep breath. "Averie, my dear, I have something to tell you. Everyone has been hiding a secret from you."

"What are you talking about?"

"There are two souls in your body. Your form not only houses your identity but the personality of Huxleigh." I continue.

"Oliver, have you lost your mind?" Averie turns away from me and folds her arms. "And here I thought we were coming to an understanding, but now you come up with outlandish statements."

"I need to speak with her."

"Who?"

"Huxleigh."

"Oliver, stop saying that!"

I grab her by the arms and turn her to face me. "Averie, you need to be set free. I need to speak with Huxleigh."

"Get away from me. Oh, my head." Averie pulls out of my grasp and touches her palm to her forehead. "Those headaches again. I shall never be free of such pain."

The headaches were the signal the transformation was taking place.

"Huxleigh!" I call. "Huxleigh, come out! We need to speak."

Averie starts breathing heavily as I encourage Huxleigh to come forth. Averie screams and falls onto the tapestry clutching her head. Her breaths change from gasping to something different. I move closer towards her bent frame. It is laughter soft at first but then louder into cackles.

Averie throws her head back and I see a change has been made. Averie's soft eyes now have a hardened look. Her kind expression is sinister and reeks of evil.

"Ah! Free! Free!" She gets to her feet. "Oh, how I hated being locked away." She stretches her arms over her head and looks around. Her eyes widen as she takes in the magnificent display of expensive treasures.

"The treasure of Yelena," she whispers, clutching her hand to chest.

"All for you, my dear," I reply.

Huxleigh turns around and narrows her eyes at the sight of me. "You!" She sashays over to me so she is in front of me. "Oliver, you called me forth."

"Yes, I would like to speak with you."

"About what?"

"Since the day you surprised me in my bed chamber, I have not been able to get you out of my head. I think we can make a powerful couple. We have the same personalities."

"We?" Huxleigh pulls her dark hair over her shoulder.

"Are you not in love with Averie?"

"All the time I spent with Averie I was hoping you would appear. Averie does not know you exist, does she?" I interrupt.

"Of course, she doesn't! That's why Lord Harrington hired Dr. Morris. It was to help cure her multiplex personality disorder and get rid of me. He wanted Averie to be whole again. But she cannot get rid of me. She is weak and she is delusional. After Dr. Morris had fallen in love with me, he told Averie her headaches were a medical condition. But it was really me trying to get out. He advised Averie to go to sleep every time she felt pain. When she is asleep, she is in a weakened state, which makes it easier for me to come alive."

"And you and Dr. Morris conspired together to find the bracelet and the treasure?" I ask.

"Of course! Then we planned to sell it and use some of that money to see about finding a way to make me in control all the time. Now why would you want to talk to me and not Averie?"

The Gate Bracelet murmurs to me. "Let's just say that Averie is too good for my soul. I need a woman who is not afraid to get her hands dirty."

Huxleigh raises an eyebrow and smirks. "I knew that day I bashed you on the head it would knock some sense into you." She moves closer to me.

"And it was Dr. Morris who tried to kill Mr. Jenkins in the library." I add.

Huxleigh smiles. "I would have done it myself if Averie had not taken control. We knew there was a second copy of *Strange Case of Dr. Jekyll and* Mr. *Hyde.* We did not want to risk anyone else having a copy and solving the puzzle. Dr. Morris would have succeeded if you and Averie had not decided to enter into the library."

She steps closer to me. "Now about this alliance you want to form. What would Dr. Morris say? He has grown quite fond of me."

"I killed your lover," I reply. "I also took care of Lord Harrington."

"Then I guess the treasure is ours, my dear, and so is this

castle. I believe now we can be the couple you desire. And I never have to let Averie come back?"

Huxleigh runs her fingers down my arm and I ignore her. The thoughts running through my brain are too hard to keep up with. What if this did not work? I had to try. I see my reflection in the mirror on the opposite wall. Leaning against the wall just behind me is a golden sword.

Huxleigh's face is inches from mine. She runs her fingers through my hair. "I knew you would be perfect the moment I saw you." She leans forward and plants her lips onto mine, and I say a silent prayer that statement uttered by Persephone so many nights ago rings true. I wrap one arm around her waist and with my free arm I lean back and take hold of the sword behind me.

Before Huxleigh realizes my intentions, I plunge the sword into her chest. She screams and pushes back . Her hands fly to the steel impaled into her flesh. Blood coats her dress and drips to the floor as she stumbles back.

"You tricked me!" She screams.

"Just as you tricked me!" I reply.

Huxleigh's eyes roll upward into her head as she staggers backward and falls onto the elegant tapestry where she lies still.

"Oh, I hope this works," I crouch next to Huxleigh and feel for a pulse. There is none. I wrap my fingers around the handle of the sword and pull it out of her flesh. It is coated in red. I throw it to the ground.

The Gate Bracelet burns against my wrist. I place my hand against her cheek.

"Soul for a soul! Averie come back to me!" I cry.

In *Strange Case of Dr. Jekyll and Mr. Hyde*, the serum of transformation did not work. But with the magic spell foretold by Persephone, if a soul broken into two could be eliminated, then one soul would form again.

Seconds pass and I fear I have taken a soul I did not want. Then I see the blood stains on Averie's dress start to fade. The blood pouring from her wound stops and closes. She takes a deep breath and starts coughing.

"Averie, my love!" I cry. I help her to her feet and pull her close.

"What happened?" Whispers Averie holding her head. "My headache is gone."

The Gate Bracelet whispers to me that Averie's headaches will never return.

"You are cured, my dear," I reply. "You have one personality now."

There is one more thing that I must do. I walk over to the mirror and stare at my reflection. I think about someone I have not seen in a long time, someone who deserves this palace and all its enchantments.

"Soul for a soul, come back to me," I cry.

A wind rushes through the enclosed hexagonal room. It scoops some of the coins out of the chest and takes them into the air. The golden gems spin in a vortex faster and faster until they fall to the ground. The chimes of gold hitting the stone ring throughout the crypt.

A figure stands before me. She has my eyes, my smile, my disposition, and my courage. She holds her arms out to me, and I run into her embrace. She smells exactly as I remember: lavender and jasmine. She is beautiful.

"Mother! I missed you so much," I cry, tears forming into my eyes.

"Oh, my beloved son! I am here now," she replies.

"Oliver," Averie's voice floats to my ears. I turn and walk towards her.

"I wanted to tell you something but you were so intent on finding the treasure I did not get a chance."

She takes my hand. She runs her fingers along the Gate Bracelet that holds me prisoner. She reaches to her neck and takes off her necklace. I see at the end is a pendant of a key.

"A stranger placed this on my crib when I was a baby," Averie continues. "I never knew what it was for, but now I know."

Taking the key into her hand, she inserts it into the heart-shaped padlock of the Gate Bracelet. The lock takes the key and she turns it. The ornament falls from my wrist and clatters to the floor.

I take Averie into my arms and kiss her.

I am free.

November 1, 1888
4:00 p.m.

The magic of the Gate Bracelet wove its spell around the castle. None of the servants, guards, or guests remember Lord Harrington and Dr. Morris. Their identity has disappeared along with their souls.

Averie and Old Man Beige were reunited as granddaughter and grandfather. Since Averie was now the sole heir of Oakenfield Castle, she invited Old Man Beige, my mother, and me to continue to live at the palace.

I proposed marriage to Averie and she accepted. We will be wed in the spring. Next month I am planning to take her on a trip to London. We agreed to sell a portion of the treasure and use the money to help the homeless in the city.

I am outside in the gardens watching the sun set behind the mountains. It is a cool November day, but the chill is somewhat comforting. Since I have been freed from the grasp of the Gate

Bracelet, it sits in my pocket. A reminder of how far I have come. Also, it spills a few more truths I must take care of.

"Well, well, well, Oliver, that was not so bad, was it?" A familiar voice chimes behind me.

I turn around and see Persephone standing close to me. She comes towards me beaming.

"I knew you would figure it all out," she says. "Are you happy?"

"Happier than I could have ever thought possible, Persephone. Thank you." I reply.

It is hard to believe that two months ago I was homeless and living on the streets. Now I have a home full of happiness. I am betrothed, I have my mother, and a new life I cannot wait to start living.

"Well, then," replies Persephone, holding out her hand. "I believe we can pass your gift onto the next soul who needs aid."

I pull the Gate Bracelet from my jacket pocket. It has been a bittersweet relationship with this ornament, but I am ready to let it go. I place the trinket into Persephone's palm.

"Good luck, Oliver," replies the mysterious woman. "I wish you all the best." Waving her hand, a black cloak and hood surround her body. A long scythe appears out of nowhere. She flashes me a white smile and disappears.

Across the garden I see Old Man Beige painting the sunset. I remember what the Gate Bracelet had whispered to me and I walk over to him.

"Hello, Oliver," he calls as he sees me.

"You were the one who created the clues," I state. "You were the one who used the book *Strange Case of Dr. Jekyll and Mr. Hyde*."

Old Man Beige smiles at me. "I knew you were a clever young lad." He puts his paintbrush down. "When I learned that Averie was my granddaughter, I found a way to be hired at Oakenfield Castle. I learned all about Yelena's treasure. You see, the treasure always existed, but the story surrounding it was not true. Yelena never got her daughter taken away from her. In fact, she and her daughter fled right here to Oakenfield Castle where they were taken in by the Viscount who loved them as if they were his own family. When he died, Yelena did not feel it was right to keep the treasure for herself, so she hid it away in the castle and made up the whole story as a way to deter people from the fortune. No one wants to look for a treasure in a place where a grieving woman lost her child. What no one knows is there were two diaries that Yelena had written. One was a fake she created to deter people from coming to the castle. The second was real. Lord Harrington had possession of the fabricated diary whereas I found the real one during my explorations of the castle.

When I found out a few years ago that Lord Harrington had a possible lead on the Tear of Erisa, I knew he did not deserve such a prize possession, for he was not a good man. I decided to create a few clues of my own to make it more difficult to find."

"You chose *Dr. Jekyll and Mr. Hyde*." I reply.

Old Man Beige smiles. "That is one of my favorite books. I am grateful Averie is cured, and I am happy to have her in my life again. Dr. Jekyll and Mr. Hyde had a tragic end, but I felt it did not have to be this way with my granddaughter. I knew you could take the circumstances and transform them into a happy ending.

I smile and clasp my hand on his shoulder.

As I walk back towards the castle, I see Averie step out onto the balcony. Her beauty radiates in the light of the setting sun, and I feel my heart flutter. She waves and blows me a kiss.

Persephone had been right. This venture has been worth my while. In the final analysis, I found a treasure more valuable than diamonds or gold. I found Averie. Now I am home.

The End

Death Keeps Watch

I am a man
I don[1] black
Protector of women
I wrap my fingers around the throats
Of those who are unjust

Raven Tartal is dead

October 10, 1890
9:15 a.m.

She is beauty, the light that strokes my heart with joy. Hair long and dark like her namesake. An eternity of passion I agree to share. Now the radiance burns in agony and cadences beat in melancholy. For true love stirs up masculine desires and unconditional loyalty; however, when the heart is broken, suffering becomes a torment with a passion of its own!

I watch them lower my fiancée's coffin into its final resting place. Raven Kinborough Tartal was the love of my life. She was the most captivating woman I had ever met.

Her smile was infectious and her laugh was contagious. I could not keep my eyes off her, and her confidence was boundless. Now her heart has ceased to beat, and mine is dead.

I stand a bit back from the crowd. The sun is bright in the sky and its rays are warm despite the chill that travels on the wind. It is unfair! The day is so beautiful, yet Raven is dead in her grave. I blink back tears that are attempting to escape the corners of my eyes. My lashes become bars imprisoning the drops, and my spirit forms a lock around my heart.

I choke back a lump forming in my throat. It is not appropriate for a young man to show emotions.

A shadow falls over me as a figure steps to my left side.

No, I silently beg, *not here, not here.*

The penumbra belongs to Bancroft MacQuoid, my soulless father.

He places one hand in his pocket while the other hand grips his cane firmly. His arrogance inflates his presence as if he were blown up like a hot air balloon.

"Atticus," he hisses.

"What are you doing here?" I whisper. The word *father* does not apply to Sir Bancroft MacQuoid. He has not been a father, and has never been a loving parent, since the day my mother gave me life. It was at the time of my birth that she went to meet the Lord.

"Still got the morbs[2] for that bricky[3] young lady," presses my father.

"She has a name," I retort.

"Yes, yes, Atticus, but you know she just did not fit your style. You are a man of wealth, Atticus, a man of status, a man of prosperity. While bricky Miss Tartal may have been brave, she was weak. Rhonwen is much more suited to your station in life."

"We are at the funeral of my beloved, and you have the nerve to bring up another woman's name!" I hiss. My tears melt into fury. It is just like him, selfish to the core, only caring for the stature and wealth of a woman whom he uses as a veneer. While in the shadows, he is a lying, cheating, gal-sneaker[4] of a man.

"Pish posh, Atticus. You are one-and-twenty years old. What do you know about love? That Tartal girl was beneath you, a middle-class woman whose only asset was her beauty which she used to marry rich. Your whole life is ahead of you. Don't waste your tears on one such as her."

I clench my fists and fight back the urge to knock my father's teeth out of his mouth. It should be Bancroft MacQuoid in that coffin, not my darling.

I turn and stare at my father directly in his face. I look at his dark eyes, his parish pick-axe[5] I wish to pommel with my fist! I keep my voice as steady as my temper would allow.

"Leave! Now!" I hiss.

My father bites his lip to keep the mourners from seeing his smirk. His eyes dance with happiness at my misery. "Very well, my son. I will see you at home. Remember what I said." He hands me a handkerchief from the breast coat of his suit. "If you must cry, do so when others are not looking. I shall be poked up[6] if I am to hear rumors around town of my patrician son wallowing in misery over a merchant's daughter." As he walks off I hear a chuckle in his throat.

I turn to see Raven's grandmother sobbing at her granddaughter's tombstone. The elderly woman raised Raven since her parents had died. Now that the light in her life has been taken, she is all alone.

My jaw clenches as fury and mourning twist into a conundrum that rips through my heart and dulls every nerve. My beloved's death does not have the feel of truth in it. She was young, healthy, and strong; she loved me and looked forward to a future together with a home and children. Her death is too soon. Too soon.

I look down at the red handkerchief my father has given me. Red like the passionate love I felt for Raven; red like the rips upon my heart that will never be healed; and red like the blood I wish to open upon my father's skin to run the rivers of sweet victory.

I see a gaslamp has been placed on a lonely stump near the burial site. The flames that burn within the glass globe entice me into an unfamiliar and unholy mood. Clouds overhead obscure the sun, throwing darkness on the cemetery. I hear the preacher offer words of comfort, but their effect is not reaching my heart.

Raven Kinborough Tartal was supposed to be Mrs. Atticus MacQuoid, not an iron grave marker with a birth and death date written across its surface.

The flare of the lamp attracts me as it shimmers in the onset of darkness, and I am overcome with passion against the spark of death that has taken the one I love. The flicker of the flame casts shadows that dance on the grass. It reminds me of the way my father's eyes filled with delight at the sight of seeing pain in my soul.

As my mind returns to the ritual of the burial service, I drop the unwanted handkerchief into the gaslamp and feel happiness as the flames consume the silk the way I wish death would consume my father. I shall like nothing more than to see that disgusting man suffer.

---

1. **Don**: wear
2. **Got the morbs:** temporary melancholy
3. **Bricky:** brave
4. **Gal-sneaker:** a man devoted to seduction
5. **Parish pick-axe:** nose
6. **Poked up:** embarrassed

October 10, 1890
8:00 p.m.

I walk into the MacQuoid mansion at exactly eight in the evening. The chimes of the grandfather clock toll my arrival. I have devoted hours after the burial to comforting Raven's grandmother. Poor dear, after having to bury so many family members, she is the last of her lineage.

I hear the crackling of the fire in the hearth and look up to see my father sitting on the leather sofa with his back to me. I feel the shadows along the walls are dancing in delight at my misery.

"Well, well, well," my father sneers, "about time you came home. What were you doing, waiting to see if your deceased mistress would awaken?"

I pull my black leather gloves off one finger at a time as I attempt to calm the fury that rages in the pit of my stomach. "I

173

know you love your dying duck in a thunderstorm[1] mistresses, Father but I am not a gal-sneaker. Raven was my future wife."

My father gets up slowly from his seat and walks over to me. "I will ignore that comment as I know you are in mourning." His eyes rove over my dark suit.

"Just because you avoid it does not take away from the fact it is true," I hiss.

"Why do you mourn for that young woman who is far beneath your social status? I will admit Miss Tartal was a bit o' strawberry[2], but marriage? Atticus! You are among the highest of London society. I could not visualize her giving the MacQuoid name the respect it deserves."

"Father, you knew I was going to marry her with or without your blessing. I had her grandmother's permission, and that was all I needed. I am a man now, and your opinions mean nothing to me."

"Well, since your "fiancée" is grinning at daisy roots[3] and not coming back, I think it is time for you to choose a proper wife who will stand by your side in matrimony, and who will not succumb to some indefinable illness before she takes her vows."

I clench my fists and shove them deep into my pockets, for the thought of pushing him into the fire is developing into an overwhelming urgency.

"Rhonwen Dankworth will make a fine wife for you and bring honor to our family name. I have spoken with her family, and they are in agreement as is Miss Dankworth. Since your wedding date has already been announced as October 31st to all the best people, you will be able to take your vows in three weeks' time."

My eyes widen and speech evades my lips, for I cannot fathom how this man has ever been blessed with the gift of being a father. How is it possible that we even share the same blood? I want nothing more than to cop a mouse[4] on his sunken face.

I move closer and whisper "just because you decided to marry three days after my mother died giving birth to me does not mean

I will follow your example, Father. Your secret life of lotties and totties[5] is not for me."

I find myself suddenly in his grip as he grabs the collar of my suit. But I am stronger, and tear his hands away. I glare at him daring him to hit me.

"What happened to your mother happens to a majority of women in labor. It was a risk."

Before I am able to respond, a feminine voice calls the name "MacQuoid." My stepmother Cedrica MacQuoid, also known as Widow Sallow, enters the room. I bite back the urge not to groan as my stomach turns. I hate that woman. Her skin is pale; her hair the color of sun; and her eyes are those of a storm cloud on the way to bring horror to the lives of unsuspecting victims.

"Bancroft, I need to speak with you, in private, if you please." Her eyes look down on me as if I am a bug. Her heel would love nothing more than to squash me. "Katja has food for you, Atticus, if you choose to eat."

I nod curtly and turn to leave.

"Atticus," my father calls to me. I look back. "I do hope all the mirrors in the Tartal house have been covered. I would hate for something unfortunate to happen to you."

"Perhaps it is you who needs to look in the mirror, Father." I shot back. "I fear blood is on your hands." For a second I see a flicker of terror flash across my father's face. I leave the room wondering why those particular words have come out of my mouth.

---

1. **Dying duck in a thunderstorm:** unattractive
2. **Bit o' strawberry:** attractive, pretty
3. **Grinning at daisy roots:** dead
4. **Cop a mouse:** to get a black eye
5. **Lotties and totes:** ladies at large, on the town

October 10, 1890
8:30 p.m.

I step into the kitchen to find Katja sweeping the floor. She is an old Greek woman, with long white hair and a mysterious personality. The townsfolk believe that Katja has a mystical aura about her. It is rumored she is able to predict the future. Although many think she is out of her mind. Even though Katja is my maid, in my heart she is the woman who raised me after my mother's death. She is the only maternal figure I know.

My father hates her but keeps her around because she is the best cook in town, and no one can tolerate the mercurial moods my father can suffer. Katja is the only person who has been willing to take care of me. My stepmother refuses any gesture of kindness. Cedrica wants nothing to do with the offspring from a previous marriage. Once the wedding band was placed on her finger, she seemed to have undertaken an obsessive pledge to produce a proper heir who in time would inherit all my father's fortune. To her dismay, her womb repeatedly failed her. I remain my father's only child. Cedrica has a son of her own named Dempster from her former husband who is now deceased. My stepbrother is three years older than I, and we do not have any particular liking for one another.

Katja looks up and a smile crosses her wrinkled face, "Oh my dear," she hugs me. "How are you enduring? I know death is not easy.

"That disgusting pig wants me to marry Rhonwen Dankworth,"

"Hush, do not worry. Right now, you are in mourning. You must take care of yourself."

"There are no words, Katja."

"I know dear, I know. Are you hungry at all?"

"Not really, but I could eat a little something."

"Good," the old woman hobbles over to the pot on the hearth and ladles some mutton stew into a bowl. The aroma from the meat makes my stomach cry in desperation, and I am aware of how hungry I really am. I take a spoon from the drawer and raise a bite to my lips.

Suddenly, a force rips away the tasty morsel from the intended target of my appetite. The bite falls to the floor and the bowl of deliciousness is overturned. I look up to see Katja with a faraway look in her eye, and fury etches across her rosy cheeks.

"Do not eat the food!" cries the elderly caretaker. "It has been poisoned!"

"What are you saying?"

The white-haired woman leans closer to the pot and sniffs. "I sense someone's guilty fingers have contaminated dinner and invite death to our door."

I smell nothing but the aroma of sizzling food that I will not be eating. My stomach growls in protest.

Katja grabs my wrist, "Someone wishes you dead."

I see her eyes glaze over, while physically in the kitchen her mind is elsewhere.

"Shall I call a constable?" I inquire.

Katja's eyes snap to attention and she looks at me, "You mentioned blood on the hands tonight because your conscience speaks the truth."

"How do you know that?"

"There is a secret your father keeps from you, and it is time you learn the truth. Tomorrow you must go to the countryside on a journey that will take four days by horse and carriage, and venture east across a wide river until you see a tall Scots pine. There you will find the start of your quest towards a confession."

She squeezes my hand and her eyes become calm again. "Aye, fatigue flows through me. My body is not what it used to be. I must take to my bed. Promise me, Atticus that you will be careful and stay in control of your emotions. For anger makes the heart lose its reason."

"I have so many questions," I state as my mind falls into an abyss of confusion.

"I cannot answer them, for you will have to learn the answers on your own."

Katja walks off. I am left alone in the kitchen with my thoughts and a pot of poisoned mutton.

I am a man
I don black
To seek the truth
One must start in the past

October 11, 1890
12:15 a.m.

My dreams materialize into flames. In my vision, I am the fire that plays upon the hearth. My anger crackles and consumes the logs as I see my father and my stepmother in a heated discussion in the parlor.

"I do not understand why your father did not leave Dempster money in his will?" Cederica is demanding.

"Why would he? Dempster is not his biological son, Atticus is," replies Bancroft. *"You know my father was not fond of you, he was not even fond of me. But he loved Atticus very much."*

My grandfather died last year and left all of his wealth in a trust for me, the true heir of the MacQuoid fortune. Now that I am twenty-one years old, it was my plan to use the money to wed my beloved and make a home for myself and my family.

My stepmother paces the room.

Bancroft frowns as he continues the discussion with his wife.

"Your family possesses a fortune equal to mine. You are confessing to me that in the testamentary dispositions your former husband did not leave a trust for Dempster?"

"He did. The lad has pilfered away almost all of it," replies Cederica.

"That is not my problem," growls Bancroft. *"That is your responsibility. It is utterly reprehensible that a young man of twenty- four years, and only heir to his family's fortune, should be almost penniless. That is because he wishes to party, drink, and have relations with wagtails[1]. Then you wish me to give him money or squander the trust set aside for Atticus? Absolutely not! Do not be vazey[2]. If we had had a child together, that would be a different story. But for many years your womb seems incapable of producing a proper heir, so do not bother me anymore with this humdrum. My concern is my own bloodline!"*

Cederica glares daggers at my father as he walks out of the room.

Atticus a sweet voice calls.

I wake to find myself in my own bed chamber. With a sinking feeling, I realize that my dream has not been a dream, but apparently a vision my soul has shown me of events that have transpired while my eyes were closed in slumber.

Atticus the voice calls again. I know that voice. My heart craves the bearer of that melodic harmony.

Raven. How I long to touch your lips against mine one more time.

Atticus the voice calls for the third time. The door to my room opens and I see a shadow beckon me into the hall.

I follow and realize I am still in my funeral attire. Stepping out into the hallway, I look for the voice to guide me. But it has gone silent.

"Raven?" I call.

Instead, I hear the quick pattern of footsteps coming from below. Peering over the balcony I see my father open the front door and step out into the night.

Now where is that skilamalink[3] gibface[4] going? I think. *It is just past midnight.* Quick as an arrow I sneak down the stairs and out the door behind him.

I trail my father across town until we reach the East End neighborhood. This is quite disturbing, even a trifle unsettling, as the East End is everything that is not part of my father's wealthy world. This district is home to back-to-back housing, narrow alleys, poor lighting, violence, and robbery. My arrogant aristocratic father would not be caught dead in this community in the daylight. Trouble is the only inhabitant that haunts this part of London. The East End is no place for a man of means.

No wonder he has a cloak over his head, I think to myself as I try to make sense of his dissipated behavior.

Bancroft rounds a corner and knocks at the door to a flat. I stay in the shadows of the alleyway.

The figure who opens the door is a woman in a shabby dress, her face heavy with make-up. My father darts inside and the door closes behind them.

"What on Earth," I mutter to myself. "Why that hornswoggler[5]! And he made a fuss over Raven's bloodline, yet here he is nanty narking[6] around in the beds of these women while his wife is home in the MacQuoid Mansion? However, I must admit I feel no pity for Cederica. Any woman who can marry a man three days after his former wife dies in childbirth can lay down the knife and fork[7] as far as I am concerned. And my father, who participated in such an act of betrayal, can lie down in the grave with such a one as Cederica.

Above my head, the gaslamps begin to flicker. The flames are extinguished and the alley is cast in darkness. I simmer in the gloom.

Most children idolize their father. I hate mine. I am an object of possession. What makes things worse is that now that I have finally entered manhood, all he cares about is whom I intend to marry to continue the bloodline and increase the family coffers.

"That man deserves a visit from death," I hiss under my breath.

At that moment of recognition, the flares in the gaslamp resurrect themselves and fill the alleyway in an eerie light that manifests ghastly shadows on the brick walls.

"Such a pity when a man is so self-absorbed that he chooses not to see the hurt of his only son," a mystical voice states behind me.

I turn to see a little old peddler woman standing behind me. Her white hair is covered in ashes and she is dressed in black. An ivory shawl is draped over her shoulders.

"Atticus MacQuoid," her wrinkled face creases in a smile, the lines around her eyes deepen as she gives me a wink. She holds a staff that resembles a serpent.

Chills run up my spine and goose bumps break out along my skin. Something about this woman seems familiar, yet I cannot put my finger on it.

"Who are you?" I ask my voice low. I have never seen her before, yet I feel this lady has been a constant visitor to the lives of people whom I know.

"A friend," the woman replies, "I am called Persephone. You do not know me, but I know you. Ever since you were a babe I have watched you live a life of cold coffee[8]. No fatherly love, no nurturing of a mother, raised by blood that is not your own, and now the one person you loved with all your heart is dead. I think it's time for a bit of suffering, don't you?"

She comes closer and looks me in the eye. "What appears to be is not always what is. Your father holds a dark secret that will change your life forever and fill you with rage. Your stepmother and stepbrother are candles to the devil[9].

"I do not understand," I reply puzzled.

"You are a good man, Atticus. Kind, humble, loving, generous. Despite being born of wealth you have not allowed your social status to turn you into your father. That is why I am going to help you."

"Help me?" I ask but Persephone ignores me.

The peddler pulls a small box out of a bag. She opens it to reveal an elegant gold pocket watch. My eyes widen.

"A pocket watch," she states my thoughts. "The symbol of manhood and mark of social status." She closes the box before I can take a closer look and places it into my hands. "Guard it well, for it has the ability to alter life. But there is one caveat. It takes a soul for a soul. Life always comes to an end. In every end there is a new beginning." She smiles mysteriously as if she holds secrets I do not completely understand. "It is time for you to turn away from this place. You do not belong here. Return to your home. You are in for quite a shock over the next few days."

I look down at the black box wrapped in gray ribbon. "I-I do not understand..." My words trail off into silence.

Persephone is gone.

---

1. **Wagtails:** promiscuous women
2. **Vazey:** stupid
3. **Skilamalink:** someone who is secretive and shady
4. **Gibface:** an ugly person
5. **Hornswoggler:** fraud or cheat
6. **Nanty narking:** having a grand old time
7. **Lay down the knife and fork:** die
8. **Cold coffee:** bad luck or misfortune
9. **Candles to the devil:** evil

October 15, 1890
12:15 p.m.

After my interaction with Persephone, I decide to embark on the quest Katja foretold to me.

Four days pass as I journey into the deep countryside. England is a beautiful display of the autumn season; trees and bushes offer a blazing display of orange, red, and yellow. From the carriage, I walk along a well-traveled path until the roaring of a river comes to my attention.

I remember Katja's words. I pull a compass out of the pocket of my waistcoat. The black box from the mysterious Persephone brushes against my fingers. I feel a chill rush down my back. The small package arouses my curiosity, but I have a mission of my own. With the compass in front of me, I head east, and begin moving in search of a Scots pine.

A cold breeze ruffles my jacket and my hair. It is as if the wind is trying to speak to me, but I do not understand its language.

Katja had mentioned that my conscience had spoken the truth. What did my inner soul know that the rest of my body is unable to understand? I think about the poisoned mutton stew. Who would want to kill me? And why? Thoughts race through my brain like sweeping gusts of wind.

I think about Raven. I miss her dearly. She has not even been dead for a week, and my father is already trying to arrange my wedding to someone else.

However, the events surrounding my lover's death are peculiar. Raven's grandmother has told me that my beloved appeared healthy throughout the day of her death, then towards the evening, she felt unusually ill. She had headaches and began to convulse, which made Raven's grandmother think evil spirits had gotten hold of her. Then Raven dropped to the floor, dead.

I shake my head and stop as a large Scots pine looms before me. I observe the green needles and touch them with my fingertips. The stiff points dig into my skin like tiny knives, and I welcome the pain as a way to camouflage my heartbroken sadness.

I hear a rustle in the bushes behind me. I turn around and see nothing. Perhaps it is a small animal roaming the woods.

Chop chop chop.

The sound of an ax against wood shakes me from my dismal state.

"What is that?" I whisper.

I hear a rustle in the brush but again I see nothing.

I continue down the path and peer through the bushes into a clearing. A quaint stone-and-stucco cottage meets my eyes. The two-story dwelling has an asymmetrical pitched room with half-timbered studs along the upper level. Dual chimneys feature elegant brickwork. Well-maintained flower beds surround the house displaying flora of every color and shade.

Two young men are chopping wood. Their backs are to me, but they appear to be around the same age as myself.

Why would Katja want me to come all this way to see two men chopping wood? How is that supposed to reveal the truth?

The men place their axes down. One wipes the sweat from his brow, and the other one rubs the back of his neck. They turn to face each other and I see their full profile.

My eyes widen and my heart begins to thump faster in my rib cage.

Those men are wearing my face!

Thoughts race through my brain. What evil brew is this?

> *I am a man*
> *But not unique*
> *I am one, but my face is three*
> *What is this bombastic complexity?*
> *What wickedness bestows this turnabout?*

I turn to leave in silence but a tree root unearths from the ground and blocks my path. My foot catches on the gnarled bark, and I fall forward into the clearing.

Instead of disappearing, I am now on full display for the two men who share my face.

They begin to walk over to me.

"Are you alright?" asks the first man. His voice trails off when he sees me look at him.

"Begorra!" cries the second lad. "His face is ours, dear brother."

I get to my feet and brush the dirt off my trousers. "Why do you have my face? What bitter broth has boiled this fix?"

"Carriwitchett[1]," replies the second man with a shrug. "That is an interesting question." He turns to his brother.

"The real question is who are you?" asks the first man, "It is you who is trespassing on our land."

"Boys, what is all this chitter chatter out here. Stop killing the canary[2]! We have work to do." An old woman who reminds me of Katja comes out onto the stoop. She is short and plump with long gray hair pulled back. A black band wraps around her head, and her clothes are covered with dirt. She is holding a broom in her hand. She gets a clear look at my face and gasps. The broom falls to the ground with a thud.

"Holy Ghost!" she cries putting her hands to her mouth. "The oldest son of Arantxa returns."

"Mother, what foolishness you speak of?" asks the first man.

"That is my mother's name," I reply.

The gray-haired woman clambers down the steps and rushes over to me. She touches my face with her hands. "Look at you, Atticus, such a fine young man you have grown to be."

"You know my name?"

"Yes, how could I not? I helped birth you, after all," the woman beams. "My name is Demelza."

I feel a tightness forming in my chest, and my breath comes in rapid gusts. Somehow I sense that everything I have ever once thought true about my life has been a lie.

"Mother, who is this gentleman?" asks the first lad.

The woman turns. "My dear sons. I have been keeping the truth from you for so long waiting for a sign. Today I received that for which I have long waited. This is your brother Atticus. Atticus, these are your brothers Ridley and Winthrop. The three of you are identical triplets."

"Triplets!" I exclaim.

"That is unheard of," cries Ridley.

"But not impossible," finishes Demelza, "Now come inside, gentlemen. Evil lurks in these woods and waits to hear the truth. I will put on the pot for tea."

"Here I thought I was just a twin," says Winthrop as we all walk into the house. "Now there are three of us. Are you sure three is all there is, Mother?"

Demelza hushes him and gestures for us to sit around the small wooden table while she puts the tea kettle on the fire.

The inside of the house is primitive and a world away from the elegance and glamor that fills my life. However, this house has one element my grand edifice lacks. Love.

I sit on one of the unmatched chairs and look across at my

two brothers. I feel as if I am looking into a mirror without the shimmer of reflection. We are all so similar to each other, six feet in height with short black hair and brown eyes. Defined cheekbones, strong jawlines, and a muscular physique round out our identical appearance.

Demelza places a teacup in front of all of us. Putting a cloth around a floral kettle, she begins to pour the hot contents into the glamorous cups. I watch the steam rise into the air and wonder if my sanity is disappearing along with the fragrant mist.

"You do not have to worry, Atticus, the tea is not poisoned." I jerk my head to look at her in confusion. She merely responds with a wink.

"Mother, what is going on?" cries Ridley, "how is it possible this man is our brother, yet he appears to live in a castle with those fine garments?"

The kind woman wrings her fingers together and bows her head. "My children, I am afraid I have been keeping a dark secret from both of you. I have raised you both as my sons, but you are not my sons. Your mother is the same as Atticus, making you triplets, which as you know in England, is quite rare."

Ridley and Winthrop's faces fall, and they look down at their tea. I feel a twinge of envy run through my blood. At least they had someone like a mother who gave them love. All I experienced was disappointment and neglect. Thankfully, I still have Katja.

"Who is our mother?" whispers Winthrop. "Where is she?" He turns to look at me.

"She is dead," I reply, and avert my gaze to the hot contents that I have no desire to drink.

"What a morbid response," replies Ridley.

"Boys, mind your manners," sighs Demelza as she settles herself at the table and takes a sip of her tea. She closes her eyes in thought, and, after opening them, begins to tell her story. "Your mother's name was Arantxa Lloyd. She was a beautiful woman of the gentry class. All of you resemble her. She married Bancroft MacQuoid who was a young business man looking to elevate his position in society. Over time his wealth began to increase, and he soon worked his way into earning a bank full of money and a minor title."

"Wait," I interrupt, "my father was not born rich?"

"Not in the slightest. Your father acquired his wealth after his marriage. Your mother was the one with money. Once Bancroft became wealthy, Arantxa became pregnant with their first child. It was rumored throughout the years that your father had not been faithful, but your mother, kind-hearted as she always was, gave him the benefit of the doubt."

"How do you know all of this?" I ask.

"I was your mother's maid as well as her midwife. No one knew her better than me. When your mother was almost nine months, tragedy struck. I was outside the house tidying up when I heard a scream. Bancroft and I entered the room to see Arantxa had fainted and was suffering convulsions. It appeared that the child was coming before its time, and something was wrong. I laid her in bed where she shook and was in and out of consciousness. Before she died, she begged me to save her "children," which I thought odd that she would say such a thing.

"I made the decision to bring the child into the world not in a womanly way. I had never performed a cesarean birth, and the fact the patient was no longer alive made the situation much more serious. To my surprise, when I opened her up, I pulled out not one, not two, but three little babes. It was a shock to the whole MacQuoid estate. First was Atticus, then Ridley and lastly Winthrop."

She takes another sip of tea. Her hands shake as she replaces her cup.

"Our mother knew there was more than one of us?" I ask.

"Yes, women always have a way of knowing those things. It was your mother who named you. She had written three names for boys, and three names for girls. I took the liberty of honoring her wishes and naming you three in the order she wrote them.. I will never forget Bancroft's face when he saw those three infants wrapped in their swaddling clothes. It was like he had seen three ghosts. Thankfully, Katja and the other servants of the house were helpful because your father would not even touch his own children."

"Why?" asks Ridley.

"I have no idea. A few hours after you all had been born, Bancroft told me that he was only keeping one child. The world could not know that his deceased wife had given birth to triplets. He said it was bad luck. He said he would keep the first child because he needed an heir. Then he would pay me to make sure the other two children disappeared from the face of the world."

My brothers and I all give each other the same look. We have only met thirty minutes ago, yet, we all share the same facial expression. I can tell my brothers do not like our father, and that fills my heart with joy.

"I told Bancroft I would not murder innocent babe. He said if I didn't do it, he would hire someone who would. Later that night, Katja and I made a plan. We had become good friends over the years, and we knew we needed to keep the two unwanted infants safe. It was decided we would hide them and tell Bancroft we had killed them. I would resign from his service, since my skills as a midwife were no longer needed. I would take the two brothers and bring them to my cottage far away from London and raise them as my own. Katja agreed that she would watch over the first born. We knew one day we wanted to reunite you, and it appears that day is today."

"Blimey, our own father does not want us?" murmurs Ridley looking at Winthrop.

"He wanted to kill us," adds Winthrop.

My jaw clenches and my hands ball into fists. "That is just like that pompous fool to be only out for himself. I am not surprised. This is the kind of thing my father would do. After all, he married my stepmother three days after our mother was dead."

Ridley slams his fist on the table. "That man deserves death."

Winthrop puts his head in his hands.

Demelza gets up and pats each one on the shoulder. There are tears in her eyes. "I am sorry I kept this secret from you, but in my heart I will always consider you my sons. I will leave you all to talk." She opens the door and goes out into the garden.

I cross my arms and feel a numbness beginning to weave its way through my veins. Blood pounds in my ears. Resentment fills me. I have always wondered what it would be like to have a sibling. Now I have two and we are triplets."

"Your father sounds like a monster," begins Winthrop.

"You mean *our* father," I reply. It is odd to see myself sitting across from me times two, only in different clothes. To see words coming out of a mouth that looks like mine but is not mine is something I will have to get used to. "To be honest, I envy you both, dear brothers. It appears you grew up in a house full of love, while I grew up abandoned and horribly mistreated. At least you have a woman who may not have been your mother but wants you. Alas, the woman who should have been a mother to me wants nothing to do with me."

"So, Ridley and I are supposed to be dead," says Winthrop, "What do we do next?"

"This is too much to take in," adds Ridley.

I stand up. "I must return home, my dear brothers, but I will be back. I feel we all need time to think about this momentous discovery, and make a plan."

As I leave the house, I see Demelza cutting roses from a bush.

"Demelza," I walk closer to her. "Thank you for saving my brothers' lives. I must admit, I envy them and wish you had taken me, too."

The old woman's face breaks into a smile and the wrinkles around her eyes crease. "Ah, Atticus, I wish I could have had you, too, but your father needed an heir. I know Katja is grateful for all these years devoted to you. I am truly sorry you had to endure such neglect from the gentleman, but it is all coming to a well-deserved end."

"I still do not understand why he wanted Ridley and

Winthrop dead. I would have thought my father would have been happy to have sons to carry on his legacy."

Cutting another rose, Demelza holds it up and eyes it closely. "A rose is a symbol of life. Its petals are soft and alluring like the good times we are given. When you focus on the long stem, this can be seen as the journey of life. If you start at the base of the stem and work your way up, you see all the thorns poking out. Those are the obstacles and challenges of life. The moments of confusion, the moments of anger, the moments of sadness, the moments where we do not understand why this is happening. But if we do not give up and continue up the stem, we reach the top where the beautiful rose presents itself."

She holds the rose out to me. Awkwardly I take it and rub the stem between my thumb and index finger.

"Each of those thorns can represent all the tragedy, pain, and misfortune in your life, Atticus, but you are closer to the top of the stem. Soon you will be nestled in between the petals where happiness and peace will find you."

Unsure of how to respond, I say, "My fiancée loved roses. They were her favorite flower."

"Then take it to her. I'm sure she will appreciate the gesture."

I clear my throat. "I'm sorry to say, she is dead."

"Oh, Atticus, my heart feels your pain," Demelza replies. "Soon you will find yourself in the petals. Take it to Katja and tell her we need to have a chat."

I nod and tuck the rose in the inner pocket of my waistcoat.

"Oh Atticus," Demelza calls. I turn around as she catches hold of my arm. "To answer your question, a week before you and your brothers were born, your father was told by an old peddler woman that the number three would destroy him.

You can imagine his shock when his deceased wife gave birth to three babes." She pats my cheek. "Do not worry, dear, the answer will become clear."

I walk into the woods pondering her words. The number three would destroy my father? How? Absent-mindedly, I reach into my pocket and touch the rose. The softness of the flora reminds me of Raven's lips against mine. I wave the thought away before sorrow can penetrate my soul.

---

1. **Carriwitchett:** a made-up word reflecting a puzzling and perplexing
2. **Killing the canary:** shirking work

October 19, 1890
5:00 p.m.

I enter the MacQuoid mansion. The edifice is silent and nobody appears to be home. This is a blessing to me. After the recent events, I want nothing better than to place my fingers around Bancroft MacQuoid's throat.

Dim light shines through the parlor window. Something out of place catches my attention. I bend down to see clumps of dirt on the paneled wood floor.

That is strange, Katja should have cleaned this up already. She loves a neat and tidy house.

"Katja?" I call, but there is no answer.

Removing the rose from my pocket, I walk through the house into the kitchen. A horrific sight meets my eyes.

Katja lies on her side in a pool of blood with her back to me . I drop the rose to the floor and rush to her aid. Rolling her over, I see a knife has penetrated her flesh just below the rib cage. I gather her in my arms.

I yell for one of the other maids but no one is home. My fingers grasp Katja's wrist looking for a pulse, but I feel no beats against the skin. Slowly I lay her back on the floor, taking a cloth from the table. I remove the knife from her body and place it on the floor behind her. I cannot bear to see her like that.

One of the maids comes through the backdoor and enters the kitchen. She screams at the sight of Katja. I yell at her to call the constable. Her footsteps patter out of the kitchen.

I feel a pressure around my wrist. Looking down, I see Katja's eyes open which baffles me because I had not felt a pulse. I am not sure how it is possible for her to still be alive, but I hold her nonetheless.

"Atticus," she whispers.

"Katja. Do not speak. We are going to save you."

The old woman shakes her head. "I will return," she chokes. "Use the pocket watch and r-remember the number three." Her eyelids begin to close.

"Katja," I ask in a hushed voice, "tell me who did this to you."

Again, she shakes her head, and I feel the life leave her body. Her hand falls to the floor.

Anger makes my tears run hot. First Raven, now Katja.

Shoes on the floor enter the kitchen. I look up to see my stepmother and father looking at me.

"Good gracious," cries Cedrica. "Who could have done such a thing?"

My brain goes numb. Why is it that all the good people in my life are gone, yet my unhappy fate suffers me with these villains? I do not know why, but in my viscera I know these two people standing before me are responsible.

"Maybe you can answer the question," I shoot back.

"What are you talking about my son," snaps Bancroft, "you're not trying to say your stepmother here committed murder?"

"Or maybe you did," I continue, "After all, you have a habit of wanting others dead who do not serve your purpose."

I see a flicker of fear flash in my father's eyes as if he knows what I am hinting at. Then the image disappears. He balls his fists, "I do not like what you are saying here, Atticus. I would mind my tongue if I were you."

"Or what? Are you going to make sure I disappear, too?"

Bancroft's fist raises in the direction of my face, but I duck, grab the collar of his jacket, and slam him against the wall. I am no longer a little boy, and his beatings no longer subdue me. Now I am as tall as he, an adult male, and anger strengthens me.

"Your days are numbered," I hiss. Then I let him go and storm out of the room.

October 21, 1890
10:30 a.m.

I sit at my desk and look at my reflection in the mirror. I do not recognize myself. My eyes are swollen with tears, and my face wears the scowl of a man who is about to do all the things that good men are advised against doing. My mother was taken from me before I had even had a chance to meet her. My siblings were hidden from me. The woman who had raised me now lies murdered. My fiancée, the love of my life, is dead.

I feel a bubble welling up in my chest as though I am trapped in the complexities of life and cannot escape.

It is time, a strange voice whispers.

It sounds like my deceased lover. I look around, but no one is in view.

I turn back to the mirror, only this time my reflection does not mirror me. I see myself with the pocket watch in one hand and a bloody knife in the other.

Use the pocket watch my reflection tells me, then the vision fades, and I see myself again.

Pulling out the black box I place it on the table. With careful hands I undo the gray ribbon and open the gift from Persephone. On a small satin pillow lies a pocket watch. It is a hunter case watch made of gold. In the center of the cover is a red ruby in a fancy cut, and the entire outside of the watch is encased in black diamonds. When I press the button, the cover pops open and reveals the watch face, which features Roman numerals with a second-hand dial that quietly ticks. In the middle of the watch face is a design that looks like two tiny bones crossing one another. There is a bit of transparency on the face that shows the gold gears grinding back and forth. I close the cover, and as it clicks into place, I feel a difference about me as if I am here but not fully here. My mind is full of anger and rage. The truth is coming through, and I know what I have to do. The pocket watch is accompanied with a long gold chain which can be fastened to the inside of a jacket. I put the timepiece into my waistcoat and head out the door on my way into town.

As I walk along the busy streets, I feel the watch pulsing against my breast. Its ticks are beginning to clear up the confusion and reveal the mysteries that have been hidden for far too long.

"Atticus," a voice calls. I turn around to see the woman my father wants me to marry: Rhonwen Dankworth. She is accompanied out of a carriage. I grumble and roll my eyes.

"Atticus!"

Here this woman stands in her red dress with her beautifully-tailored hat on her brown braided hair. While others may consider her attractive, she is not my Raven, nor will she ever be.

"What can I do for you, Miss Dankworth?"

"Oh, Atticus, no need to be so formal! After all, we are to be married in ten days. Exciting, isn't it?"

"I beg your pardon?"

"I'm sure your father told you. He and my father have arranged our marriage, and we will be wed on October 31st. Soon we shall be husband and wife." She gives me a wink and bites her bottom lip. "I assume you are curious to see what is behind all these bustles."

My wedding day! The nerve of this lunatic woman! Determined to marry me, and my fiancée is newly dead. I pause - this is exactly what my father did when my mother died.

A voice whispers in my head. *She has blood on her hands.*

It is the pocket watch speaking to me. I look at her pale fingers. I do not see any blood, but I understand the message.

"Rhonwen, I am not sure what it is my father told you, but I am not marrying you on October Thirty-first, nor will I ever marry you. Good day, madam."

As I turn to go, I see her face flush, and her eyes narrow. "I suggest you reconsider your answer, Atticus. Only a foolish man would choose not to marry me. We are a match made in heaven, and you should accede to your father's wishes and put a ring on my finger. Fortune might be in peril when people do not know what is good for them, and I am good for you."

I smirk, "I will take my chances." Then I walk off into the morgue, my destination.

October 21, 1890
11:00 a.m.

D r. Wiktor Wiśniewski is in charge of the morgue. I enter with a storm raging inside me. Before he could turn around, I hit him over the head. Not enough to kill him for he is not the intended victim.

I check his pulse. It is there. I hear his breaths. It will be a few minutes before he comes to, and that is all the time I need.

The pocket watch tells me exactly where to look. I walk over to a lock box and break the seal with my bare hands. My strength has increased. The pocket watch fills me with determination.

As I shuffle through the files, I find a document that contains the post mortem results of Raven Tartal. After reading through all the details, I find two certificates of death that contradict themselves. I quickly learn that Dr. Wiśniewski originally found traces of arsenic in the stomach of my beloved. However, the second report notes that she died from illness. Apparently abandoning his professional ethics, the medical examiner lied. One of these reports is untrue. But why?

Within my pocket I feel the presence of the watch imposing its power upon me. My mind shifts into an illusion between reality and truth.

No longer am I in the morgue with an unconscious doctor at my feet. Instead, I see myself in my father's study at the MacQuoid mansion. Bancroft sits behind his desk and looks at the figure who has her back to me.

"Has it been taken care of?" asks my father.

The woman nods. "Just as you said it would."

MacQuoid reaches into his desk drawer and pulls out an envelope full of money. "Here, for you."

The woman shakes her head. "I do not need any money. You know Atticus is the only thing I want."

Bancroft flicks the money toward her, "And you shall have him. Take the money, anyway, and buy yourself something fancy to wear for your wedding. After all, the blessed event will take place in a few weeks." He stands up and looks out the window. "I cannot thank you enough for taking that foolish young girl off my hands. I cannot believe my son was going to marry a woman like that. He will be better and more powerful with you by his side."

In the flicker of the gaslamp the woman's face comes into view. It is Rhonwen! She smirks and smoothes out her dress. "You realize, good Sir Bancroft McQuoid, these young lads' brains are not fully developed, and sometimes you have to eliminate the trash to show them you mean business." She laughs. "Raven's grandmother did not even notice when I poured the arsenic in her soup. If the old woman accidentally eats it too, then they both will be dead. But wait. Will not the medical examiner be able to detect the arsenic?"

"Do not worry your pretty little head about it, Dollface. Let me handle Dr. Wiśniewski. Wealth goes a long way. Just worry about your wedding vows to my son."

. . .

Once again I feel the power of the pocket watch. My mind clears and I am back in the morgue. I snap the file shut. My malicious father paid the medical examiner to hide the truth of Raven's murder. I feel myself transform into someone I am not, into a beast thirsty for revenge upon the people who have stolen my happiness. Groans sound behind me. Dr. Wiśniewski is regaining consciousness. I whisk away from the smell of death like a draft in the chilling noon air.

Go to your brothers, my pocket watch whispers.

I obey its command.

October 26, 1890
12:00 p.m.

Truth dances on the lips of others but is not revealed.

I stumble through the woods, a change occurring through my soul and body. My mind fills with visions as the pocket watch speaks to me. An illusion appears before me.

Within the vision, once again I see my father's study, but this time, Rhonwen is not present. Instead, I see my stepmother bursting into the room.

"What is your point in marrying off Atticus?" she huffs. *"Dempster should be your only heir."*

"He is not my heir. If you're going to continue to annoy me about this topic, then kindly go about your own business this night," replies my father.

Cedrica walks over to him. "Remember what the old peddler woman said a long time ago, how the number three will destroy you? Atticus is still one of the three, and you must destroy him if you are to maintain power of the estate."

"I will take care of Atticus on my own terms. Thank you, my dear. In the meantime, calm your money obsession. I know you are only trying to help your drunken son. You want to use Atticus' trust from my father to set up your son for life. This will never happen, so long as I am alive. If you bring it up again, I will find a means to silence you forever."

"Oh, so you can get rid of me like you did your wife and marry another one of your little mistresses?" snaps Cederica.

My father gets up and begins to walk out of the study. "You had no problems with it when you agreed to marry me three days after Arantxa's funeral. You knew what you were getting into. So why complain now? Everyone has their turn."

He closes the door.

With the closing of the door, the illusion disappears. The Scot's pine emerges before my face, and I almost run into it. A rustle sounds behind me. My brothers emerge from among the trees.

"Atticus, you really did not see that tree?" asks Ridley.

"My mind is elsewhere."

"Are you alright?" asks Winthrop. "You look a bit pale."

A feeling of dread sweeps throughout my body. Somewhere, sometime, somehow, something is wrong, as if a good soul has departed before its time has come.

"How long have you been out?" I ask.

"We have been hunting for most of the day," replies Ridley, gesturing to the bow in his hands and a quiver of arrows at his hip.

"Where is Demelza?" My heartbeat intensifies.

"At home."

"We need to go there at once. I feel something is amiss." A shiver runs down my spine. Within my jacket the pocket watch whispers danger has entered the small cottage.

Together, we race through the woods to the home of my brothers. As we enter the clearing, flashes of red and gold meet our eyes. Flames lick the roof of the cottage, trickling down the sides, and spreading towards the front door.

"Demelza! She must still be inside!" cries Winthrop.

Without hesitation, I run to the wooden door and throw it open. Smoke enters my lungs, but I do not feel it. The pocket watch tells me the flames will not hurt me. I enter the cottage as flames envelope me, but do not harm me. Fire fills the room as if some manipulation of evil has worked its malicious mischief upon all the walls of the loving home.

I see Demelza collapsed on the floor. I pull the cloth off the nearby table and wrap her in it. I carry her outside as the architecture of the structure begins to deteriorate and collapse around me. I remain unharmed. The pocket watch burns close to my soul.

I emerge from the flames unscathed and lay Demelza upon the lush grass. My brothers and I crouch around her lifeless body. I pull her upward into an embrace only to spy two bullet holes in her chest.

Upon my soul, I swear by all that is holy, I shall learn the identity of the monster who has taken the life of the only mother my brothers have ever loved.

October 30, 1890
11:00 p.m.

Four days have passed since the death of Demelza. I am home. Within my waistcoat, I feel a burning near my heart. I reach for the pocket watch that displays eleven in the evening. Time is a cruel ally. Only a few hours exist until the hour of my wedding. How I miss my lovely Raven. Our wedding day has been our death. Now it will be a day of revenge.

How curious that all these deaths seem connected to my family in some way. The pocket watch whispers the long-awaited truth that my ears yearn to hear. Salty tears drip from my lashes onto the black diamond casing of the watch that I hold in my hand. I am not of sound mind. The only emotion my body suffers is anger.

I witness the gears turn through the glass. I cannot bear the sight of the mechanism that speaks to me of the hours stolen from my darling. The lid of the watch closes. I feel it snap into place. It is almost as if time has taken on a life of its own. Now I have an ally for retribution.

A soul for a soul, Persephone's voice hisses in my head.

Suffocation throttles my breath. I must leave the MacQuoid mansion. It is time for me to set into place the wheels of justice.

October 30, 1890
11:30 p.m.

My feet take me to the doorstep of the Dankworth estate. Rhonwen will be home alone. My knuckles rap at the door. I hear someone light a candle, and after peering through the keyhole, Rhonwen opens the door for me. Deep within the chambers of her home, a clock chimes eleven-thirty. It is the eve of my wedding to Raven, but Rhonwen stands before me.

"Atticus," she invites me in. A smile spreads across her face like that of a cat about to devour a tasty morsel. "What a surprise. You could not wait until our wedding day?"

Bombastic woman!

I give her a wan smile and step across the threshold. The door closes behind me, and she leads me into the parlor where the fire glows brightly and the lamps illuminate the shadows that wait for my next move. She stretches across the settee like a feral feline as if inviting me to take her in my arms. I hold back my disgust.

"Rhonwen, there is not going to be any wedding," I begin. "You believe it is acceptable for you to marry me after my fiancée mysteriously dies? It has only been three weeks."

My self-appointed betrothed wrinkles her forehead. "What do you mean mysterious? She died of illness, which is hardly mysterious. Pish Posh! It does not matter to me. Atticus! I want you, and whether we wed in a few hours or a few months, makes no difference to me. Raven Tartal is still dead."

"You poor misguided soul. You want to marry me so badly that you would kill for it?"

"What is the matter with you, Atticus? Why do you tell such lies?"

The pocket watch speaks to me softly as I pace in front of the fireplace.

"Lies? You believe there are no lies? I beg to differ, my darling. My father was angry that I proposed to Raven, and he felt my union would not be a good match. He wanted a woman of rich, aristocratic flair to be my wife. Because you were a friend of the family, you took it upon yourself to devise a plan to bring about the death of Raven. My father must have told you that he married my stepmother three days after my mother died, and it gave you hope that if you murdered Raven, I would follow in his footsteps."

"I think you had better leave," hisses Rhonwen.

The pocket watch continues to murmur, and I reveal what it says. "You thought you were exceptionally clever. You knew Raven's grandmother sold jams which she mixed in her own kitchen, so you placed an order and told her it was for one of your social gatherings. When you arrived at her house to pick up your package, you spied a pot of stew on the stove. Taking advantage of the fact that Raven's grandmother momentarily left the room, you saw your opportunity to put arsenic into the food knowing that it would be eaten by members of the household."

I glare at her as she shifts her weight on the settee.

"I do not like what you are saying," she complains.

"You are a murderess, and you expect me to marry you when you brought about the death of the woman I loved? My fiancée? What are you thinking? You believe that I am my father?"

Rhonwen's eyes narrow. "Quite a dizzy[1] you are, Atticus," she whispers. "You are, however, a fool. You accuse without evidence. You speak without foundation. We could have had a good life together, but you have chosen to be a pompous imbecile. Now I suggest you leave before I call the authorities to report the intrusion of a trespasser."

The pocket watch tells me she has a trick up her sleeve.

I nod my head and turn towards the door. The hair on the back of my neck rises as I feel her reach for the fire poker and attempt to ambush me with an untimely death.

I whirl around and grab the heavy wand with one hand and wrench it out of her malicious grasp. I throw it, and it clatters to the floor. With my other hand, I grab the nearby vase, and bring it down upon her skull.

She falls to the floor. Water and fallen flowers scatter around her lifeless form.

A soul for a soul

The clock chimes midnight. A new day has begun. My day has begun.

I hear a scuffle outside. *They have arrived.*

Opening the door and stepping out into the darkness, I see my brothers emerge from the shadows into the light of the street-lamps. The pocket watch has called them to me.

"My dear brothers, how kind of you to join me. Come, we have much work to do."

---

1. **Quite a dizzy:** A very clever gentleman

October 31, 1890
12:00 a.m.

Dempster Sallow stumbles out of the nearby pub. The young lad is up a pole[1] as he clings to the walls that lead him into the alley. He trips and falls on his stomach at my feet. In a drunken haze, he struggles to push himself up. As he reaches his knees, he looks up and sees me standing over him.

"Atticus w-what are y-you doing here?" slurs Dempster as he finally rises to full height.

"The same reason you are here," I reply, "looking for the truth. However, I am still searching for answers while you are trying to drown away the guilt of what you did."

The pocket watch pulses against my chest and I listen.

"I d-did not do anything"

"Dempster, you are a murderer."

"What bloody lies you speak. You must be arfarfan'arf[2]. Atticus, you talk about me, and it is you who must be nipping at the bottle. There are no lies."

I look at the glassy whites of his eyes. "No, Dempster, you are broke. You wasted all your money on drinking, women, and expensive gaming clubs. You were desperate for money, having lost an entire fortune at the tables. It was then that you turned to my father. You wanted my money. You and your mother hatched an invidious plan to eliminate me. All these years, Cederica never quite believed that my brothers were dead. Her suspicions grew over time.

On the day that I ventured into the country for the first time, she had you follow me. It was at that time you discovered the cottage, and realized that my brothers were still alive. You saw their existence as a threat to the inheritance you lusted after so badly. You made up your mind to go back later to kill two innocent people. However, when you arrived at the cottage a second time, my brothers were not home. They were out hunting. Demelza surprised you and you shot her in the chest, so she could not tell my brothers you were here."

A sly grin spread across Dempster's face. "What are you going to do about it? You think yourself to be a copper?" He reaches into his pocket and pulls out a gun. "You think you're so afternoonified[3], Atticus. Everything is always about you, and you think I am supposed to stay in your shadow? Well, now, I will end you, and all of your money will go to me, because your father will have no choice."

A twang echoes against the walls of the dingy alley, and Dempster falls to the ground.

Dead.

His gun clatters along the pavement. Two arrows protrude out of his back.

Ridley and Winthrop appear at the opposite end of the alley. They clutch bows in their hands.

Target practice is an amusing sport.

My brothers look at the malicious evil doer.

"What a dirty scoundrel, killing an old woman," sneers Ridley.

"Well, people always get what they deserve," replies Winthrop, "Demelza did not deserve this fate." He bows his head.

"Do not worry, brothers, all is not lost." I pick up the gun and place it in my pocket.

A soul for a soul the wind whispers.

"Let us pay our next murderer a visit. Time is my ally. Midnight is my hour."

---

1. **Up a pole:** drunk
2. **Arfarfan'arf:** Drunk
3. **Afternoonified:** smart

October 31, 1890
1:00 a.m.

Predawn on All Hallows Eve is such a tasty hour for death. My pocket watch reads one in the morning. Standing in the shadows of my stepmother's room, I see Cederica pull back the curtains and look out at the night sky.

"Hoping to find forgiveness for your actions?" I inquire quietly.

Cederica whirls around to see me standing before her. "Atticus, do your manners escape you? How dare you step into a married woman's bedchamber at night? Especially your stepmother?"

"Oh, please! Cederica! You are no mother of any kind to me. Any woman who can plot the murder of an entire family has allowed polite considerations to escape whatever claims she might have to social standing. Your integrity died long ago."

She steps closer to me. "You dare accuse me of a deed so malicious?"

I listen to the pocket watch. Time is my ally. It speaks truth.

"My words are not an accusation. What I utter is true. Any woman who marries a man three days after his wife dies is not a woman of fine feeling. You were my father's mistress for many years, and you did not care that he was a married man. Admit it, Cederica, you were always jealous of the fact that I was Bancroft's only heir. Try as you might, your womb failed you for your sins. You have always believed if I were dead, my father would have no choice but to bequeath my trust fund and worldly possessions to Dempster."

I see a flicker of fear flash across her eyes.

"It was after Raven's funeral, Cederica. You made a point about food in the kitchen, drawing my attention to some evil you had prepared for me. It was Katja who sensed something was wrong. She knocked the bowl out of my hands. You knew I would be the last person to eat anything that night. It was you who had poisoned the dish. When you realized that Katja had interfered in your plan, you killed her."

Cederica glares at me. "Lies you speak. I shall be sure to tell your father that you have lost your mind and should be examined by a doctor."

"Many years ago, when Katja told you and my father my brothers were dead, you did not believe her. But you had no proof, and you had no way of knowing where Katja and Demelza had hidden my brothers. Behind my father's back you paid investigators to try to find them. You knew it would be easier to kill two newborns than two grown men. After many years of searching, you eventually gave up. Then the other night you overheard Katja suggest to me that I should go into the woods to find the truth. You had an inkling that this journey might lead to my brothers, so you sent your dissolute son to follow me. When Dempster reported Winthrop and Ridley were alive, you told him to kill them. But instead, he killed the wrong person."

Cederica trembles before me. "I will not tolerate such accusations!" She turns and heads towards the door.

I draw a knife from my pocket and settle it into her back. She drops to the floor like a pile of bricks.

Stepping over her lifeless body, I head out the door and down the stairs. Katja's death has been avenged. Now it is time for the grand finale when three sons will confront their father. Time is my ally. Revenge is sweet.

October 31, 1890
2:00 a.m.

Sir Bancroft MacQuoid stands in front of the fireplace, watching the smoke rise up into the chimney.

"Hello, Father?" A voice that sounds familiar but is not familiar calls to him.

He turns around to see Ridley standing before him, but he thinks it is me.

"Atticus, what are you doing up? It is two in the morning."

"I could say the same for you, father. Why awake so early? Your guilt eating you alive?" Another voice also familiar but not familiar speaks behind him. Winthrop appears.

Sweet victory fills my soul at the sight of my father's face when he sees two of me materialize out of the shadows like ghosts. His body freezes and his eyes widen as if he has seen the spirits of the

217

past rise up against him. He looks from Ridley to Winthrop. I step from the shadows.

"Hello, Father," I call. Now the voice is tantalizingly familiar.

We stand in a triangular formation with my father in the center. Bancroft's glance leaps from one to the other to the other. We three are formidable.

"What's wrong, Father? Disappointed to see the sons you sentenced to death still alive? Do you not wish to meet Ridley and Winthrop? Or have you forgotten that we are three in one?"

Ridley and Winthrop wait patiently for my command as my father stumbles over his words muttering something like, "I didn't know they were alive. The midwife deemed them dead at birth."

I shake my head. "You are a liar. You have been a gal-sneaker your whole life. You married my mother when you were a poor ragamuffin. She was the one with the money. She loved you and believed in you. When you sought your pleasure elsewhere, you wanted to marry your mistress Cederica. Over time you had acquired wealth of your own. Cederica was born with a title to her credit. You felt your acquired wealth rendered our mother unworthy. You believed you would be endowed with a title over-time. How curious, Father. Time is not your ally."

I pause as the watch whispers a truth that makes my heart clench and fury rise up to my lungs. My breath is heavy.

"You chose to murder our mother while she was pregnant with your children. You slipped strychnine into her tea. As the poison took effect, you made others believe she had gone into labor early. Upon her death, you had the midwife perform the birth in a most unconventional way."

I lick my lips awaiting the spillage of his blood.

"What nobody knew was that a few days earlier, while you were out purchasing the poison to kill my mother, an old peddler woman stopped you on the street and told you the number three would destroy you. You had no idea what it meant until you saw Demelza pull out not one, not two, but three babes from your dead wife's organs. You knew that triplets were a sign that you would somewhere in time be annihilated, so you vowed to end us. But you cannot."

"These lies you speak are most untrue. My own son is turning against me."

"The lies are strangling you now, Father. You have turned against me. Not only did you kill my mother, attempt to kill my brothers, but you murdered my fiancée."

Bancroft's eyes speak the truth, but he remains silent.

We begin to move closer to him, the start of his death procession.

"You plotted with Rhonwen Dankworth to poison Raven as you poisoned your own wife. Your reputation is your undoing."

"You ungrateful fool," Bancroft hisses. "With the death of Raven, I rescued you from imbecility in the eyes of aristocratic society. How could a man of your stature marry a woman beneath you? You think I would allow my only son to create a union with a woman like that?"

"You murdered my mother!"

"Your mother was an ungrateful person just like you!"

I reach into my pocket. I nod to Ridley and Winthrop. I am ready to end this.

My father breathes heavily, and I see the chain of his sins wrap around his throat. I know he lacks remorse.

"It has taken twenty-one years but tonight the power of three destroys you for the years of wicked deeds you have wrought unto others," I cry.

The flames in the gaslamp glow brighter.

Together we raise our knives. A bullet is far too easy. We want this to be personal. We want him to feel the pain he has caused us for too long. In unison we come at him from all sides and drive our knives deep into his heart. He falls to the floor dead.

The pocket watch keeps time and now brings justice. A soul for a soul.

October 31, 1890
3:00 a.m.

My brothers and I stand together in the parlor clutching the bloody knives in our hands.

The pocket watch burns against my chest, and I hear Persephone's voice on the wind. *It is time for the exchange, bring forth the souls.*

I drop my knife next to my father's body and spread my arms outward. Through my fingertips I summon the bodies of Rhonwen, Dempster, and Cederica into the room. Their frames appear next to my father.

Ridley knocks the gaslamp off the table and it falls in front of them. The glass shatters and the flames begin to devour the floor. Winthrop takes the fire poker and pulls out one of the flaming logs near the sofa so it catches quickly.

The walls of fire mirror my joy. I plan to burn the McQuoid

mansion to the ground. We exit the edifice and I know it will become ashes soon.

"Where are we going?" asks Ridley. He and Winthrop are on my heels.

"To the cemetery," I reply. "I have souls to claim!"

A soul for a soul
An equal exchange
Through the depths of darkness
We find the light

October 31, 1890
3:30 a.m.

The full moon casts light on the graveyard as we stand amongst the tombstones. I feel as though a heavy burden has been lifted from my shoulders. Yet I continue to crave happiness.

I hold the pocket watch out before me as the moonlight illuminates the black diamonds in the gold.

With this watch you can bring the past to the future, Persephone's voice whispers in the darkness. *Soul for a soul.*

I walk until I reach the headstone of my beloved. The words Raven Tartal jump out at me.

I place the watch against the marble.

"This soul I claim. Come back to me," I whisper.

A rustle of leaves sweep up and swirl into a vortex. When the foliage drops, there before me stands the lovely Raven Tartal, looking as beautiful as she was the last time I saw her.

Overcome with emotion, I rush to her and take her in my arms. I stroke my hand through her glossy hair and kiss her forehead.

"Atticus," she says groggily, "what is happening? Why are we here?"

"It is a long story," I reply, "These are my brothers." I point at Ridley and Winthrop. "Again, a long story. Wait here with them, I will be right back."

I race against the tombstones until I find the two markers I need. At each gravestone I repeat the phrase. "This soul I claim. Come back to me."

Soon Katja and Demelza stand next to my brothers. Their faces beam with pride as though they know I have righted wrongs.

I feel a lump rising in my throat. I swallow. There is one more person I need to save. My heart thumps loudly. With trembling legs, I stumble along until I fall at a headstone. It is covered with leaves and overgrown vines. I swallow the lump in my throat. The stone looks forgotten and I am nervous. It has been so many years.

I place the watch on the marble and say the words. "This soul I claim. Come back to me."

"Atticus?" a soft voice whispers. I turn around to see her standing before me. Just as Katja had described to me many times.

My mother is beautiful like the rising sun. Her long black hair runs down her back like a waterfall. Brown eyes shine like stars in the night. Reaching her arms out to me, I run to her like a small child. Her skin is soft and she smells of lavender and jasmine. For the first time in twenty-one years, I meet my mother.

She calls out to Ridley and Winthrop who join in the hug, as well.

"My beautiful children," she whispers. "At last, we meet."

"How do you tell us apart, mother?" asks Winthrop.

Arantxa gives a sly smile, "A mother can always tell her children apart. Just because I have not been in the physical world does not mean I have not been watching over you."

I feel wetness drip down my cheeks. My heart no longer seeks revenge, but instead is filled with joy. The pocket watch finally falls silent.

The exchange has been made. *Soul for a soul.*

Later that day on All Hallow's Eve, I keep my wedding date. I marry my beloved Raven in a secret ceremony with only those closest to me in attendance.

November 5, 1890

MacQuoid Mansion burns to the ground taking the souls of Bancroft, Cederica, Rhonwen, and Dempster to the grave. Death is ruled an accident as a consequence of an unattended gaslamp. This time Dr. Wiktor Wiśniewski speaks the truth.

As the sole heir of the estate, I receive a fortune, and I have more money than most of the titled people in London.

No one questions the deaths of the villains nor comments on the resurrections of the innocent. Time has truly been my ally. To this magic the pocket watch bears witness.

I move to the countryside far away from London. There I build my own estate. A new MacQuoid mansion. An edifice full of kindness, love, and generosity. My wife, my mother, Ridley,

Winthrop, Katja, Demelza, and Raven's grandmother who miraculously never touched the poisoned soup all live with me, and I have more joy than I ever thought possible.

~

October 31, 1891
One year later....

All Hallow's Eve is a happy day for me.

I watch from the window and see everyone gathering in the gardens to celebrate my one-year anniversary with Raven. The happiness on the faces of the ones I love brings joy to my heart.

"Atticus," Raven calls up to me. "Everyone is waiting."

"Coming, darling." I turn the valve of the gaslamp on the dresser. The flame dies and the glass globe is empty.

I head down the hall to the grand staircase. Just as I am about to descend, I stop and stare at my reflection in the mirror.

"Happiness suits you, Atticus," a familiar voice calls. I see Persephone appear behind me. I turn to her and the wrinkles in her face deepen as she chuckles.

"Did you get exactly what you wanted?" she asks.

I glance at the ashes in her white hair and on her clothes. "Persephone," I answer. "I got more than what I ever thought possible."

She chuckles and holds out her empty palm to me. "Then I believe we can pass this gift onto the next soul who needs a hand."

The pocket watch appears in her palm. The black diamonds sparkle within the rays of sunlight. I pat my empty pocket. Since the day I resurrected the souls, I have kept the watch in my breast pocket as a reminder of how blessed I am.

I nod. "Yes, my good woman."

Persephone laughs. Her soft chuckle turns into a cackle. The pocket watch glistens and then transforms into a long scythe. A black cloak and hood replace her peasant attire.

She gives me a wink and with the twist of her cape she disappears.

I am alone at the top of the stairs.

I put my hand to my face then laugh at my realization.

Death has been keeping watch over me.

The End

Death Brings a Brooch

October 31, 1892

My eyes open in darkness.

Where am I? I struggle to get up and my head hits something hard. *Ouch!* My lower body feels limp. It is difficult to move.

"Good heavens! Where am I?" I mutter. Twisting my body around I am confined in a suffocating space.

Upon my face, I sense the presence of delicate lace. My arms are confined in a blanket of some sort. I run my fingers along the inside of the linen and learn that it is tied with bows.

What is this wickedness? I am wrapped nicely like a gift. But I feel this is a present nobody would want. Struggling, I pry my arms free and pull down the veil that covers my face. Darkness surrounds me bringing with it feelings of sadness and despair.

I raise my hands upward and touch something solid. I struggle to turn over, but my body rubs against another surface. I am imprisoned. My sweaty palms bang at the hardness above me. It feels like wood.

"William!" I called my husband's name. "Where am I? I cannot see." There is no reply.

"Marion! James! Mabel! Phoebe! Louise! Peter!" I call my children's names but only silence greets me.

My heart beats rapidly against my chest, and I can hear my pulse echoing throughout the box as I thrash in this cage. My lungs crave air.

My fingertips brush against the fabric of my dress. *Silk?* I grasp at the cloth. *My best dress? Wait, this is not my best dress. This is... this is the shroud I made for when I...What is this madness?*

"Where is everyone!" I yell.

A green light begins to glow on my chest, illuminating the darkness. Looking down, I squint, and lift the object. A round brooch is attached to my dress.

What is this jewel? Has someone bestowed a gift upon me? This is not mine.

I peer at the glimmering object on my chest. It is the profile of a woman carved on a white shell against a dark background.

"How strange," I murmur. "Where did this brooch come from?"

As the green light fills the space I am in, my eyes focus on the surroundings, and I realize I am in a satin enclosure. My body is on a cushion, and a pillow is underneath my head. I am in a bed of forever slumber.

Is this a coffin? Am I dead? No, it cannot be!

I clasp my hands to my chest and feel my heart slamming against my fingers. My mouth gasps air into my lungs. *I am not dead.*

I scream and bang on the casket. "Help! Anybody there? Help!"

I have been buried alive. If I do not get out, I should see the Gates of Heaven standing before me very soon.

Tears prick at my eyes. "Oh Lord, help me!"

I hear a murmuring in the gloom but I do not understand its words.

"W-Who is there?" I call. "Oh my God, how did this happen? Save me!"

As if in answer to my prayer, the cameo brooch glows brighter, and the words are clearer.

Break the coffin.

I try to hear who is speaking.

Get out!

I feel a pleasant sensation travel along my spine and spread throughout my body. My muscles feel refreshed. I am strong. My hands clench into fists.

In one powerful motion, I smash my fist into the roof of the coffin. An action that had been unproductive a few moments ago now gives results. I do not know what has come over me, but it appears my body works better than my brain. A crack in the wood shows, and I continue the same action. Fractures in the coffin grow wider, and fragments of dirt fall around on me. I throw the veil over my face as the musty smell of fresh soil fills my nostrils. Ripping a section of the funerary box to the side, I am met with a wall of dirt. My body responds while my brain remains numb. My hands behave as shovels propelled by an unexplainable force. I claw and fight my way through the dirt as I leave the coffin behind and continue upward.

My body moves through the soil as if guided by a mysterious presence. I can't breathe but I feel powerful. I feel strong. The ground becomes easier to move as I battle to freedom.

In one final motion, I punch my fist upward and I feel it break through the ground. A breeze brushes my fingertips. Moving my other hand skyward, I grab the edge and hoist myself out of the soil. Crawling on all fours, my sweaty body collapses onto the ground. My chest heaves as the cool air fills my lungs, my heartbeat slows, and my stiff muscles begin to ache.

The dewy grass brushes against my cheeks and I inhale the

fresh scent of the ground. It is as if the Earth has exhaled and now breathes life back into my body. I sense movement near me. I blink and see a pair of worn leather shoes in front of me, and I jerk my head up. A shadowy presence looks down on me.

Pushing myself to a kneeling position, I lean back on my heels so my eyes can focus on the figure that stands before me. It is a woman. A peddler woman. She is clothed in black with an ivory shawl draped across her shoulder. Her white hair is covered in ashes and her wrinkled fingers grip a staff that resembles a serpent.

"Victoria Taylor" the woman says. Her voice sends chills up my spine. Her presence has an air of familiarity, but at the same time distant. I cannot put my finger on it, but I feel as if she has been a part of the dark times of my life. "It is about time you woke up." She shakes her head. "Over two weeks. I think that is the longest it has ever taken someone to wake up. I was beginning to think the brooch was not working."

"Who are you?" I ask, finding the strength to get to my feet and stand at an equal level to her. "Are you an angel?" I grab at the brooch pinned to my dress. "You put this on me?"

"Careful, dear," replies the woman. "Such action could have devastating results." She chuckles as if she finds herself amusing. "I am an old friend." The lines deepen in her face as she smiles. "I am Persephone. I have watched you grow from a tiny child into a wife and mother of six."

I wrack my brain trying to bring forth a memory of this woman, but I come up empty. "I do not remember."

She winks at me. "I am not a person you would want to remember."

"Where am I?"

Persephone gives me a knowing look and spreads her arms wide. "Look around, dear. You look chilly. Here take this." She pulls her ivory shawl from her shoulder and wraps the garment around me. Goosebumps break along my skin. I am chilled to the bone.

Clutching the shawl around my body, I turn to center myself

with my surroundings. It is night-time and the full moon shines among the stars. I am in a graveyard. The elaborate monuments and headstones stand like sentinels as the mist surrounds the graves.

"Why am I here?" I whisper.

"Pull that shawl tighter, dear. One could potentially catch a chill if she had just climbed out of her grave." Persephone answers.

I furrow my brow and look at her.

"See for yourself," she points at something behind me. I turn and see the hole I climbed out of. Just behind it, I see a headstone. Carved into the marker I see a name. *My name*

Victoria Louise Taylor

My head feels woozy and my heart bangs against my rib cage. My breath is stuck in my throat. Moving closer, I fear what I will read.

Sacred to the memory of
Victoria Louise Taylor
Of London
Who died October 15, 1892
Aged: 40 years
Born October 15, 1852
Wife of William Roger Taylor

I wipe my fingers over the words as if trying to scrub them away. *Dead? How could I be dead?* I move my hands and clasp them over my heart. The gentle thrum calms my nerves.

"I am dead," I whisper.

"Not anymore," replies Persephone.

"How did I die?"

Persephone waves her hand and the hole I had climbed out of disappears. "You were murdered by someone you trusted." She clicks her tongue. "And the day of your birthday, too. Forty years old is quite a milestone."

I stare at her, unable to move. I hear her words, but my brain is unable to comprehend what she is saying. I clasp my hands to my chest; my throat feels tight and I am barely about to form the words. "Murdered? By whom?"

Persephone winks at me again. "That my dear is for you to find out."

The old woman waves her hands and my surroundings become a blur.

October 15, 1892
12:00 a.m.

My eyes open. A full moon is above me. A glowing orb in a grim sky. I move my fingers back and forth in the dirt. I rise into a sitting position and scan my surroundings.

I recognize my Grandmother Emily's neighborhood. I am in the alleyway between two row houses. My granny's house is on the left side of me, and her neighbor's is on the right.

"What happened?" I rub my temples. "Where are we?"

I move to get to my feet. As I place my hand on the ground to support myself, I feel my fingers touch something wet. As I rise to full height, I bring my palm closer to my face. It is covered in red. *Blood.*

"Ah, how I love the early hours of the morning. No people. No noise. So peaceful and serene." A voice distracts me from this revelation. Glancing up, I see Persephone still standing before me.

She looks at me, and the creases around her eyes deepen as she chuckles. Holding out her hand to me, a cloth magically appears in her palm. I take it and wipe my hands while murmuring a thank you.

"What day is it?" I ask.

"October Fifteenth."

I pause, "But didn't you say it was-"

"October Thirty-first," finishes Persephone. "Yes, I did say that. However, the magic of Revenge works in strange ways, and I have reversed the narrative. We have gone back in time to the day you died, the day of your birthday. By doing this, you have been given the gift of time to learn how you ended in such a predicament. This is the place where you died." She points to the droplets of blood on the ground. "You see the blood. That is your blood." She waves her hands over the stains and they disappear. "The past is now the present. No one will have any recollection of your death. You have been given a second chance."

I stand before her unable to comprehend anything this woman has said. *Time travel. Second chance. This woman must not be of sound mind!*

"I don't believe you." I reply, pulling the shawl tighter around me.

"Ah, time travel does make one forgetful. You are staying at your Grandmother Emily's house, Victoria. She is not well. In the early morning hours of your birthday, an intruder entered the home and dragged you out to the alley. There your life was taken."

My breath accelerates and butterflies flutter in my stomach.

Persephone walks over to a pile of crates stacked against the wall. Reaching behind one, she pulls out an object. As she comes closer to me, I see it is a dagger.

She places the weapon in my palm. "This is the object that killed you. Your murderer is full of pride over your death. But I make the rules. Not this evil fool. Revenge is a delicate subject.

Not all revenge is justifiable, but your death deserves to be avenged."

My brain seems to suffer the onset of a demented spell. *Murdered here. No it could not be.*

She closes my fingers around the knife and clasps my fist in both her hands. "Keep it close. Your murderer may try to strike again."

"Who killed me?"

"That is for you to find out. In order for you to keep your life, you must work for it."

"Who are you?" I ask again.

A smirk crosses her wrinkled face. "An old friend, a cherished companion to misery. Do not disappoint me, Victoria Taylor. All that I seek is a soul for a soul."

She reaches forward and touches the brooch pinned to my chest. "Oh, and one more thing, Victoria,- if by the stroke of midnight on October Thirty-First, the exchange has not been made, you will return to the grave. And I might not be able to save you a second time."

"I do not understand." I say.

Persephone shakes her head. "My dear, in order for you to remain alive, you must take the life of the person whose pride took yours."

My hands fly to my mouth. *Kill? I am not a killer!*

I open my mouth to protest, but flames in the street lamps grow brighter and Persephone is gone.

I break out in a cold sweat. I look down at the knife in my hand. There is only one person in this world who would want me dead. Only one person, but he is dead himself. Or is he? Has time reincarnated my worst nightmare, too?

Picking up my dress, I run the remaining streets to Stonegate Cemetery. I burst open the wrought-iron gates and sprint among the tombstones until I find the one I seek.

A raised square base stands before me. On top is a statue of an angel as tall as me. Its wings fan out while the head tilts down towards its hands. Behind it rises an enormous Celtic cross. Inscribed on the base are the words:

Sacred to the memory
Luther Frederick Marrow
Of London
Who died July 7, 1876
Aged: 24 years
Born October 31, 1851
Faith, Fate, and Family

I quiver as I see his name. A flood of bad memories I have tried to shut away come pouring through. *He is still dead.* I feel a weight has been lifted off my chest. *He is still dead.*

However, disgust sits on my tongue unable to be swallowed. Luther always thought himself so important. It would surfeit his pride to have a grandiose monument almost seven feet tall. The inscription stated everything that Luther was not.

This is the grave of my first husband. I have been resurrected on his birthday. If Luther is still dead, then I am at a loss for who could have taken my life.

I am a woman
Time has reversed
But not everyone
Is immune to the curse

October 15, 1892
6:00 a.m.

A wooden floor presses against my face as sunlight streams through an open window. I try to move, but I am confined. My eyes snap open and I thrash my arms.

Have I returned to the grave?

Pulling my sweaty body into a sitting position, I see I am tangled in a pile of blankets. My breathing slows as my heart rate calms down.

I have been having a dream. Just a dream. I must have fallen out of my bed during the middle of night.

I lean against the bed. I see portraits of my parents, and I realize I am in the guest room of my Grandmother Emily's row house.

The nightgown feels soft beneath my fingers, and I check my pulse. The little beats against the skin calm me, and I run my fingers through my hair.

It was a dream. A very bad dream.

Something brushes against my chest. I look down and my heart sinks. The cameo brooch is attached to my garment. The woman with no eyes stares back at me. The dark background that surrounds her sends chills down my spine.

It was not a dream!

My stomach twists into knots and my anxiety increases. A brown cloth peeks halfway from under the bed. Leaning over, I pull it into my lap and open it. With trembling fingers, I pick up the dagger Persephone gave me only a few hours ago. Dried red blood is caked to the shiny blade. *My blood.*

I fear I am going to be ill, but I hold myself together. This dagger had penetrated my skin and...

I leap to my feet and undertake an examination of my entire frame. I search for a scar, a mark, something to indicate where this weapon took my life. There is nothing.

I shiver. I don't even want to think about it. I was grateful to be alive. The thought of my children growing up without a mother was too much to bear.

Placing the knife into the nightstand, I slip beneath the silk sheets upon my comfy bed. I smoosh my face into the pillow and try to think.

Shouldn't there have been a sign someone was trying to kill me? Shouldn't I have seen something suspicious?

The past few weeks leading to my birthday seemed normal to me. But there had been much worry on my mind. Granny had fallen ill, and we had the upcoming harvest on the farm. I was torn between two worlds, distracted by my responsibilities as granddaughter, mother, and wife.

I pace back and forth. I have been here in the East End of London for the past few days while William was home taking care of the children in Hampshire. Nothing seemed out of the ordinary.

A cough interrupts my thoughts.

"Granny!" I call out. Opening my door, I see Grandmother

Emily in the kitchen. One hand grips her cane so hard her knuckles are white. Her other hand forms a fist that is against her lips as spasms wrack her frail body.

Putting my arm around her, "Granny, are you alright?"

She looks at me. Her eyes widen and her little body shakes like a leaf. Screams erupt from her lips, and I fear she may faint.

"A ghost! Victoria! In her grave! Now a ghost has come to take me, too! Get away." She moves her cane and attempts to whack me in my shins.

"Granny! It's me, your granddaughter, Victoria."

I see the whites of her eyes as they moisten with tears. "Victoria is dead! Who are you?"

I release her and step back in shock. Persephone had stated that the hands of time had been turned backward. Why is Grandmother Emily still saying that I am dead? She should not remember. Did Persephone lie to me?

Guiding her to the chair in the parlor, I sit her down. "Granny, I'm not dead." I take her wrinkled hands and place them on my chest. "See, my heart is beating."

Snatching her hands back, Grandmother Emily narrows her eyes. "Impossible. I found you lying in the alley outside almost two weeks ago, dead."

"Granny, it is October Fifteenth, my birthday."

"No, it is not." Leaning heavily on her cane, she gets up and hobbles over to the calendar on the wall. "I mark it every day. W-What? What is this? It is October Fifteenth? Oh, my God! What is happening?" Her chest heaves and she stumbles backwards. I grab her and sit her back in the chair.

"I will make you a cup of tea."

A few minutes later, I place the tea cup into Grandmother Emily's shaking hands.

"Impossible," she murmurs. She reaches out and touches my cheeks as I sit on the footstool in front of her. "You're alive. Impossible." She places her hand on the brooch that is pinned to my dress. "I knew there was something strange about that woman."

"What are you talking about?" I ask.

"A woman put it on you at the funeral. We held the wake at your house. She was an old lady with decent clothes. But there was a little bit of soot in her white hair. She told me she was an old friend from many years ago. I asked for her name but she did not say. She walked over to the casket and pinned that on your dress. Then she whispered something into your ear. She smiled at me then left."

Persephone. I get up and look around the room at my grandmother's elaborate collection of statues and wall art. *Why has Persephone included my gran in this secret shift of time?*

"What is going on, Victoria?" asks Grandmother Emily.

"Do you remember anything about the night I died? Did you see who killed me?"

"I did not see who the person was. After you had put me to bed I remained awake reading. You know how I love my Jane Austen books. In the early morning hours, I thought I heard glass breaking. Then I heard you scream. I tried to get out of bed as fast as I could, but you know these old legs do not work like they used to. By the time I was able to walk, I saw the back door was open. When I walked outside into the alley, I found you lying there in a pool of blood. Stab wounds covered your body. I screamed for help and the neighbors ran outside. One of them checked your pulse and said you were dead. Then I fainted. Now what is going on, Victoria?"

Taking a deep breath, I tell Grandmother Emily the story of how I had woken in the coffin, to the time when Persephone left me in the alley telling me I needed to find the person who killed me.

"By the Grace of God, it is a miracle." She leans over and pulls me into a hug. "Happy Birthday, my dear. A second birthday. You have been blessed."

"I still need to find out who took my life. I have no idea where to start." My heart sinks into my stomach. "This is going to be like searching for a needle in a haystack. I do not understand why Persephone has included you in the quest I must undertake."

"Maybe, Persephone thinks you will need help. Besides, no one would believe me, if I said anything. You know everyone considers me in my Dizzy Age[1]." She chuckles.

I stand up and brush off my night dress. "I must change and head home, Granny. I will be back soon."

I feel as if I am losing my sanity.

Sixteen days or I will find myself back in the grave.

---

1. **Dizzy Age:** a phrase meaning elderly

October 16, 1892
11:00 a.m.

I take a private carriage back home. As I walk down the entrance of the long dirt path that leads to the farm, I run my hands down my new dress. My burial dress has found an appropriate home at the bottom of the Thames River. I clutch my bag with my fingertips.

I know Luther is dead, but I cannot help but feel as if there is a reason I was resurrected on his birthday.

The hedgerows that flourish under massive oak trees begin to rustle near me.

"Victoria" The bushes call to me.

I freeze and squint my eyes.

"Who's there?" I whisper. *Is the bush talking to me?* The leaves continue to shake.

"Victoria! Come here." I recognize that voice. The evil tone still haunts me in my dreams to this day. It cannot be. I approach closer and move to pull back the branch.

"Mum!" Different voices yell behind me. The sounds are light and full of joy. I turn around to see my daughters Phoebe and Louise coming to greet me.

"My darlings," I cry.

Kneeling down I feel their little bodies crash into mine. Their arms wrap around my neck.

"Happy birthday!" shouts Louise.

I cup their chins with my hands and kiss their soft cheeks. I caress their angelic cheekbones. Five-year-old Phoebe has flaming red hair just like her father. Four-year-old Louise is blonde like the shining sun that warms the chilly air. She is a younger version of Grandmother Emily.

My vision blurs. What would their lives be like if they had no mother to love them, nurture them, hold them, read them stories and cheer them when they are upset?

"Come on, mum!" Phoebe grabs my hands and starts pulling me down the path. "Everyone is waiting for you."

I let my daughters lead me away from the bush. Turning my head I give the hedgerows a parting glance, but no one speaks my name again.

We round the corner, and our beautiful cottage comes into view. It is an asymmetrical two-story dwelling with a thatched roof and round door. Now that I have been given a second chance at life, I see everything in a different light. Not far from the house is the barn where we keep our cows, pigs, sheep, and horses.

I will be forever grateful for William's grandfather leaving us this farm. Sixty acres allow us to grow crops, raise chickens for eggs, and cows for milk to sell in town.

I see the rest of my children sitting on the stoop playing jacks. My eldest son Peter is fifteen-years-old. James is fourteen and Marion is two. I run over to them and wrap them in my arms.

During the moment of our reunion, our helper Hannah walks out of the house holding my youngest one-year-old Mabel on her hip.

She locks eyes with me and freezes. I watch the color drain

from her face. By her expression, I know she knows my secret. I do not know how she knows when my family has forgotten. But I know she knows.

She mutters a quick hello and places Mabel into my arms. Then she walks back to her own cottage on our property.

As I watch her go, I see her shoulders are hunched, and she looks around as if expecting someone to jump out at her. Hannah Morgan is a mystery. A Welsh immigrant with no family and no children. My little ones had found her sleeping in the garden. Hannah was in her early twenties and told us she had left Wales in search of a new life in England. She had no money, no clothes, nothing. She claims fire had taken everything she once owned. William and I decided that Hannah could stay in the guest cottage and help out on the farm. That was three months ago.

I narrow my eyes. Hannah knows something and I will make certain I find out what it is.

**October 16, 1892
10:00 p.m.**

After putting the children to bed, I clean the dishes and my mind drifts towards Hannah. I cannot get her and the look she gave me out of my head. It was as if she had seen a ghost.

The back door opens. My husband and our dog Lolly come into the house.

"How is Mindy?" I ask. Our cow had cut her leg on the stall door a few days ago.

"She is doing better. I changed her bandage. She should be fine in a day or two. The children are asleep?"

"Not yet, they are resting." William hangs up his hat and comes over to me. He gives me a kiss and presents me with a bouquet of wildflowers.

"Oh, Will, how lovely," I cry. I open the cabinet to get out a vase.

William's reddish hair sparkles in the light of the lantern. He smiles. "I still need to give you your gift." He opens the drawer and pulls out a golden box with a bow. I sit at the table and he places it in front of me. "I know it is a day late, but happy birthday, darling."

Blushing, I unwrap the gift; it is a small satin box. Opening the lid, my smile disappears.

It is a beautiful necklace. An oval pendant on a delicate ribbon. As I look closer, I see something in the lavaliere that sends shivers down my spine. The pendant is a cameo woman of white shell, holding a rose against a gray background. The same woman on the brooch pinned on my chest.

"What's wrong, darling? Do you not like it?" William had seen my expression.

"I love it, dear, thank you, but I worry this must have cost a pretty penny. We are still recovering from last year's bad harvest."

Will's tall frame towers over my petite stature. "This year's harvest will be better." Mabel's cries ring out. "I will go check on her." He kisses my head and walks off.

That is my William, always the optimist. He has been my ray of sunshine in the hell that has been my life.

Unpinning the brooch from my dress, I hold it next to the necklace in the box.

The two brooches feature the same woman. On the necklace, the woman's profile is facing right and she is smelling a rose. Whereas on the brooch, she is facing left. The backgrounds are different. There is an aura of mystery surrounding the brooch women.

Out of nowhere a tightness sears in my chest. I bend over and grip the table for support. My throat is constricted and I wheeze. I look down at my hands and see my flesh on my fingers turns old and cracked. The skin begins to fall off the bone. Pain runs rampant throughout my body.

What is this wickedness! I am dying again!

I hear a murmuring. The same sound from when I was captive in the coffin. Only this time I hear its words. *Put it back!*

As black spots form before my eyes, I refasten the brooch onto my dress as my body shakes.

With the pin once again in place, suddenly, the hold on my body is released. Air flows easily into my lungs, and I look at my fingers to see they have healed.

I clasp my hands to my chest as I try to wrap my mind around what just happened.

Is this brooch the reason I am still alive?

With trembling fingers, I remove the brooch again. Sure enough, the same effect takes over my body. My throat cuts off my air, and my skin begins to die.

I repin the brooch and the phantasmagoria disappears.

What kind of trickery is this? What game is Persephone trying to play?

I realize the murmurs I have heard over the past few days have come from the brooch. It speaks to me through a telepathic intuition that binds us. The brooch is keeping me alive.

October 16, 1892
10:30 p.m.

With Lolly by my side, I storm across the grounds to Hannah's cottage and bang on her door. After another experience with death, I need some answers.

Hinges creak as the door opens. Hannah stands before me in her white nightgown and nightcap.

"Victoria, what is the matter?" She asks. Her eyebrows are knitted together and her jaw is tense. Her pupils are big and her eyes shift side to side. She gazes out into the darkness behind me as if expecting someone.

As I am about to reply, light from the lantern draws my attention to something on Hannah's dress. My words die in my throat and my tongue goes dry. Pinned to Hannah's nightgown is a brooch that looks identical to mine! The sight of the faceless woman staring at me fills my soul with rage.

I step over the threshold and close the door behind me. My fingers turn the bolt and lock the door. Walking over to Hannah, I place my fingers onto her brooch. I am about to rip it off and throw it into the fire.

"No!" screams Hannah backing away. "You cannot do that. I-I will-"

"You will what? Die?" I point to my brooch pinned on me.

Hannah gasps. "She gave you one, too?"

"You know something!" I cry. "The look you gave me at the house. You know I'm supposed to be dead."

Hannah is frozen before me. The words are unable to come out her mouth, but tears leak freely from her eyes.

"I-I do not know what's going on. I-I..." Her eyes roll back into her head and her body goes limp. She collapses into my arms.

I huff and drag Hannah over to the chair by the fire where Lolly has made herself comfortable on the cushion.

"Lolly," I hiss. "Lolly get down!"

The dog hops down onto the floor, and, using the last of my strength, I place Hannah into the chair.

"Hannah," I call tapping her face. "Hannah."

Her eyes twitch beneath the lids. Slowly lashes part to reveal brown irises. "W-What happened?"

"You fainted," I point to the brooch. "Who gave you that?"

"An old woman named Persephone. Back home in Wales, I was engaged to be married. One night I was home alone. My parents had gone to visit a sick friend. I—I went to bed and when I woke up in the middle of the night the whole house was on fire. There was smoke everywhere. Running to the door, I tried to open it, but it was stuck. I remember coughing and lots of smoke, then everything went black.

"When I woke up, I found myself in the garden. I do not know how I got out of the house. A—A woman was standing over me. S-she seemed so familiar, yet I cannot place her. S- She said her name was Persephone and she told me I was supposed to have died in that fire but she saved me. Someone had tried to kill me in the fire, and now I must find who it is. She gave me the brooch and told me never to take it off. Then she told me to take the first train out of town, for my help would be needed to find the killer. Then she disappeared. I was sure I was hallucinating."

"When did this happen?" I continue.

"T-Two months ago. After the woman disappeared. I went to my dear friend's house. I sent a telegram to my parents and then left town on the train the following night."

"Why?"

"I was frightened. I am not the police. How could I find a killer? Who would want to kill me? No, I had to leave. If a murderer strikes once, he will strike again."

"What happened to your fiancé?"

"I-I do not know. I-I just left."

"You left him and did not give him an explanation?"

"Oh, do not look at me like that. How could I explain to Paul that I am tasked with finding an arsonist who is also a murderer because an old lady told me so? And she gave me a brooch. He would have had me committed to an asylum for sure, or abandoned me for good."

I clench my fists. "Did Persephone give you a timeline of when you had to find the person who burned down your parent's house?"

"No. I was fortunate to come across your farm. I do not know what I was thinking." Hannah got up and stood in front of the fireplace. "You have no idea how frightening it is to think that you could have been dead."

It was planned. Persephone had set this coincidence into motion months ago. She knew I was going to die. She had sent Hannah here to help me.

Clearing my throat. I told her a brief summary of the events that had transpired over the last twenty-four hours where I was concerned.

Hannah clutched her hands over her heart. "You have sixteen days to find your killer?"

I nodded, "and you are going to help me do it."

"Oh, I cannot. I am not a detective."

I move closer to her and grab her by the shoulders. I feel my chest getting tight and my nostrils flare. "There is a reason why you and my Grandmother Emily are the only ones who remember that I died. I refuse to leave my six children motherless and my husband wifeless! You have to help me! Please!"

Hannah takes a shaky breath and nods. "I will help you."

Releasing her, I tighten my coat around my body. "Thank you! I will see you tomorrow."

I return to the cottage and sit at the table, trying to process the turn of events. I hear William come into the room.

"There you are, darling." He smiles at me. "I was wondering why you had not gone to bed." He pauses and stares at my brooch. His fingers touch the delicate pin. "My! This is pretty."

"It was a gift from Grandmother Emily," I reply quickly. "Beautiful. It will match perfectly with the necklace."

I give him a small smile and nod. Little does he know I had locked the necklace away in the drawer. One faceless woman was enough in this deathly charade. And the brooch is a tortuous reminder of my impending doom.

October 17, 1892
4:30 a.m.

Bits of moonlight stream through the window pane and make a design on the wood floor. I stand at the cookstove and slide the bread into the oven.

I was tossing and turning all night. Sleep an evasive foe. The impending thought of an eternal slumber has left my body unable to rest. Soon the little ones will be awake. Their chatter and laughter are a delight I appreciate. Who knows how much longer I will be able to hear it?

Get it together, Victoria.

Wiping my hands on my apron, I walk over to the Belfast sink and glance out the window. I see a light bobbing in the predawn hours. It is held by someone walking towards the barn. Leaning closer, I see that it is Peter. He carries a fishing pole and steel container. James walks next to him. Their figures waver before me.

Fishing this early? I have known my older boys to get up earlier to do their chores, but four-thirty?

Moonlight gives me visibility as I open the door and head out to the barn with Lolly on my heels. Colorful leaves decorate the tops of the trees. Chickens in the coop fill the air with their clucking.

I enter the barn. It is empty.

"Peter! James!" I call. There is no answer. I could have sworn I saw them walk inside.

Our animals are starting to wake. My white mare Eliza pokes her head over the stall door. I rub her muzzle and say 'good morning' to each of the animals. I hear Lolly barking outside. I walk out of the barn to see my dog barking at something in the dirt.

"Lolly, what is the matter with you?"

As I approach closer, the brooch pinned to my chest shimmers.

Near the bush, I notice a shape has been painted in the dirt.

It is the letter L!

I tap my fingers on the red paint that makes the shape. I sniff it. It smells like rust. Blood!

L for Luther! No, it cannot be! He is dead!

My head feels woozy and my vision starts to blur.

As I open my eyes I find myself back at Grandmother Emily's house.

A shadow stretches out on the floor behind me.

An arm goes around my neck with a hand covering my mouth stifling my scream. Another arm goes around my waist, and I am dragged toward the kitchen.

My teeth sink into the stranger's palm and the fingers move so I can scream to my gran for help. I struggle and thrash. My arm hits a vase knocking it to the ground. Glass shatters everywhere, but the person is much stronger than me. The body that holds me feels masculine, and the embrace is familiar, but I cannot place it.

As he drags me like a rag doll, the kitchen door is open, too. I am carried into the alley between the houses. My body is slammed against a brick wall. There is an arm against my throat. Black spots dance in front of my eyes as I cannot seem to get enough air into my lungs.

"You thought you could leave me didn't you?" I hear a voice as dark as a demon.

A sharp pinch in my stomach. He releases his grip on my neck and the air flows back into my lungs. My hands fly to my abdomen and I feel wetness against my fingers. I struggle to see who my attacker is but it is too dark. The dim lanterns in the alley shed enough light that I can see it is a tall figure dressed in black with a hood over his head. I will my legs to run, but he grabs me again. A pinch enters my arm and another pinch to my chest. Tears stream down my cheeks. My insides burn, my wounds feel on fire, and the strength leaves my body.

He throws me to the ground. "If I cannot have you, then no one can." I cannot hear the rest of his words over the buzzing in my ear. I taste dirt on my tongue. Pain wracks my body, but I feel too tired to scream. His footsteps run in the opposite direction as I hear voices approaching from the entrance of the ally. I see my hand through my half-opened eyes. It is covered in blood. I am covered in blood. My blood.

October 19, 1892
10:00 a.m.

I am on a mission. While Hannah watches my children. I ride my horse into town, to the East End of London. I hear the clip-clop of horse hooves reverberate off the cobblestones. People hurry this way and that. Vendors stand on the street corners selling roasted chestnuts, flowers, and newspapers. Finally, I reach my destination to the building that says Mortuary.

I cannot ignore the signs I have been given. Resurrected on Luther's birthday. The initial L painted in blood outside my barn. The evil voice. There is no way he could be alive. I was the one who had identified his body. I need to look at his file again.

I walk to the door and try the handle. It is locked.

The brooch whispers to me to try the back door. I hurry down the side of the building to the rear entrance where I find the key hidden in a flower pot.

I let myself in. I do not have much time. I am sure the mortician Dr. Adamson will be back soon.

The inside of the building is a ghostly gray, and a dampness sinks deep into my bones. Metal tables are laid out before me. I see a white sheet covering something that appears to be the outline of a body. I shudder.

I slip into Dr. Adamson's office on the opposite side of the room. There is a filing cabinet behind his desk.

I open the drawers and ruffle through the names on the labels. I do not see what I am looking for.

You must go to the basement. The brooch whispers. *There you will find what you seek.*

I see the door to the basement on the other side of the room. The light from the windows is helping me see, but I know I will be surrounded by darkness once I enter the underground chamber.

Reading my thoughts, the brooch begins to glow. The green light illuminates the room. My problem is solved.

Running to the basement door, I throw it open and hurry down the stairs into the small subterranean room. Shelves upon shelves of boxes meet my eye. An earthy scent fills my nose. I have no time to waste. I pull boxes from the shelves and place them on the metal table at the center of the room. Throwing back the lid I begin to shuffle through the dates.

Not here.

I open the next box and spill a stack of files onto the table.

Ouch! Papercut. Not enough time! Not enough time!

"Looking for something, dear?" A familiar voice calls to me.

Turning around, I see Persephone standing before me. Smiling, she holds a file out to me.

"How did you get in here?" I ask.

"Oh, dear, nothing can keep me out when I choose to go somewhere." She shakes the file before me. "Take it. I think this is what you are looking for."

Grabbing the paper, I read the name Luther Marrow scrawled

on the edge along with the date July 7, 1876. The date that changed my life forever. The date that freed me from the grips of a tainted love. I feel my stomach start to churn, and the tightness in my chest makes it hard to breathe.

"A name can bring forth so many memories, can't it, dear?" Persephone looks around the basement and pulls her shawl tighter around her. "Not many of us get a second chance to face our past and have a different outcome." She reaches over and touches the brooch pinned to my chest. "It has such a beautiful emerald glow, doesn't it?"

"What kind of bewitchment have you cast on this jewelry?"

Persephone does not answer.

"You gave the same one to Hannah."

"I did."

"You did not give her a date for her to find who killed her. But I have a death date?"

"Her situation is different from yours. She was not the intended victim. She just got in the way. She is a vessel of information that you will need."

Persephone reaches out and strokes my cheek with her hand. Her skin is ice against my flesh. A shiver runs down my spine, and goosebumps break out on my body. I feel as if I have plunged my face into an icy river.

"It will all make sense soon, dear. Now head back home." Then she is gone.

"I have to clean this mess first." I look back towards the metal table. All the files are back in their boxes and the crates are stacked neatly on the shelves again.

The file is in my hand. My shaking fingers stroke his name written in fancy script.

"I hate you," I whisper to the silence.

October 22, 1892
9:00 p.m.

I *cannot open it.*

Fear has stilled my resolve.

I sit on the settee of Hannah's cottage with Lolly. Seeking an escape from the October chill, the dog settles herself beside the warm hearth. Hannah is in her kitchen rummaging through the cabinets.

Open the file, Victoria. The brooch whispers.

I can't.

You must. Your life depends on it.

Closing my eyes with quick hands I open the bag and pull out the file. I grip the sides of the folder tight and open my eyes. I see his name. The name I wish with all my heart I could forget.

Luther Marrow
October 31, 1851 - July 7, 1876

Seeing the letters combine to form the identity of the person I hated most on this Earth fills me with rage. Luther Marrow, a liar, cheater, an outlaw who made me suffer from his abnormal and abusive behavior every single day. An evil soul. The most horrible human being to walk this Earth. A demon.

I met Luther when I was seventeen years old. I was walking along the streets of the East End of London when he ran into me, nearly knocking me over. With his dark hair, brown eyes, angelic cheekbones, and muscular physique, I was quite taken from the moment our eyes met. Little did I know he was an eighteen-year-old on the run from robbing multiple wealthy people's houses.

I was so mesmerized by his charm, his wit, and romantic words towards me that I would do anything for him. After a year, we were married. Little did I know his personality was nothing more than a facade. Once the rings and vows were exchanged, that's when the mask fell off and my life turned upside down.

We lived in a small flat on the East End of London. I had Peter at nineteen and James at twenty. I pictured a beautiful life together with Luther. My reality was the complete opposite.

Luther would disappear for hours then reappear stinking of tobacco and cheap whiskey. He spent his days drinking, gambling, breaking the law, and sneaking around with a mistress or two. I had too many arguments with Luther that involved anger, threats of violence, and items tossed against the hearth and walls.

I was so in love with him. But some days it felt as if he had married me to have a shield to camouflage his identity so that he could skulk about with unsavory thugs and wanton women. After six years of hell, Luther died when I was twenty-three.

Taking a deep breath, I flip open the file and peruse the page. I see his death certificate.

I see the report of the postmortem done on his body after the authorities had pulled him from the river. His body had been quite mangled by the rocks after the shallow undertow had dragged him half a mile. But the description matched. Five foot seven inches, muscular stature, black hair, green eyes...

I flip over the next paper and a photograph of his mug shot stares back at me. With trembling fingers, I hold it up to the light of the lamp. There he is with his brooding expression. His eyes mocking me, getting joy from my pain. He took our vows as a joke while he ran to the beds of different mistresses while I was home taking care of our two young sons. He barely supported us with the money he robbed from others. Unbeknownst to me, he had been in and out of jail more times than I could count.

I turn the photo facedown and slam the picture and the file onto the coffee table. *There that settles it. Luther has to be dead. All of these occurrences are simply coincidences.*

Read it again, the brooch whispers.

"What?" I say.

Read it again. Use your brain, not your emotions.

Groaning, I reach for the paper giving the postmortem description when my arm hits the lantern and I almost knock it over. The glow from the flame illuminates a paragraph on the paper that I had overlooked.

Leaning closer, I squint and read to myself. As my eyes take in each word and sentence, I feel my breath strangling in my throat. Luther's body had been smashed against the shallow rocks multiple times obscuring his face. When it came time for me to identify him, his features were so mangled, I went by his general appearance. I was in shock at the time and under the care of a physician, for I was out of sorts. From there the doctors finished the postmortem examination. Now sixteen years later, I see things clearly.

While the description of the body matched Luther's general appearance, I had forgotten some key features of my first husband. Luther had a six-inch scar running down his stomach. It was from when he was a boy and had fallen off a fence impaling himself on a loose nail. The last two teeth on the bottom and top of his mouth were gold. Lastly, on his right elbow he had tattooed my initials V.M. Victoria Marrow.

I read the description of the body multiple times. Even though the river had mangled Luther's face, the key features would still be identifiable. The description claimed the body had silver teeth in its mouth. There was a scar on the upper back which Luther did not have. And there was no mention of a tiny tattoo on the elbow.

Black spots start to form between my eyes, and I lean back on the sofa. The paper drops from my fingers and flutters to the floor. All this time. All this time. How could I not have known? How could I have been so stupid?

"Victoria, are you alright?" calls Hannah. She sits beside me. "What is wrong?"

I open my mouth, but my words fail to come out. Try as I might, my lips refuse to form the realization that would put my safety at risk. All these years it was a comfort knowing that the demon who had hurt me and terrorized me was gone.

Finally, I manage a soft whisper and Hannah leans closer to hear my words. "Luther is still alive. It was the wrong body."

"Are you sure?"

I reach forward and pick up the photograph. I place it into her hands. Hannah glances down at the picture and her eyes widen.

"This is Luther!"

I nod.

For a minute, I think Hannah is going to pass out, but she grips the side of the settee and composes herself.

"What is wrong?" I ask.

Hannah takes a shaky breath. "I know your husband, Victoria. Luther is my step-brother."

"Step-brother! What are you talking about?" I cry. "He told me he was an orphan and he did not have siblings! Why didn't you tell me you knew him?"

"You just said his name was Luther. You never told me his last name. There are a lot of people with that name," replies Hannah.

"Ugh, Luther was always a liar," I groan.

"My mother died when I was a baby," said Hannah. "My father raised me. Years later, he met Luther's mother Erin, and they fell in love. Luther was seventeen when they married. Erin had left Luther's father because he was an alcoholic. His father died a month before their wedding. From what my father told me, Luther blamed his mother for the death of his father. Then he left." Hannah's eyes blazed. "He would come back periodically and threaten Erin to give him money. If she did not do what he said, he would throw a fit. One time Luther broke into our home when we were out and stole a lot of money and valuables from my father."

"Did he ever mention he had a wife and children?" I ask.

Hannah shook her head. "No, as far as we knew he was single and with a different female each week. After the robbery, he must have left Wales and come here to England because we never saw him again."

I stand. This was too much to take in. I told Hannah it was getting late, and I would talk to her tomorrow.

As I walk across the grounds back to the cottage, two hooded figures appear before me.

"Mum!" They call and their hoods fall back to reveal my sons Peter and James.

"Peter! James! What on Earth are you doing out this late?" Everyone had been sleeping when I left the house to see Hannah.

I walk closer to my sons and see they are cast in an eerie white light. Their figures waver before me as if they are ghosts.

"You lied to us," sneers Peter. "Excuse me?"

"You told us, our father is dead. He is not dead," replies James.

"What are you talking about?" I look closer at my boys, with the moon as my only light. Their eyes seem far away as if they are under the power of something evil.

"Our father is down by the lake," replies James. "He has been watching us all these years."

I feel the hairs on the back of my neck stand on end. A scalding pain blazes through my heart.

"Get back in the house at once." I cry.

"He is coming for you, Mum. Be careful." My sons disappear and I am alone.

Have I gone mad?

A particular odor fills my nostrils. It is smoke.

Picking up my dress, I run in the direction of the smoke. It is coming from the lake. As I reach the top of the hill that overlooks the point, I see our fishing shed is on fire.

The flame licks the sides of the shed, tasting the wood, and collapsing the structure. The blaze illuminates the dark sky and throws light onto someone standing in front of it.

It is a man. Five-foot-seven, muscular stature, black hair. His back is to me and his arms are crossed. My heart beats faster and the hairs on the back of my neck stand on end. I would recognize that figure anywhere. It was the man who had once been the love of my life but had morphed into the most evil person I had ever met. It was Luther!

Just like it was not possible for me to crawl out of my grave, it is not possible for Luther to be alive. But he had survived a jump into the churning waters of doom. It must be the wickedness that lives in his soul that keeps him alive.

My feet are frozen to the ground. I cannot move. I am numb. My eyes are fixated on the man who tried to destroy me. My chest aches, my stomach churns, my body breaks out into goosebumps, and my breath comes in short gasps. Time has slowed down around me. I no longer hear the crackling of the burning shack. I do not see anything but Luther.

Behind me I hear a noise. It is barking. Lolly comes running next to me. She stops and barks at the figure by the flaming shack. Luther turns and sees me standing on top of the hill. Our eyes meet. He flashes me a wicked grin and disappears into the woods.

I hear his words ring in my ears from that July Seventh day. *Just remember that you are mine forever, and if I cannot have you, no one else can.*

A husband
A liar
A cheat
A woman scorned
Death becomes me

October 23, 1892
2:00 a.m.

Fear confines me to my bed. As I lay among the pillows and blankets, I think back to the events that transpired after I saw Luther's evil face disappear into the woods. I am asleep but not asleep. My eyes close and my mind dreams of the horrific day Luther supposedly died.

July 7, 1876

"Stay back or I will kill her." Luther's strong arm is around my chest pulling me close to him while the barrel of a gun presses against my temple. The authorities surround us as we stand on the steps of the savings bank. Our sons were at Grandmother Emily's house. Luther had promised me a romantic day together as the way things used to be. He told me we had to stop at the bank first because he had to make a deposit.

As we left the bank, the authorities surrounded us, stating they were arresting Luther for robbery, blackmail, and murder. Luther pulled out a gun and decided to use me as a hostage. The police backed off, and we ran into the alley. Coming out the opposite side, Luther stopped a passing carriage and threw the driver into the street. He demanded that I get into the driver bench of the wagon. Luther hopped next to me, took the reins and headed out of town.

"Luther! Stop! Where are we going?"

He does not answer me.

"Who did you kill?"

No answer.

"I want to get out!"

He grabbed my arm tight and I winced from the pain. "You are not going anywhere. You are my wife, and you will do as I say. After all, you vowed to be with me through whatever comes our way."

"I did not promise to support your criminal antics. We have to go back. You have to turn yourself in!"

"No, sweetie, I am not going back to jail."

"What about our sons?"

"They will be fine. Grandmother Emily will take care of them."

We rode out of town. The horses galloped down the dirt roads. Luther moved the reins urging them to go faster. Turning around, I spied the constables on horseback following us. But they were in the distance. As we rounded the turn, they disappeared from view.

The wagon rocked back and forth as we approached the bridge. One of the horses was spooked by the bridge and stopped abruptly. Turning to the right, the wagon wheel caught in a rut in the road, flipping over, breaking the harness. The horses went running into the woods.

I felt my body slam against the hard dirt. My arm hurts. I hoped it was not broken. Luther was by my side yanking me to my feet. "Let's go!" He pulled me close and we began to walk onto the long bridge. I looked up into his face and realized he had this getaway planned all along.

The overpass crossed a large ravine with churning water that swirled below us. I heard gunfire behind us. Turning around I saw horses carrying the police galloping towards us. In front of us on the other side of the bridge, more horses carrying policemen came towards us.

"We are trapped, Luther. It is time to give yourself up. You can't get away with this any longer."

He released me as the policemen started yelling for us to stop. Looking left and right, Luther grabbed me by the shoulders and pulled me close.

"I will be back. Just remember that you are mine forever, and if I cannot have you, no one else can."

He planted a kiss on my lips. "We will see each other again. I will be back."

Running to the railing, he grabbed the ledge and hoisted himself up.

"Luther! No!" I screamed

He leapt off of the bridge. It seemed as if he fell forever before his body hit the churning waves. Disappearing under the surface, he never came up again.

I wake up in William's arms.

"Honey, are you alright? You were screaming." I feel his calloused hands stroke my head.

"I had a nightmare," I whisper. My fingers clutch his forearms as my body trembles.

"It is alright, my dear. You are safe."

I lie back on the pillow wishing I could believe him. How could I tell him that my nightmares were images of the past that had come to the present? The papers in the file had declared Luther dead. But Luther is not dead. Luther is malicious. He is a conniving manipulative soul. I feel Death could not defeat him.

I hear William gently snoring again. Sitting up, I turn and look at him. He had been a Godsend. A year after Luther died, I met William through Grandmother Emily. A year later we were married. William knew of my traumatic past with Luther, even though I had not told him everything. Some wounds are too hard to reopen.

October 26, 1892
8:00 a.m.

For the past few days, I have lain here plagued by memories as the weather mimics my feelings. My head pounds and my muscles feel as if I have been run over by a herd of cattle. Every time I close my eyes, I am haunted by images of my life with Luther. I can feel his fingers at my throat, I see his malicious eyes looking into my soul. I hear his evil laugh. I can neither eat or sleep. Nightmares fill my slumber. All the years of our marriage, I was Luther's puppet.

In one of my dreams, I relived the day I died. Only this time, as I am thrown to the ground, I turn and look up at my killer. He steps into the light of the lanterns. A lock of black hair escapes the hood, I know it's Luther, even before I see his green eyes narrowed in anger and his cruel mouth pursed in distaste.

Sitting up in bed, I open my eyes, gasping for air. Persephone stands at the foot of my bed looking at me.

"Victoria, there is no time for slumber. You only have five days left."

"I-I..."

"I know, Victoria. The wounds people leave never truly go away. Undeserved pain inflicted on good people can last for a lifetime. But we cannot let our scars become us. We must loosen the grip others have on us. We must be strong. Five days, Victoria, five days." In the blink of an eye she is gone.

The door opens and William comes in. "How are you feeling, my dear?" He places a hand to my forehead. "Your fever is gone." He puts a bouquet of flowers on the nightstand. "I picked these for you to bring you some cheer. I stopped by your Grandmother Emily's place while I was in town. She is requesting for you to come see her. I told her you would come if you felt up to it. Do you want me to fetch a doctor?"

I look at William. I am bewildered. Throughout all of this craziness over the past few days, my husband has not taken notice of my erratic behavior. I am convinced that Persephone cast some kind of magic when she turned back the hands of time.

"I am fine. I will go tomorrow."

William nods and leaves the room.

I simmer in the security of my blankets. William had said that lightning struck the shack by the lake and burned it to the ground. Had Luther been hiding in there this whole time? The rain put out the blaze before it could spread to the trees. However, I am not convinced. I think Luther started that fire on purpose to send me a message.

How I wish Luther had been in that shack when it burned to the ground. Then all my worries would be gone.

As I stare at the porcelain clock on the table, I swear to myself that I will not tell William anything about Luther's return. This is my problem, and I am going to resolve it myself. Five days. Five days.

October 27, 1892
2:00 p.m.

A full day has passed and I am true to my word. I have returned to London.

I get out of the carriage and walk down the bustling streets, then take a right to where the row houses signify the entrance to the East End. I have no idea why my Granny chooses to live here. Narrow alleys breed poverty, thievery, and violence. Since marrying William, I have tried over and over again to convince Granny to leave the East End and live with us. She refuses every time stating that as long as she is healthy, she can manage on her own.

I cross the street and head up the steps to the house at the end of the row. I call, "Granny! It's me, Victoria!" I knock on the door, and it opens at my touch.

"Granny?" I step inside and close the latch behind me.

"Granny, are you home?" The house is quiet. Granny's bag is gone. She must have gone out.

"Hello, wife," a deep voice calls, a voice that I had not heard in a very long time. My heart sinks into my stomach. Whirling around, as I stand in the hall, I see him on the stairs. Green eyes, dark hair, wicked heart, with a face that has not been marred by the river.

It is Luther!

My knees grow weak but I hold myself together. He walks down the remaining steps and stands before me. My saliva feels thick in my mouth.

"Shocked to see me? I've missed you."

"You're supposed to be dead." I say.

"I know, I know, but the authorities do not look for you when they believe you are dead."

"What are you doing in Grandmother Emily's house? Where is Granny? What did you do to her?"

"I have not done anything to Grandmother Emily. Really, Victoria. You consider me a monster. Grandmother Emily left long before I let myself in."

He takes my elbow and leads me to the kitchen where he pulls out a chair at the table. "Come sit, Victoria. I promise I won't hurt you."

Luther had never been one to keep his promises.

Narrowing my eyes, I sit down. Luther sits across from me. "I had it all planned from the beginning. I was going to fake my own death. I knew I was facing jail time and I had no plans to go back. My partner Nigel and I, you remember him, had a plan for me to jump from the bridge into the water. You never knew I was a strong swimmer. Nigel would be waiting for me in a boat and we would leave the country for Scotland."

He stares at me with his piercing eyes and I feel as if he can see into my soul.

"I did not tell you, because I could not risk the authorities getting to you and making you talk. You are weak and would crack under immense pressure. Nigel and I had been robbing banks and taking advantage of people for seven years. Our last bank heist in Charing Cross gave us a sizable fortune and left a few people dead. However, one of the people we had deceived recognized us at the bank and gave our names to the authorities.

"The day before our plan to disappear, I learned Nigel had been stealing money from me. When he picked me up in the boat, we got into an argument, and Nigel tried to kill me, so I took his life. I figured it was the perfect plan. Since we were of similar body composition, I knew the police would not question if they pulled Nigel's mangled body out of the river. They would think it was me! Since I am a wanted criminal, they would not investigate because they would not care. I pushed his body off the boat and then continued through the currents until I was far enough away, and then I made my escape to Scotland."

"Why didn't you stay there? Why did you come back?" My face grows hot as the flame in the gaslamp that burns on the table.

"I am in need of more money. Plus, I left something behind when I disappeared that I need now. I am currently wanted by the authorities in Scotland. I figured my return would be a nice surprise. But you have betrayed me, Victoria."

"What?" I cry. "You were supposed to be dead, Luther!"

"Tisk, tisk, always making excuses. Did I not tell you the day I jumped off the bridge that I would be back? Did I not tell you that we would be together again? I thought you were smart enough to understand what I was telling you. But instead, you ignored everything I said. You went and lived your life. You got married and had more children. I had people keeping tabs on you."

"You're not innocent, Luther I am sure you were busy in the beds of all the Scottish women. Maybe you have a few secret children of your own."

He smirks at me.

"That does not matter, Victoria. What does matter is that I am still alive. Which means you are still my wife."

"You were declared dead, Luther!"

"That does not mean anything. I can make the claim that I suffered from loss of memory for years. Now I have regained clarity and I want to be with my wife. I'm sure whatever his name is...William Taylor...is it? I'm sure he would love to know that his wife's first husband is still alive and will make his life hell.

A fire burns in the pit of my stomach. "You are evil," I hiss.

"However, I will make a deal with you. If you do something for me, I will leave you alone and disappear forever."

"Why would I help you? You tried to kill me." The moment the words are out of my mouth, I want to swallow them again. I had forgotten that we had gone back in time. The brooch warms my chest.

Luther tilts his head and looks at me. "Kill you? Now why would I do a thing like that? I did not kill you. You are still very much alive. I told you your mind is not well. You are unstable."

This had been my life with Luther. He was always asking for favors, always wanting me to do something for him and never giving me anything in return.

"What do you want, Luther?" I sneer.

He leans closer. "My brooch."

"Brooch!" My hand immediately flies to the pin on my chest. "This brooch!" My heart hammers against my chest. I cannot give it to him.

"Not that cheap brooch, you fool. What would I want with that ugly pin on your bosom?" sneers Luther. "I have a brooch that I borrowed from a wealthy Duchess. It looks similar to yours, but mine is covered in diamonds and rubies. It is worth a fortune now. I kept it in a small black box in the back of the wall clock we had that hung in our front parlor.

"I do not remember where that is." I reply.

"Find the brooch and give it to me. Then I will leave, and you will never hear from me again. You can have your new life, with your husband. Who needs you, anyway?" He stands up and walks towards the back door.

"I'm sure you need some time to search for it, since you were always so forgetful. I will give you until my birthday. If I do not have it by October Thirty-first, then on November First, I will be at your door to inform your husband that his marriage has been a sham. Also, I cannot guarantee Grandmother Emily will be safe if I do not get that brooch."

"You wouldn't dare touch her," I growl.

"Make sure you get that pretty pin, and do not even think about keeping it for yourself. If I find you tricked me, I will kill you, too." He opens the door and looks back at me. "By the way, you look very lovely. Time has made you even more beautiful. If you get tired of your stupid husband, you can come back to me. We can leave the country together. I am thinking I might travel to the United States, next. We will see each other soon, Victoria."

As he disappears out the back door, I hear the front door open. Grandmother Emily calls my name.

An innocent love
Now turned sour
How do I kill the past
When it won't die?
The day of my death date
Approaches near
Once frail now strong
Will the exchange be made in time?

October 30, 1892
10 p.m.

"Victoria!" A familiar voice calls. "Wake up!"

I groan and ignore the voice. It has been a tumultuous few days. My husband, my children, and Hannah have all fallen ill and are in bed. Since I had come back to life, William acts as if he is under some sort of spell. The same with my children. I feel it might be Persephone's doing. I think she wants me to do face this terror on my own.

While caring for everyone, I have been searching for the missing brooch that Luther desires. I am not planning on giving him the jewel, but I feel it could be used as a bargaining tool.

Luther and I had lived in a small flat when we were together, but I could no longer afford the rent after his death.

I took my two children and was welcomed into Grandmother Emily's home. When I married William, all my belongings had been packed in boxes and brought to the farm. I know I had discarded many unwanted items because I did not want to remember my life with Luther, but I know I did not throw out that clock where he says the brooch was hidden.

"Victoria! Wake up!" A hand is on my shoulder, shaking me. I open my eyes and see Persephone standing before me.

"It is two hours until October Thirty-First and you are sleeping!"

I jump up. A shiver runs down my spine. "What are you doing here? Have you come to get me?"

"Not yet. There is still time. I have come to deliver something to you that I think will help ignite the passion that seems to be missing." She places a mysterious envelope in my hands.

"I don't understand." I begin. Persephone is gone.

I get out of the bed, dress, and go downstairs to the parlor before I look at the envelope.

I see near the top it has already been opened. A piece of paper is inside. Pulling it out, I begin to read its contents.

October 1, 1892

My Dearest Granny Emily,

I thought we had an agreement. October 3 at 10 p.m. I will be at your house. Make sure you have the monthly amount available. If you refuse to continue our agreement, I cannot guarantee the safety of your granddaughter. I will not stay away. She may not be married or alive much longer.

Goosebumps break out along my skin. I clutch my hand to my chest. The handwriting and tone of the letter tell me only one person could have written it.

Luther!

I crumple the letter in my fist. How dare Luther threaten an old woman! I want to wring his neck.

Victoria! Time is ticking. Make the exchange. The brooch whispers.

I blink and a small bag appears on the tea table in front of me. It is the magic of the brooch.

Look inside.

I lean forward and open the bag to find a bundle of letters.

They are already open.

One by one I pull out the contents and see a variety of dates from the beginning of this month all the way back to sixteen years ago. The last letter is dated six months after Luther supposedly died.

All of the papers have the same message. Grandmother Emily has to give him money for him to stay away from me.

Otherwise, he will make good on his threats.

Blackmail!

A sharp pain sears in my heart. I knock the bag to the carpet and double over in pain. Wincing, I place my hand on the arm of the sofa to steady myself.

I remember how Luther had taken advantage of me all these years. He had tormented me, telling me I was not good enough, telling me if I did not follow his guidance I would not have anything in life. No other man would want me.

My mouth clenches and my nostrils flare as tremors move throughout my body. The brooch falls from my chest and clatters onto the coffee table. I scream. The woman carved in shell stares at me with no eyes. A single tear leaps from my lashes and falls onto the woman. My chest starts to ache, and I feel my flesh starting to crack. A sense of urgency is released from the brooch. Calling me, telling me it is time for revenge.

If by the stroke of midnight on October Thirty-first, the exchange has not been made, you will die. And I might not be able to save you a second time. Persephone's voice echoes on the walls.

I know what I must do now.

Picking up the brooch, I reattach it to my dress. Warmth flows through my body bringing a sense of clarity to my soul, and my body heals itself.

Yanking the bag of letters from the floor, I toss the packet into the fire. The flames snake around the brown bag. Dark cracks form along the seams hot with red embers. Pieces slowly break apart. The sight of the blaze brings joy to my soul.

After making certain my husband and children are safe. I reach into the drawer and pull out a knife that Persephone gave me that night in the alley. It is the dagger Luther used on me. Only this time, I will return the favor!

I put my coat on and step into the night, closing the door behind me. The cold October air hits me in the face, awakening every fiber of my being. There is not a star in the dark sky. The only thing that illuminates the heavens is a bright moon. The yellow glow mixes with the green glow of my brooch.

It is time to hunt a man.

It is time for revenge.

October 30, 1892
11:00 p.m.

The bell tower chimes as I walk to Grandmother Emily's house. The brooch has not only given me the power of strength but the power of speed as well. In the blink of an eye, I find myself in the East End of London. This side of the grand metropolis is still alive at this time of night. It is the hour where humanity submits to its evil desires. The hour where secrets run rampant through the streets. The hour where unexplained circumstances occur. I am at the heart of Death's hideaway.

Opening the back door of Granny's house, a horrific sight meets my eyes. Grandmother Emily lays before me in a pool of blood. I scream and cover my mouth.

Rushing over to her side, I kneel next to her.

"Granny! Granny!" I call. It appears she has been stabbed.

Her eyes open upon hearing my voice. She grabs my arm.

"My dear,"

"Granny! Who did this to you?"

"I-I have a s-secret I must tell."

"I already know, Granny, I know about Luther. I know he has been blackmailing you."

I noticed my brooch was glowing brightly. The magic of the lady with no eyes allows my Granny to be coherent and speak.

"It was my fault. I was trying to protect you. Sixteen years ago, he came to my house looking for you. I told him to stay away from you, and he said that he would only do so if I made it worth his while. I paid him some money to stay away, yet he kept coming back. Each time, his demands were more. I saw how much happier you were after he had died. I could not let you be unhappy again."

"You paid him for sixteen years? Granny, where did you get all that money?"

"Ah, my dear, there is much you do not know about me. Your grandfather was my fourth husband. My three deceased husbands all had great fortunes they left to me, as I was their only living kin. I suppose Luther did some digging into my finances, which is how he knew of my sizable fortune."

I glance at the wall splendid with art and statues. "But why do you live here in the East End? Surely you could have afforded a better place to call home?"

"Looks can be deceiving. By living here, no one would ever suspect how wealthy I was. Living in this area has allowed me to help many people who need it."

She grabs her side and gasps.

"Granny, did Luther do this to you?"

"I refused to pay him."

"We have to get you help." I rise to leave, but my dear Granny grabs my arm again.

"No dear, no time. Here. Take it."

With trembling hands, she reaches into her pocket and places a glittering object in my hand. I look down to see the brooch Luther desired.

"Granny! How?"

"You left the clock at my place when you moved. Years ago, it fell off the wall and revealed the hidden package. I have been keeping it safe ever since. I knew Luther wanted it. I heard him speak to you in the house when I was coming home the other afternoon. That was when I knew I could no longer keep up this charade of payments." Her eyes start to close.

I hold her tight in my arms. "Granny! Stay with me!"

"Oh, my dear, do not worry. If you play your cards right, I will be back." The green glow of my brooch dies and her eyes close.

Gripping her wrist. I frantically feel for a pulse. There is none.

"Granny! No!" I cry. I cover my mouth so the sobs do not escape my lips. Tears burn the corners of my eyes, while fire blazes in my heart.

Standing up, I open my hand. Sitting in my palm is the brooch. The exact replica of mine and Hannah's. Only the woman is covered in diamonds. Behind her is a background of rubies. The edge of the pin is trimmed in gold. It is the most exquisite piece of jewelry I have ever laid eyes on. I place it in my pocket.

Positioning each hand under my Grandmother Emily's armpits, I drag her body to her bedroom. I cannot leave her on the floor. The brooch has given me strength and anger fuels me. I hoist Grandmother Emily up and place her in her bed. Pulling the covers up to her chin, I plant a kiss on her forehead.

"I will bring you back, Granny." Closing the bedroom door, I set out on my quest!

The brooch glimmers hot against my chest. I feel my skin burn.

Luther had taken my Granny. Just as he had taken me.

I feel the knife in my pocket.

I know where I have to go and I know he will be there.

October 30, 1892
11:30 p.m.

I push back the iron bars of Stonegate Cemetery. The barrier lets out a scream in the stillness. Mist encircles the ghostly tombstones ranging from tall to small. Wind whistles among the graves, emitting a mournful tune that sends chills up my spine. Despite the fact the graves look at me in silence, I sense spirits spinning about me, as if in encouragement.

Soon, I believe I shall be entrapped in chaos.

A sickening feeling whirls in my stomach. Relief mixed with curiosity fills my soul as I notice my grave no longer exists. Nevertheless, I tremble at the memory of clawing my way upward out of the shroud, the casket, and the suffocating soil. I have no wish to return to the eternal darkness.

I walk among the graves until I see the tall, stone angel and Celtic cross loom before me.

My heart leaps to my throat. There among the death stones, arches, crosses, and angels. I see him...

The bane of my existence.

The torment of my life

The blight upon my soul

I pray that tonight, it shall be him who resides beneath the rocks and dirt.

As all are my witnesses.

I pray tonight, Death will take him!

Luther turns and smirks at me as I approach. "Well, well, well, Victoria. What a nice surprise. I see for once in your life you did not let me down. Do you have what I asked for?"

I hold up the elegant brooch. "You mean this?"

Luther's eyes light up with greed. "Yes, yes give it to me."

I stare into the face of the man who terrorized me for so many years.

"No!"

"What did you say to me?"

"I am not giving you the brooch. You killed my Granny, you fool!"

"No, I did not! What are you talking abou, you crazy woman!"

The brooch speaks to me. I clench my jaw. "You dare lie to me!"

"It is not my fault she did not keep her end of the deal.

Now, are you going to give me my brooch or not?"

"It is not your brooch! You stole it!"

Luther reaches into his coat pocket and pulls out a small handgun. "I do not have time for idle chatter. Give me the brooch or I will kill you, too."

Even though my brooch has given me strength, my legs tremble. I cannot think. I cannot focus. All I see is the shiny barrel of the gun pointed at me. My mind comprehends the distinct chance I can die in mere seconds, and my family will never know what happened to me.

I see his finger squeeze the trigger, and I leap behind a nearby tombstone.

Bang!

The gun goes off at the same time Hannah jumps out from behind a gravestone and whacks Luther in the side with a shovel that had been used to dig a recent grave.

The gun leaps from his hands and scatters somewhere along the grass. Luther stumbles backwards but gains his balance.

"Foolish girl," before I can react, he grabs me and throws me to the ground. He rips the diamond brooch from my hands and runs off down the row of tombstones.

"Hannah, thank you" I cry, getting to my feet. "What are you doing here?"

"I could not sleep and I looked out my window to see you leaving the farm. I saw you move at breakneck speed and my brooch allowed me to do the same. I followed you here to the East End. I had a feeling you could use some help."

Luther is getting away. I tell Hannah to stay in the graveyard, and I run after him. This is my battle to fight.

Willing my legs to move faster, I see his fleeting shadow dodge from tombstone to tombstone. My lungs burn but anger fuels my chase. I see him running towards the gates.

He pushes at the latch, but the iron bars do not budge. They are locked. Luther tries again, but they will not offer escape.

He slams against the gates again. The magic of the brooch has locked us together in this Realm of Death!

"Dammit!" Screams Luther. He turns around and sees me approaching him.

"You're not going anywhere!" I yell.

He sneers at me. "You pathetic weakling! You think you're going to stop me? You are a fool! You couldn't support yourself without me. That is why you had to find a new husband to take care of you!"

He turns and begins to climb the iron bars to get over the fence.

He will not get away! It has been sixteen years! I am not the same person!

I run at him. Strength fuels my muscles. I grab his legs, and the power of the brooch allows me to rip him off the fence and throw him to the ground.

He winces as he crashes onto the grass.

"I am not weak," I hiss. "You are a murderer! You tried to take my life, Hannah's life and the life of Grandmother Emily!"

"Hannah?" Luther gets to his feet. "I was not trying to kill Hannah! What are you talking about? When I set the fire to the house in Wales, I was trying to kill my own mother! She is the reason my father is dead. My mother drove my father to an early grave. Then she goes on to marry another man like the wench that she is, and she thinks she is going to get away with it! You're telling me, my mother did not die! You're telling me I did not kill my mother!"

"No, you did not," I reply. "Hannah was home alone at the time you set the fire."

"It was not my fault Hannah was in the house. That is her fault."

"You also killed Grandmother Emily!" I yell.

"Your Grandmother Emily was holding out on me. I had a feeling she had the brooch all along, and when she refused to give it to me, I took her life. And since you insist on arguing with me, I might as well kill you, too. I am getting sick of listening to your voice. William was a fool to marry you! You are not worthy of life. Your parents should have never given birth to you."

His verbal assaults fuel me. The brooch has given me a power that I have not known before. I do not feel myself. I am ready to silence the man who broke me.

Luther grabs my arm and throws me onto the grass. He brings his fist down, but I roll out of the way. Jumping to my feet, I smack my hand across his face. I grab his wrist, twisting his arm behind his back and I pin him against the tombstone. Reaching into my pocket with one hand, I pull out a knife that I have kept hidden. The dagger that was used to kill me.

Raising the weapon, I drive the blade into his back, piercing his heart.

He screams. His body starts to go limp. I release my hold and watch him drop to the ground- dead.

A calmness flows over me, and I feel a weight lift from my shoulders. The brooch glows in approval. I will not die.

The exchange begins. A soul for a soul.

October 31, 1892
12:00 a.m.

In the distance, I hear church bells chime midnight. I stand over Luther's body.

It is finished.

I look up to see Hannah walk over to me. She covers her mouth as she looks at Luther.

"He.. He is dead?"

I nod.

"I knew you would not let me down, Victoria." A voice rings out. Persephone appears before us. "You found the strength within yourself to face your past and conquer it. The exchange has been made."

"Not exactly," I reply.

Persephone looks at me. "What do you mean? Your life has been restored."

I am nervous speaking to such a powerful creature, but the brooch gives me courage.

"Luther took three lives. He took my life which you restored. He took Hannah's life, which you also restored. But there is one more person whose life he took that has not been restored."

Persephone crosses her arms and raises an eyebrow at me.

"You needed Hannah in order to understand Luther's past and give you the motivation to extract revenge. You are asking me to restore three souls in exchange for one soul?"

"I am sure you have seen through the years what a horrible person Luther was. He did so much hurt and damage to so many people. His soul is the equivalent of hundreds of souls. And in his pocket is a diamond brooch worth quite a fortune."

Persephone walks to Luther and reaches into his coat pocket. She pulls out the diamond and ruby jewel, and holds it up before her. It glitters in the moonlight.

She sighs, "Yes, Luther was evil. I did let Hannah live, so I suppose I can make one more exception. You are giving me this diamond brooch as an exchange. I will have a use for such a special gift. Very well. You may bring back her soul."

She waves her arms and disappears with Luther's body.

With trembling fingers, I clasp the breast pin, and I feel its warmth against my skin.

Parting my lips, I call out into the night. "The soul of Grandmother Emily Price. I claim! Come back to me."

A beam of light spikes into the air from the brooch on my chest. The luminescence circles the graveyard. It forms a green vortex that spins and twirls. When it stops, standing before me is Grandmother Emily.

"Granny!" I yell. I run into her arms.

"I knew you would do it, Victoria!" Granny hugs me and Hannah. She looks over at Luther's tomb. "I see the evil villain is back where he belongs. Good riddance!"

I smile. It was a unique exchange, three souls for the price of one.

Once full of fear. I am now strong. From the depths of Hell, I rise. Revenge has been my weapon and I am now at peace. I will never endure mistreatment again. I have found myself. I am reborn.

A soul for a soul.

November 7, 1892

Luther is finally dead and freedom flutters in my soul. Like waking up after a nightmare.

My life seems back to normal now. My husband and I were outside playing kick-the-ball with the children.

Grandmother Emily finally agreed to move into our home, and I am so grateful to have her so close to me.

I see Hannah coming up the path with a suitcase in her hand.

I walk over to her.

"I came to say goodbye," says Hannah. "I am going back to Wales. I sent a telegram to my father a few days ago and he told me that Paul is not seeing anyone. I am going to go home to talk to him. I do not know how I can explain all of this madness, but I hope he forgives my sudden departure and will offer his hand in marriage."

"I am sure he will," I reply, giving her a hug as I see a private carriage coming down the road.

"I will write, I promise. Oh. Here," she places in my hand Persephone's brooch. "I will not be needing it anymore and I certainly do not want to see that ever again in my life."

Laughing I give her one last hug and watch her board the carriage.

"Phoebe kicked the ball into the barn!" yells Peter.

"I will go get it," I reply. I walk into the barn and close the door behind me. The building is empty with all the animals outside. I walk past the lonesome stalls in search of the ball.

How far can a five-year-old kick a ball? I think.

"Is this what you seek my dear?" I look up to see Persephone standing before me. In her hands is my children's toy. She lets it fall from her hands and it rolls to my feet.

"You are quite clever, Victoria Louise Taylor. In all my years I have never had anyone convince me to make an exchange of returning multiple souls for the price of one. But I suppose it was worth it. You look much happier now, and I do have a diamond brooch to add to my collection of jewels." She beams at me

"Persephone, I feel better than I've felt in years. I feel at peace."

"That is wonderful, darling." She pulls her shawl around her shoulders and holds out her hand to me. "Then I believe we can pass this gift onto the next soul who needs help."

I nod in agreement, reaching into my pocket I place Hannah's brooch into her palm. Then I unfasten mine and give it to her.

The three beautiful brooches lay in Persephone's wrinkled hand.

"I still do not understand why you brought us these jewels?" I ask.

"Ah, my dear, look at these brooches, for they are not only articles of jewelry but lessons as well. These pins represent how one evil person can ruin the lives of so many good people as you saw with yourself, Grandmother Emily, and Hannah. But if we all unite together, we can conquer the darkness in our lives. This you all did."

"Thank you, Persephone."

"Just doing my job," Persephone chuckles. The brooches glow in her palms and merge together, changing shape. The jewelry transforms into a long scythe and her shawl grows longer until it is a black cape. Persephone pulls the hood over her head. She winks at me then disappears.

I walk outside to join my family. My heart fills with joy.

Death has brought me more than just a mysterious brooch.

It has brought me a second chance at life. I am finally free!

The End

Acknowledgments

To my readers. Thank you for choosing my book. I truly appreciate you. Thank you for believing in me.

Thank you to my sister Ashley for the hand-drawn images featured in my book. You are a talented artist and I cannot wait to feature more of your drawings. You are a beautiful person inside and out. One day you will have your farm with all of your animals.

Thank you Dr. Edith A. Kostka for helping me edit this beautiful book. I could have not made it through this process without you. You are a talented author and I cannot wait for your books to be out in the world.

Thank you to Emily at Emily's World of Designs for creating a stunning cover and for helping me throughout my author journey. Thank you for having patience with me and guiding me through this process.

A special thank you to my beta readers: Ashley Testa, Lyndsey Hall, Emily Katzenburger, Stephanie Whitfield, and Illona Nurmela. Thank you so much for your feedback and challenging me to be a better writer. I could not have done this without you.

Thank you to the following authors who have become my personal tribe. You are talented writers and beautiful people. Thank you for helping me navigate this publishing journey.

Thank you for taking the time to answer my thousands of questions. I truly appreciate you all.

- Jennifer Kropf. Jen, I truly appreciate our friendship. I am so happy we became friends through the Bookstagram community. I am glad I joined your Facebook group. You have given me a wealth of knowledge and wisdom about the publishing and author industry. I could not have done this without you. You have inspired me to become a better writer. Watching you grow as an author has motivated and inspired me more than you know. You are a talented novelist and a beautiful person inside and out. I am honored to know you.

- Ashley Steffenson. Ashley, thank you for being one of my first author friends. I couldn't have picked a better person to navigate this first-time author journey with. You are a wonderful friend and thank you for always being here for me. I am so proud of you. It has been an honor to watch you become a published author, a successful businesswoman, and a wonderful mother. I cannot wait to see what is next for you.

- Bekah Berge. Bekah, you are one of the strongest women I know. I am in awe of how you have persevered through the trials and tribulations of life. No matter what you are going through you always have a positive attitude. The fact you are able to publish book after book despite all the challenges is truly inspiring. Thank you for being a wonderful friend. I will forever be cheering you on.

- Stephanie Whitefield and Lyndsey Hall thank you for being wonderful people and wonderful friends.

I want to thank Alice Ivinya, my Enchanted Anthologies coauthor. Alice, thank you for taking a chance on me and allowing me to be a part of the Enchanted Anthologies Series when I was not even published. I truly appreciate your kindness. Thank you for helping me to take the first step into the author world. You are such a caring and generous person.

Thank you Rhianne for helping me format my book. I am so thankful for your generosity and kindness. I am happy we have become friends. I cannot wait until you offer your formatting services to the world, and everyone can benefit from how talented you are.

Thank you to my Enchanted Anthologies and What's In A Name coauthors. I have learned so much from all of you.

Thank you Bethany Atazadeh, your YouTube series on publishing helped me so much.

And lastly, thank you to YouTube. I would not have been able to get through this process without the wealth of knowledge from so many creators who take the time to upload videos to this platform.

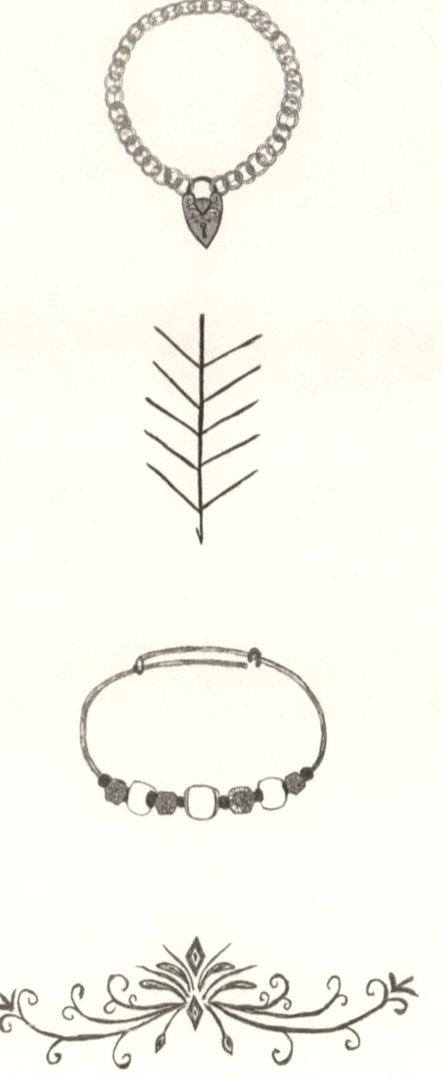

N.D. Testa is an Italian-American author who lives in the United States. She creates magical realms for others to escape to and enjoy. Her goal is to write stories that bring joy, happiness, and hope to the lives of many.

When she is not hard at work writing, N.D. Testa spends her time riding horses, working out, traveling, snowboarding, and looking for her next adventure. She is fluent in multiple languages, loves animals, and is obsessed with fashion and fitness. She always ends her day with a cup of tea.

N.D. Testa also writes under the pen name N.D.T. Casale.